JOHN F. WATSON

The Final Journey

First published by Emoter's Gap 2023

This novel is entirely a work of fiction. The names, characters and incidents portrayed in it are the work of the author's imagination. Any resemblance to actual persons, living or dead, events or localities is entirely coincidental.

First edition

ISBN: 9781803528694

Typesetting by Antony Wootten

This book was professionally typeset on Reedsy.
Find out more at reedsy.com

'Words are the only thing which lasts forever.'

WILLIAM HAZLITT.

Chapter 1

1918

Through half-closed eyes, Ruth roused, the fuzziness of a deep, untroubled sleep reluctant to leave her mind. For a split second a sliver of fear shot through her. Strange surroundings; old-fashioned wallpaper; paintings hung on the wall of places, and people, she did not recognise, a blocked off fireplace. Where was she? Her brain began to clear as the shafts of early morning sunlight eased the last remnants of darkness from the small bedroom and a sense of relief flowed through her as remembrance hit. Now, with eyes fully open she found herself staring into the dark, luminous gaze of Jim, her husband of just a few hours. He studied her closely, a hint of a satisfied smile twitching at the corners of his mouth.

"Good morning, Mrs Styles," he said tenderly. "Welcome to Honey Bee Nest Farm, your new home and our new life." Resting on one elbow he brushed the tousled hair from her face, lowered his head and kissed her. When their lips finally, and reluctantly, parted, Ruth sighed. "Promise you'll wake me up every morning like this, for as long as we both shall live?"

"I promise I will, Ruth," and the passion of the previous night ignited again.

Afterwards, Ruth lay with her head on his shoulder, a hand across his chest, the thud of his heart feeling strong under her fingers. For a moment they lay in silence before Jim whispered in her ear, "Ruth?"

"Yes, Jim."

"Was it... you know... how was it for you?"

"Jim, it was wonderful. You took me to another world, a world of pleasure that I didn't even know existed." She clutched the covers tight under her chin, shy to reveal her nakedness under the sheets. "I was nervous though, Jim. I have imagined this moment for such a long time, that I was afraid I might be disappointed when we, you know, *did it.*" Ruth giggled to hide her embarrassment, then became serious. "Or that you might be disappointed with *me.* All these uncertainties raced through my mind." Ruth stretched under the covers. "I didn't need to worry. It was better than I ever imagined it could be."

A self-satisfied smile spread across his face. "Keep talking, Ruth. You're saying all the right things." Jim fell back on the pillow, relieved at the reassuring words from Ruth. "Funny how doubts creep into your mind, 'specially over something so natural. I mean, everyone does it. Animals do it. It's what makes the world go round." He turned his head, the smile still plastered to his face.

"Well, it certainly made my head spin." Ruth rolled onto him and with lips close, she whispered, "I think I must have married the world's greatest lover, Jim Styles."

Jim replied with a mischievous grin and a glint of devilment in his eye. "Yep, it's possible, Ruth but I'll need a lot more practice."

Their laughter was muffled as Jim dragged the sheets up over their heads. Finally, he made the effort to jump out of bed, washing and dressing quickly. Ruth watched his every move, remembering the small, painfully thin boy dressed in rags when they had first met at the orphanage. How he had changed in just a few short years. But, there again, they both had.

Once into his clothes, he wandered over to the low window and gazed outside. "Ruth, I can't quite grasp what's happened. It hasn't sunk in yet."

With his attention outside, Ruth quickly slipped into her dressing gown, padded over to stand behind him, slipping her arms around his waist. They watched as the village below slowly came to life, as slivers of red from the rising sun, pierced the thin clouds to find the base of the valley.

Resting her chin on his shoulder, he stroked her hair as it fell across his chest and Ruth said, "I know exactly how you feel, Jim. When I first opened my eyes this morning, I felt a stab of fear." He looked at her. "Honestly, Jim, I couldn't remember where I should be. In a strange room and someone alongside, in bed with me."

"And?"

"And it was the best feeling I have ever experienced." Ruth hugged him. "But after the excitement of our wedding and Josh's return right on the point of taking our vows, I just knew everything was going to be okay. Now we have our whole lives stretching in front of us and I don't intend missing a minute of it. And do you realize, Christmas is on its way. Our first Christmas together."

He stared into her eyes, "Well, if Christmas is coming and all this work to do, I better get out there, 'specially if we haven't a minute to spare."

Ruth laughed. "Now who's making fun, eh? Right, I'll follow you down. Do you want to do breakfast or feed up outside?"

"Daft question, Ruth? I'll feed up."

"Okay, darling husband. What are you waiting for? Off you go."

With a glint in his eye, he said, "I'm waiting to feast my eyes on what that dressing gown is hiding."

Ruth coloured up. "Aw, come on, Jim, give me a day or two to feel comfortable in front of you. Don't forget you are the first ever man in my life." She waited awhile before saying. "Not that I have much experience in this sort of thing, but from what I just saw, you have a beautiful body, Jim Styles."

Jim swaggered out of the bedroom, a broad smile on his face as he dashed outside, the sharp morning air catching his breath.

Once the bedroom door closed, Ruth began to dress, annoyed with herself for feeling embarrassed. In her eyes, their intimacy should be free and relaxed. There to be enjoyed. But it was early days. She looked ahead to the day when she could just throw all her inhibitions to the four winds and be as free as a bird. She wanted to experience and feel the same freedom, excitement, and emotions within this small intimate bedroom as when outside riding and exploring these wonderful, rugged moorlands.

Chapter 2

With farming, the stock always came first and were to feed and look after morning and night, so there was no chance of even a couple of days away for the newlyweds. Sam, who helped out on the farm, had offered to work a weekend for them but neither Jim, or Ruth were prepared to fritter money away that they could ill afford.

With Sunday, supposedly, a day of rest and all yard work done, Ruth hoped a ride up onto the high moor with Jim would be possible. A favourite of hers was the bridleway that skirted the rim of the dale, following the now relatively quiet railway. Many houses stood empty, some falling into disrepair now the mining boom was over but Ruth still found it a stunning ride. With breakfast over, she studied Jim, who was sat in pensive mood.

"Penny for them?" Ruth asked.

"For what?" Jim asked, looking puzzled.

"For your thoughts. You were deep in thought, I assumed it must be serious."

He laughed. "No, nothing like that, Ruth." He walked behind her chair and nuzzled into the nape of her neck. "To be honest, I was thinking of last night."

Ruth turned and kissed him. "Hmmm. Hopefully, there will be many more to come."

"Well, why wait for night, we can go now." His hands were persistent.

Rising from the chair she pulled him close and whispered, "Patience, Jim Styles. I don't want you tiring of me. So, trust me, wait until nightfall and I will be all yours again." The kiss lingered, Jim finally pulling away.

"My god, you are a strong-willed woman." Turning on his heel, he headed for the door. "I'll finish outside and then we'll saddle up and go for a ride together."

Ruth's face lit up. "That's brilliant, Jim. There couldn't be anything better for me." Jim turned and caught her eye. She added, "well, okay, maybe only one thing. I'll soon be done in here and ready for when you finish outside."

Packing sandwiches and a drink, Ruth changed into her riding clothes and entered the stable, the warmth and smell enriching her senses to what lay ahead. By the time she had the horses saddled, Jim was ready to go. Quickly slinging a coat on, he led the way up the loose, rocky gully through the woods, their mounts scrabbling for grip, before breaking clear and out onto the moor top. A bright day with just a few clouds skimming the horizon but a keen wind bit at their cheeks. Once hitting the well-ridden track on the open moor, they eased the horses into a canter, then a full-blooded gallop for a couple of miles, before easing back to a trot.

Drawing their mounts to a halt for a drink and a breather at a small stream trickling down the moor side, Ruth dismounted and said, "God, Jim, there cannot be a more exciting life than this. I can't believe it's happening. I keep pinching myself to make sure it is real."

"Oh, it's real enough, Ruth." Jim answered, "but I understand how you feel, 'specially when you think where we came from. How lucky was that?" He shook his head in disbelief. With horses watered and rested they mounted and resumed at a leisurely pace, marvelling at just the sigh of the wind and the quietness surrounding this rugged terrain. No more clanking engines, railway tubs, or gangs of working men out on the line. Even the chimney that once belched fumes into the atmosphere was almost redundant.

At the highest point of their ride, Jim reined his horse in when Ruth caught sight of a kestrel, hunting the moor for a kill. "Look, Jim. D'you see it?" She pointed excitedly into the distance. The bird, motionless, a stark silhouette of a cross in the clear blue sky had eyes only on its prey, hovering silent and deadly. Ruth dropped her voice to a whisper. "Imagine how powerful that bird must feel. The owner of all it surveys." Ruth spread her arms out in a gesture of enormity, her eyes bright with pleasure from this spectacular setting. "See how deep the valley is, Jim. At this very moment, I feel as free as that bird, as if this valley is ours alone."

Jim smiled, enjoying the scene as much as Ruth. Nudging his horse closer, he flung an arm around her shoulders. "Well, in a way, Ruth, it is. If we can ride up here and experience such freedom as this whenever we feel like it, then it's as good as owning it."

Suddenly, a gasp from Ruth. The bird dropped from sight like a stone before sweeping back into view with dinner in its talons. The sight took Jim's breath away, as he said, "ah, Ruth, what a marvellous sight. Nature in the raw." Jim put a hand up to shield his eyes from the sun, watching the bird fly into the distance. "But it just shows that life in the animal world can be just as cruel as ours."

Dismounting, Ruth spread a small rug on the base of the old cross and out in the middle of this desolate moor above Roston, they were about to enjoy what they laughingly called their honeymoon meal. Surrounded as far as the eye could see by the straggly black stalks and lack-lustre hue of the heather, far from ready to emerge from its winter dormancy, silence reigned, only the occasional raucous call from the moor birds.

Unpacking their snack, Ruth asked, "have you any history on this old cross, Jim?"

Jim bit into his sandwich. "Only what Albert told me. He says history and folklore seep out of every nook and cranny of these dales if you are prepared to listen and learn." Between mouthfuls he told Ruth that, where they sat, was the site of a bronze age burial mound thousands of years old and the original name for the cross was Ain, or One Cross but now known locally as Ana.

Ruth screwed her face up. "*Ugh,* I wish I'd chosen a more suitable place for our meal, Jim. I feel uncomfortable knowing we are on top of a burial site. It's not really showing respect for the dead, is it?"

"Not to worry, Ruth. I don't think it'll be bothering 'em underneath." The gap-toothed smile appeared. "After all, thousands of years have passed and some arche... archeol..."

"Archaeologist," Ruth offered.

"That's the word I was looking for," Jim said with relief. "I didn't even know how to pronounce it properly, Ruth."

"Maybe not, but you'll remember now," she said.

"Well, anyhow, they've all been excavated by now and most of the stuff will be in museums." Finishing the last of his sandwiches, he said, "oh, and a bit more information from Albert, he told me the cross was a marker stone for the monks trekking these moors from Lastingham to the Abbey at Roston." He stood and brushed himself down, feeling quite knowledgeable. "This isn't the original, though. All that's left of that one is the top of the cross and that's in the crypt of St Mary's at Lastingham, just over the hilltop there." He pointed down into the next valley. "So, that's your history lesson for today, Miss Schoolteacher."

Ruth felt a warm glow inside. "That makes me feel good, Jim, when I hear it out loud like that." She glanced up at the sky. The sun was beginning to dip and the clouds, scudding low on the horizon, were bringing a chill to the late afternoon.

Jim felt it as well. "Come on, Ruth, let's head back before dusk. We still have quite a bit to do."

"Okay, I suppose we should." Reluctantly, Ruth packed the saddlebags, mounted, and allowed the horses to amble steadily along on the way home. Jim was right, it was back to reality tomorrow. As the once vivid blue of the sky changed to grey, the dusk of the evening eased gently down just as they entered the velvety darkness of the wood. It felt surreal, as though the night itself was alive, tangible and could be reached out and touched.

"Careful as we go here, Ruth. This path has washed away badly this winter." The horses were occasionally losing their footing as the loose rocks slipped from beneath them on the steepest part of the descent. "You don't want to be using this on your own, it's getting dangerous. Maybe take the longer route from now on."

"Will do, Jim," she replied. But Ruth found this part of the ride exhilarating.

Laid well back in the saddle, transferring her weight to the rear, making it easier for the horse and feeling every muscular movement of the animal under her, picking its own path was a remarkable experience she never tired of. Night had certainly fallen quickly, so once back home, Ruth stabled the horses while Jim did the work in the yard.

Later that night, by the warmth of the fire, Ruth gathered her schoolbooks together ready for work in the morning while Jim sat at the table, catching up with bookwork. His grasp of dealing and business had always been apparent, part of his survival technique learnt at a young age. But it was learning to write that gave him the confidence to rise to the new challenge of responsibility. Ruth noticed him take the tattered old dictionary from the bookshelf, knowing he was checking the spelling of a certain word. She smiled to herself. If you want something badly enough, you will always find a way, she thought.

"There, that's invoices done for this month," he said, finally rising from his chair, rubbing his eyes. "I can understand why Albert hated it so much. If you could post these tomorrow, Ruth, that would be good."

"That's fine, Jim. I'll do that."

With the pressure, and pleasure, of the wedding over, the challenge of back to work loomed. Turning the lamp down low Jim came across and sat close, wrapping his arms about her. Ruth dare not let her mind dwell too deeply on her good fortune, as she well knew, happiness can sometimes be fleeting but, the worst of her childhood nightmares appeared to be over. And the future. Well, that was now in their own hands.

Although Jim was anxious about the decline of the mining, he didn't worry unduly as the building of Castle Moor church was about to start. The only problem was, with the wedding first and foremost on his mind, he'd forgotten to put his name forward. He just hoped he hadn't missed out.

The next day, while repairing the stable doors, Jim spied Jed Elcock walking along the lane. Well-known locally and, after retiring from shepherding, had spent many hours with Albert at Honey Bee over the years. A battered trilby, pulled well down over his shock of white hair, often hid his lined and weather-beaten features. His flapping coat, with a couple of poacher pockets sewn on the inside was tied around his waist by a piece of old rope. While chatting, Jim mentioned that his chance to lead stone for the new church may have gone.

Jed had settled on the mounting steps, his old black and white dog, Bob, nearly blind now, sat alongside. Grasping his shepherd's crook in gnarled and heavily veined hands, he said, "no need to worry on that score, Jim, your name's on the list." His eyes crinkled as he smiled. "I took the liberty of putting your name forward when those useless council feller's called round. I thought it'll be better for being on twice rather than not at all. Hope you didn't mind?"

"Mind, Jed. Not a bit, I appreciate it." Jim shook his head, kicking himself for almost missing out. "With so much going on, I'd forgotten."

"It could prove to be good earner for a year or two. You have the horses, the equipment, and the drive to make it work. All you want now is more than twenty-four hours in a day."

After a few more bits of local news, Jed made his way back to the village.

Later that night, Jim lay back on the pillow and whispered, "you awake, Ruth?"

Ruth answered but drowsily. "Yes, only just though. What is it?"

"Y'know this stone leading contract I was on about. If we get it, there could be mebbe a year's work ahead of us, on and off, if we're lucky."

Ruth raised herself up on one elbow and looked him straight in the eye. "Jim Styles, how can you talk about leading heaps of stone after such a tender, loving moment together?"

"Well, I just thought you might be interested."

"Well, I'm not," she got up on her knees, grabbed the pillow and, laughing, hit him over the head.

"Ow, ow, there's no need for that," he shouted, shielding his face, eventually grabbing her arms, and pulling her on top of him.

"God, I love it when you're angry." Holding her tight, they kissed.

10

Chapter 3

Albert and Martha's dining room sparkled with the many baubles and tinsel adorning the room. All ready for Christmas Day and as they were expecting guests for dinner, Albert had cut a small holly tree from the garden, placed it next to the fireplace and Martha had decorated it beautifully with candles and presents.

With heavy snowfall overnight, a pristine blanket of white covered the valley, broken only spasmodically by the dark, meandering lines of rough stone walls, hedges and the stark black silhouettes of trees following the line of the river. Mid-morning, the sun broke through and the billowing dark clouds receded leaving a clear blue sky. As the temperature eased, snow began its steady slide from the roof tops and the rows of icicles spearing down from the eaves like stalactites, sparkled and dripped before releasing their icy grip to fall silently into the soft cushion of snow.

Jim was just finishing feeding up in the buildings as Ruth put a bridle on Farmer and threw a blanket over his back. Putting fingers to her lips, a shrill whistle pierced the air. Nell ceased her rolling in the snow and came bounding to her side. "We're going now, Jim." A shout from within the stable. "You go on, Ruth. I'll be down later."

"Okay, don't be too long." Using the mounting steps, she leapt onto the great stallion's back. Although the sun was out, the cold was biting in the shade, stinging her cheeks and lips but this was no hardship to Ruth. A life without horses, or riding, would be unthinkable to her, always making her feel so alive. The ride down into Roston was magical. No one about. Everything so silent and still, as if the whole world had suddenly ground to a halt. At this moment, Ruth felt very special, as if her and Farmer were the only living beings on the planet, alone in this alien white world. Eventually, the spell was broken as she arrived in the village. On passing the Tavern, she was pleased to see the landlord wave a greeting. "Merry Christmas, Ruth."

"And to you, Mr Henton," She brought Farmer to a halt as the landlord wandered over.

"How are you and Jim keeping? I've not seen you for a while, young lady. We haven't upset you, have we?" There was always a twinkle in Tony's eyes when talking to the fairer sex. Ruth had finally plucked up courage to go for a drink with Jim occasionally and was now beginning to understand Tony's sense of humour.

"Goodness me, no," she said, laughing. "If you'd upset me, I would certainly have let you know, Mr Henton. You know how it is, work must come first."

"'Course it does. It's good to see you two making a go of it. You might have a hard year or two but you're young enough to stand it." Tony turned serious. "By the way, Jed told me the sheep stealing has kicked off again. Now, I know you haven't any sheep but high up where you are, it's a likely place to spot any strangers."

"Yes, Jim heard from Albert. I'm sure it's the food shortages. Everyone must eat."

Tony nodded. "I agree. The black market's a racket but there's nothing worse than hunger gnawing away inside you for changing one's opinion."

Ruth frowned. "Mm, don't I know it, Mr Henton. I'll never forget those days."

Tony studied her afresh for a moment. "It sounds as though you speak from experience, Ruth. I'm surprised, a fine figure of a woman like yourself."

She smiled at him. "Thank you for those kind words, Mr Henton. Well, surprised you may be but I certainly didn't have it easy as a young girl." She cast him a quick smile. "I'll shall bore you with it the next time we meet."

"I'll hold you to that, Ruth. But knowing you, that'll be never, cos you never have a minute to spare, do you?"

"No, I keep busy but we are in a good place to see anything suspicious as we have a good view of the open moor." Her face creased into a frown. "Do you think it could be dangerous, Mr Henton?" Ruth asked, as if for reassurance.

"There's no guarantee, Ruth. These hill farmers have it hard enough without thieving setting 'em back." He scratched his bald head in thought. "The general feeling is it's someone local, as any fresh waggoner would soon be recognized. The problem is, it 'll be done at night."

"Well, no chance of me catching them, Mr Henton as I'm usually tucked up in bed. I'm an early riser."

Tony chuckled and winked at her. "Ahh, yes, I forgot. You newlyweds like your sleep."

Ruth felt the colour rise in her cheeks, realising what she had said. "Whatever do you mean, Mr Henton?" With that, she gave him a cheeky grin, dug her heels in and rode off. "Bye, Mr Henton." Tony waved back and watched her go. It set him thinking about her childhood. That is one young lady he would never have guessed had come through difficult times.

Ruth enjoyed her chat with Tony and catching up with the local gossip. But now, she was looking forward to spending the day with the very ones who had helped set them on the right path.

Slinging Farmer's reins over the front fence where Albert and Martha lived, Ruth ran up the path, knocked and walked in, surprised to see the table set for seven, and the mouth-watering aroma that only a roast dinner can create, wafting in from the kitchen. "Merry Christmas, you two." Ruth flung her arms around Martha, then planted a kiss on Albert's bald spot as she was wont to do as he sat by the fire. "By, you're looking after yourself, Albert. I think Martha is spoiling you rotten."

Albert's face lit up. "Good to see you, Ruth. You're right, Martha is looking after me and we're so pleased the war is over. I know there'll be many heart-broken families across the land but all everyone can do is try and pick up the pieces of life and hope for peace in the future."

"As ever, you're right, Albert. When you're down, the only way is up. Jim's

13

on his way. I left him to do everything this morning. I couldn't wait to see you both, as things have been so busy. You two have been busy, as well, I see." She studied the decorations. "Who else are we expecting for dinner?"

Martha came in from the kitchen." Well, we thought, seeing as Robert and Esther have Nancy back from college, we could all have dinner together."

"That's brilliant, Martha. It'll make it special for us all. Can I help?"

"No, everything's under way, Ruth."

A sudden knock at the door and Jim poked his head in, brushing the snow off his boots on the step. "Come in, Jim. Happy Christmas to you." Martha said. Jim went over and hugged them both. "We're just waiting for the Lawson's to arrive." Another knock at the door as she spoke. "Ah, that'll be them. Come in, come in," she shouted. "Merry Christmas all. You've timed it just right." After exchanging presents, Martha disappeared into the kitchen and Ruth followed, bringing the roast turkey and all the trimmings onto the table. Afterwards they could barely move. Even Nancy, relaxed after such a feast, said, "I never realized, when I moved away, that I would miss home cooking so much, Mrs Styles. That dinner was beautiful."

"Thank you, Nancy. I'm glad you enjoyed it. Now, if you and Ruth will clear away, I'll put things back in their place, then we'll catch up with the news."

Once settled in the front room around a roaring log fire, Ruth mentioned her conversation with Tony Henton.

"How serious do you think this sheep stealing is, Albert?"

"Oh, it's serious enough, Ruth. Only a few at a time to start with but it is getting worse, especially this last year. Shortage of food and all that has brought it back. Rumour has it that it's someone local."

Jim asked, "Any ideas, Albert?"

Albert shook his head. "Not really, Jim. It'll happen at night and there 'll not be a policeman up there after dark."

"Now, don't you be getting involved, Jim." Robert spoke up, reading Jim's thoughts. "You have no sheep. It's not your problem."

"True enough but I think it's just youngsters, Robert. If it was on a bigger scale, that'd be different." In serious mood, he carried on. "If it's kids and we

14

catch 'em, then we might be able to set them straight, like Albert and Martha did for me when heading down that road." Smiling, he studied Robert. "I also think that you and Albert would see it the same way in days gone by. Am I right?"

They both nodded in agreement. "You're right, Jim. Age does make you more cautious."

With conversation light and lively, Nancy explained the excitement of her move to Leeds and the opportunities open to her since deciding to take her love of art further. Jim noticed she had also lost some of the flirtatious nature that he remembered. But, there again, time changes everybody.

While Albert and Robert reminisced, Ruth and Martha retired to the kitchen for a chat. She knew Martha had something on her mind but not sure what. Swinging the crane over the fire, Ruth casually asked about their health. "Aye well, I think Albert's beginning to feel his age a bit, Ruth."

Ruth smiled, trying to lighten the mood. "I think when the spring weather arrives, Martha, he'll be fine. A bit of gardening and if he feels like it, back to help around the yard."

Martha sighed. "I'm sure you're right, m' dear. Anyway, enough about us, how are you two coping with married life? You've had all of a month to have your first argument and then make up from it as well."

Ruth loved Martha's humour. "Yes, we've had a bit of adjusting to do but, fingers crossed, all's going well. Jim's heard of more contract work and Mr Haigh still needs me at school. I do owe him a lot for taking me on."

"The man's a good judge of character, Ruth. Knows when he has a good 'un."

Ruth smiled at the praise as Jim entered. "I've never eaten so much since last time I was here, Martha." He rubbed his stomach.

"Isn't she feeding you well enough, Jim. I'll have a word in her ear."

Saying goodbye to everyone, Jim made sure he jumped on Farmer first to return home as dusk fell. Farmer's tracks from mid-morning were obliterated by another snowfall that again muffled the sound of the big horse's hooves.

"What a lovely afternoon, Jim. Did you enjoy catching up with everyone?"

"Yeh, I did, but Albert appeared a bit under the weather. Mebbe worried about something."

"He didn't say?"

"No. He kept us all entertained with his yarns but sometimes lost track of the conversation. His intentions are still to come and help when the weather picks up."

Once back at Honey Bee, Ruth dismounted first. "I'll see to Farmer, then give you a hand feeding up?"

Dismounting, he grabbed her in his arms. "Yeh, that would be good. That'll leave us a full night to ourselves." Holding her at arms-length, he put his head on one side, a serious expression on his face. "Now, let me see, what do you think we can do later to help us through the long winter night."

Ruth returned his serious look, then pretending excitement, said, "I know, I have a pack of cards. We can play whist all night."

"Are you serious…" Jim appeared stunned until Ruth ran off laughing.

Chapter 4

1919 and a new year beckoned, free from the shackles and horrors of war. Survivors were on their way home, some to wives, families, and work. Others, the injured, shell-shocked, or worse may only find despair and sadness, unable to adjust into an ordinary, mundane world once again, their lives changed forever. One such man was Patrick Brennan, making his way back to the streets of York and the only shelter he knew, if it was still there, St Catherine's.

The streets were eerily silent, the bone-numbing cold preventing anyone from venturing out unless absolutely essential. As darkness crept in so did fatigue, into his very bones, as he trudged homeward. Wherever home was. He had no idea. So desperately tired, Patrick had nothing more to give, the biting cold draining every ounce of energy from his weary body. Lifting his head, he faced the stinging icy pellets of snow through half-closed eyes, hoping to God – if there was one – that some distinguishing features or buildings would enter his view. The city of York was huge and Patrick was only familiar with the deprived areas of the city and St Sampson's Square where he ran a market stall, before... Before what, Patrick thought. Before you took to drink. Before you lost your head, murdered your wife, went to gaol and lost your only daughter in the process. Before throwing your life, and everyone else's close to you, into chaos.

The driving snow, and his tears, were making it difficult to recognise anything but certain structures still standing were beginning to stir faint memories. Surely, he must be in Bishophill now, but with large areas razed to the ground, it was difficult to tell. So, the city had not escaped the violence of war. He tried not to think about it but he knew with the scale of the destruction around him, many must have suffered.

As further memories filtered into his mind, this spurred him to greater effort but his body was not responding. How much further. Every step, serious cramps tightened calf muscles, pain sliced up the back of his thighs and shoulders ached from the constant chafing of the kit bag slung on his back. It now felt like a ton weight. God knows how many miles he had walked. Why the hell couldn't they have allowed him to stop longer in the warm comfortable barracks? There was no one else clamouring to get in. The last couple of months had been the easiest of his life, just him and a dozen others left to clear up as the fighting men were shipped back home. Or those that were fit enough.

Fingering the few shillings left in his pocket, he gained a certain satisfaction from his determination not to spend them if it could be avoided. Unwashed, unshaven, and weak, due to lack of food, he had sustained some strength from the meagre offerings given by kind people along the way. After all, the war was finally over and the country overjoyed but communities still had their own families to feed.

Suddenly, his heart leapt. Could this be St Catherine's, looming out of the darkness ahead? Lifting a hand to shield his vision, relief swept over him, he'd finally made it. Back to the shelter that housed him in his hour of need. All he had left in this harsh, cruel world. After sleeping rough for more than a week, Patrick knew his journey was almost over. But then, self-doubt crept in. Would the shelter be open? Maybe the helpers had left, or passed on. No, surely not. Their names came back to him. Yes, Jenny. She was the fussy one. And the other, a jolly lady. What was her name? Come on, Patrick. Think, man, think. Phyllis. That was it, Phyllis, and the vicar, the Reverend Simmons. He allowed a smile, painful as it was through cracked and chapped lips but also quietly pleased with his powers of recall. Yes, it must surely be working, as there would be even more need for shelter and food after four long years of war.

His footsteps deadened by the snow, the gate swung open easily and he made his way through what used to be a well-kept graveyard but was now covered with spiralling drifts of snow. Rounding the corner, relief swept through his tired body. The wooden structure was still there and with dusk falling, slices of welcoming orange light spilled out through the badly fitting curtains at the windows like a beacon of hope.

Mustering his courage, he put his ear close to the door and heard voices inside. A gentle knock and the chatter from inside instantly stopped. Silence. Then the tap of footsteps gradually growing louder as someone approached the door. Slowly, it creaked open, lamp-light spilling out into the cold night air. Patrick instantly recognised the friendly face of Jenny, the lady who had done so much to help him the first time. Jenny was first to speak.

"Yes, can I help you?" she asked. Cautious, unsure, peering out from behind the door into the darkness. Why wouldn't she be. A stranger, knocking on the door at this time of night and only two women alone in the building.

"I hope you can, Jenny. It's Patrick Brennan, back from the war. Do you not remember me?"

The door creaked open a fraction more, the escaping light illuminating his gaunt, sunken features as she studied him more closely. A gasp of surprise as she recognised him. Grabbing both his hands she said, "Oh, goodness me, Patrick. Is it really you? No wonder I didn't recognise you. What a state you are in. Come in, come in. What are you doing outside on a night like this?" Finally, she stood back, unable to believe this forlorn figure of a man could be Patrick Brennan. She immediately sat him down in a chair before turning and shouting toward the kitchen. "Phyllis, put the kettle on, please? We have a visitor and it looks as if he could do with a few home comforts."

A few minutes passed and Phyllis paddled through with a cup of tea and biscuits on a plate and set them before him. "Well, well, well, Patrick, just look at you. What a sorry soul you are." Her face took on a worried look as she studied him. "But, at least, you're one of the survivors, m'dear. One of the lucky ones to return."

While he devoured the biscuits and tea, Patrick's dark eyes surveyed these kind, caring women before him, noting the sadness, or was it sympathy, in their eyes. "Thank you, ladies. I know I must appear in a terrible state to you both but with a good night's rest, I'm sure I'll be much better in the morning."

"Well, I'm sure you will, Patrick but," she turned to Phyllis, "have I to tell him, or do you want to?"

Phyllis smiled. "No, you tell him, Jen."

Laughing, she held her nose and said, "will you make sure to get washed before you go to bed or we'll have to fumigate the place."

"Does that mean you have a bed for me then?"

"Course there is." It was Jenny who answered. "It's a whole lot quieter now, Patrick. Many have not returned home." Her voice cracked with emotion. "My grandson was one who didn't make it back."

"I'm sorry, Jenny."

"No, it's okay, Patrick. Sometimes it helps to talk about such things. Just eighteen, he was. Wouldn't be told. Headstrong and wanted action. Well, he would certainly see that. Such a shame, all his life in front of him, like many others who have gone far too soon." Shaking her head, she looked away and dabbed at her eyes with a handkerchief. "One thing, Patrick, there'll be a better chance of work for you now as most of the country's workforce have been wiped out, or returned so badly injured, they're not capable of work."

Phyllis butted in. "Now come on, Jen. Let's have you out o' this morbid mood, or Patrick will be thinking the stormy night might be a better option after all."

"I'm sorry. I didn't mean to be morbid but sometimes it builds up in me and I just need to have a moan." She tried a smile in Patrick's direction.

He replied. "There's no need to be sorry, Jenny. I think the suffering seems to continue. We have all lost someone or something in this cruel world." He paused. "By the way, is there still just you two ladies running things and doing all the work around here?"

Phyllis answered. "Of course. What else would you expect from two stalwarts of the church. We are still the main ones." She looked him straight in the eye. "Just remember, Patrick Brennan, everything will run like clockwork, when Jen and I give the orders. Isn't that so, Jen? Even the vicar toes the line when we are here. This is our domain." A stout woman with a seemingly dominant attitude, but all part of her façade. The jovial features coupled with a wicked sense of humour meant she could never stay serious for long. And Phyllis didn't walk, she waddled, feet wide apart, as if on a ship's deck in a high storm, rocking from side to side. Patrick smiled, remembering that there was often more soup in the tray than the dish by the time it reached the customer if Phyllis was serving.

As Patrick reminisced, Phyllis continued talking. "You might find things strange to start with but you'll soon get the hang of it." Her advice was given with a smile of encouragement that lit her whole face.

Jenny noted Patrick's eyes were closing and was near exhaustion. He'd been polite long enough, now he needed sleep but first, hot water for a wash. "Right, it's time Patrick got some rest. The kettle's boiled for hot water, you know where your bed is, all clean and tidy. It is closing time and we must get back to our families." Jenny ran through and retrieved their coats, hoisting it onto Phyllis's shoulders for her. With gloves and headscarves on, Jenny ushered Phyllis out of the door. The snow had stopped and they ventured out into a bright starlit night.

"Mind how you go on a night like this, ladies," Patrick advised, adding, "I will thank you properly tomorrow after a good night's rest." Once on his own, Patrick undressed, used the rest of the hot water to wash and then clambered into bed. Heaven. A big sigh escaped his lips as he drifted into a deep sleep.

Chapter 5

Waking early, Patrick dressed quickly, not sure when anyone would arrive. He felt revived, almost human. While on his own, he searched the cabinets in the small kitchen and found a medicine box with pills and plasters in. He also found a tub of Vaseline for his cracked and painful lips. With no idea of the time, he began to acquaint himself with the workspace once again. Although still finding the cafe slightly claustrophobic, his experience of working the canteens during the war would prove useful and hoped the do-gooders respected his space. The years in prison had made him a loner. But, if it was quieter, as Jenny said, he could handle that.

Patrick was glad of his early start when the door suddenly burst open and in walked Jenny, an icy blast following in her wake. Wearing a thick, black coat, a woolly hat pulled low and a scarf coiled tightly up to her mouth, only her eyes and bright red cheeks were visible. Patrick smiled at the figure as she unwrapped herself after the walk in the early morning frost.

"Morning, Patrick." She saw his amusement. "Don't you dare laugh, Patrick. It is bitterly cold out there." Then she studied him. "Well, what a transformation from last night. Welcome back into the real world. We'll try and get those clothes washed today if we can."

"I'll do those tonight, Jenny. Have you any idea on the time?"

"Almost dinner time."

"Really?" Patrick shook his head in disbelief. "I must have slept like a log. I should be able to help you today, if needed, Jenny?"

"That's good, as Phyllis is off. It should only be steady, but I think we'll still be needed."

"As it proved last night."

She smiled. "Mmm, as you say, Patrick. As it proved last night."

It was certainly quieter but there were still many hungry and desperate people in need of a square meal. Over the next few months, Patrick kept telling himself this is not permanent, as he reverted to his role of doing the mundane job of drying pots and collecting plates. While doing so, Ruth was never far from his thoughts. Where would she be? Could she be married by now? It would be an impossibility to find her whereabouts after all this time.

But what if Guthrie was right? What if she did turn her back on him? She had every right to and he could not blame her. It was dark thoughts such as this that haunted him.

Patrick kept a tight rein on any religious views, as he knew just how necessary this kitchen was. For himself as well. People of all ages and origins shuffled in and out, all made welcome and provided with food, possibly their only meal of the day. When not washing and clearing pots, Patrick served on at the tables and noticed how many avoided eye contact. Ashamed. Unable to accept their circumstances, or the fact they could no longer fend for themselves. Patrick realized he was not the only one struggling to get a grip on life.

The canteen was a gift from a wealthy businessman, a regular churchgoer and on his death, his wife donated more money to St Catherine's to have it constructed into a usable building. Since Patrick's last spell of work here, when first out of prison, the interior had been brightly decorated and alterations made for a much better workspace.

The workforce, especially Jenny, did their utmost to help Patrick adjust to the real world again. He just wished they would hold back on the preaching and soul saving, as they often sidled over to share a table or a coffee with him. He listened patiently but remained non-committal at the end of the conversation.

But one particular lady, a regular on the staff known as Emmy, caught his attention. She had the boundless energy of a person half her age and her enthusiasm for life was infectious. For whatever reason, Thursday's were always quiet and Patrick was sat deep in thought with a coffee, when Emmy bounded across out of nowhere and drew a chair up. "Mind if I join you, Patrick?" He realized she had been waiting for this opportunity.

Not waiting for a refusal, Emmy jumped straight in. "Now, what are you looking so miserable about, young man?"

Patrick raised his head and stared into the direct, steely grey gaze of Emmy, studying him carefully. "Am I? I didn't realize I was, Emmy." He forced a smile. "I suppose when things are quiet, my mind wanders and I become melancholy." He tried to brighten up. "To be sure, it's better to be kept busy, don't you think?"

She ignored his attempt at small talk. "If you feel like talking, I'm a good listener."

Patrick thought Emmy must be seventy years old at least. Her long grey hair, tied in a bun at the back of her neck, accentuated the deep lines etched across her brow and she carried not an ounce of spare flesh on her bony body. Her eyes, sharp and set deep behind high cheekbones and pencil thin brows, missed nothing. The same could be said about her quick mind and humour. The regulars knew well enough that her tongue could cut like a whiplash and tear strips off anyone in a matter of seconds, the vicar, the helpers, the regulars, she favoured no one.

"Well, I'm not sure you can help, Emmy. It's family, you see?"

Her head tilted. "You think nobody else has a family, is that your problem, young man? You think 'cos I work here, I have no one?"

Patrick felt embarrassed. "No, no, not at all, I didn't mean that, Emmy. I just didn't want to bore you with my problems."

"No, you'll not bore me, Patrick and you are not the only one with problems either. Most of 'em who come in here, carry a load of baggage, up here." She pointed to her head. "Something you never see, all searching for what? Sympathy, salvation, a caring word?" She smiled. "A few just enter for a free meal." She took a sip of her coffee. "You know what keeps me sane?" Patrick had no time to answer as she carried on. "This place does. Don't look so worried, Patrick. I'm not here to convert you like the others but when you see the good work they are doing, it makes you think, doesn't it?" She held her head on one side again, this time waiting for a response. Nothing forthcoming from Patrick. "Hear my problems, then I'll listen to yours." Without pausing for breath, she related how her first husband died from a heart attack in his twenties leaving her with three young children to raise and no money. She married again, for security, but mistreatment followed. For the first time in her life she was frightened, terrified, and she fled with the children. Unable to support them, they were taken away and she had only the workhouse for shelter.

Emmy settled back in her chair. "I must be a poor judge of men, eh?" Then suddenly leaned forward again, defiant. "But I'm still here. Because I fought back, see."

His admiration rose for this hard as nails, feisty lady. So intrigued by her story, he had to ask the question. "What happened the children, Emmy?"

She smiled. Her face softened. "I found 'em again, Patrick. All of 'em. It took me a long time but I found 'em." She looked away before adding, "only I was too late for the youngest. I found her in the graveyard." A huge sigh escaped her lips. "But the other two keep in touch with me now and have made a life for themselves."

"Emmy, I'm sorry. I didn't mean to..."

"No, no need to be sorry, Patrick, I offered the information cos I've been studying you for a while and I know there is something bothering you that you can't lay to rest and I thought I might be able to help." She got up to go but Patrick reached for her hand.

"No, don't go, Emmy. You're right, there is something bothering me. Eating away inside me, dragging me down."

"Well, now's your chance, young man. Tell me."

Patrick hesitated, then in a low voice said, "I murdered my wife, Emmy. I've served my sentence and I should be free to carry on with my life but I don't think I shall ever escape the shackles of my crime." Tears clouded his

25

dark eyes but Emmy was not one for dishing out sympathy, or dwelling on the past.

"Well, I knew that. Everyone in here knows what you did but that isn't the problem, is it? There is something else eating away at you."

"I have a daughter."

"And?"

"I'm not sure I am strong enough to meet up with her. What I would do if she rejected me."

"Do you know where she is?"

"No, but we did have a neighbour who I tried to contact from prison," his head dropped, "but never received a reply."

"Where did you live, Patrick?"

"Lady Peckitts Yard. I'm not sure if they are still there. They could have been demolished by now."

"Well, for your information, young man, they have but I have it on good authority," she tapped the side of her nose and smiled, "that a few of the last residents found accommodation at Walmgate. You got a name to follow up?"

"I have. Molly Turner. It's possible she might still be alive."

"Well, there's your starting point, Patrick."

A prickle of excitement fizzed up his spine.

"What's wrong now? Are you one of these people who always find an excuse to put things off, because if you are, I've certainly read you wrong."

"No, it's not that, Emmy," it's the thought of rejection. I'm frightened of rejection. In my mind she is still just a nine-year-old girl, missing her father. In reality, she will be a grown woman in her early twenties with no need for a father. At present I can cling to the thought that she may still be hoping to meet up, missing me, still wanting to know me, even after all that has happened."

Silence for a while before Emmy spoke. "Is that it?"

"Yes."

Emmy placed a hand across her chest. "What do you feel in here, Patrick? What is in there?" She stabbed him in the chest with a bony finger. "That's the important bit. What is in that heart of yours, Patrick? I do not know you that well but I have never met anyone in my lifetime with a heart carved from stone and I do not think yours is."

Silence for a minute as Patrick searched for the words that had been on the edge of his lips many times. "I would like to find her again, Emmy. At least I would know."

"Then there is your answer, Patrick. You must try. If we don't try, then we don't do. And if we don't do, then we will always fall short in life. At least be man enough to try."

Patrick studied Emmy, took a sip from his now cold coffee, a smile spreading slowly across his features. "Thank you for your advice, Emmy. I appreciate it very much."

"What are you going to do, then? Sit here and sup coffee with old ladies, or get off your arse and make things happen?"

He stared at Emmy and his face crinkled. Then he laughed. A real laugh. The first one, he realized, to leave his mouth in years. God, he felt a warmth for this forthright lady. So direct, there were no grey areas in Emmy's life. Black and white. Tell it as it is. With a smile still on his face, he said, "I promise you, Emmy, I will get off my arse and make it happen."

"That was the answer I expected from you, Patrick." They rose from the table together and they hugged. "You can do it, young man. Be brave and when we meet up again you can explain the outcome." Emmy turned and carried on with her work.

Chapter 6

T he ever-optimistic Emmy had motivated Patrick and as the year
wore on, his search for Molly began in earnest. The memories
of that fateful day were still vivid in his mind and, even now, he
rubbed at his wrists, as if experiencing the tightness of the cuffs once again.
He remembered Molly taking charge and dragging a screaming child, his
child, Ruth, away from it all, shielding the child's eyes from the morbid scene.
Patrick closed his eyes but not before the tears of remorse broke free and
trickled down his cheeks.

This was when he was thankful for the privacy that his own small room
offered, allowing him to weep alone and unashamedly. But a whole river of
tears could not change the past. It was time to be brave and move forward.

As the grey light of dawn broke, Patrick wandered into the kitchen area and
boiled the kettle for his breakfast. While at the table he made plans. Usually,
he didn't take a day off as he had nowhere to go. No friends, or relatives,
his only acquaintances, the ones he worked alongside in this shelter. So, he
would make the most of his time today. The Walmgate area of York was not
far away, within walking distance for him and his heart rate quickened as
he realized what he was about to do. After shaving and smartening himself
up, the time had come to face the outside world.

The click of the door heralded the arrival of Jenny for the first shift. She
breezed in, surprised to see Patrick looking quite respectable for once.

"My goodness, Patrick, you are looking very smart. Am I allowed to ask what the special occasion is, or not?"

Patrick was slightly embarrassed. No one had ever commented on his appearance. "Of course you can, Jenny, it's no big deal. I've decided to use my day off to go for a walk and try to adapt to that big wide world out there."

"Well, good for you. It's time you picked yourself up and got out more. Get well wrapped up because it's a bright enough morning but very cold."

"Thanks, Jenny. Don't work too hard. I'll see you all later, 'Bye."

"Bye, Patrick, I'll put your soup to one side."

"Thank you." A smile and a sly wink from him brought a hint of colour to Jenny's cheeks. But, on second thoughts, it may just have been the morning chill.

Jenny was right, the cold did bite but turning his coat collar up and walking at a good pace soon got his circulation going. The streets were busier than he expected and the cabs appeared to rattle past at an alarming rate. Patrick tried to concentrate on his options, a visit to his former home had to be first on the list. If he could face this, the rest of his tasks should prove easier.

But he had not allowed for the memories as every sight, sound, and smell, all quickened his heartrate. Finally, he entered the marketplace, almost on the exact patch where his stall once stood. Images, vivid and real, flashed before his eyes. The Salvation Army preachers, the customers that frequented his stall, Ruth and her friend helping him on Saturdays.

Without warning, his legs buckled, the buildings and the people milling the market square were unreal, untouchable. He grasped a wall to prevent himself falling and a hand reached under his arm and led him to a seat.

"You okay, mister?" Patrick tried to focus on the blurry figure in front of him.

"Yes, I'll be fine now, I think."

"Bit early in the day to be drunk, isn't it?

"No, I'm not drunk. It's just a dizzy spell. It'll pass, I'm sure."

The young man shouted for someone to bring a drink over. A few seconds past and a glass of water was thrust at him. Patrick sipped it steadily and, eventually, the world gradually returned to normal.

"Thank you for your help. I used to trade here when I was younger and I think the nostalgia got to me." He tried to smile.

"Okay, you just sit a while longer till you feel up to it," said the youth and hurried off. A few minutes later, Patrick handed the glass back to the trader and went on his way, unsure of his strength to see this through. But Emmy's words rang in his ears, "if we don't try." Surely, he must try or he would never dare face her again. Or himself.

With much more resolve, he headed to where the rows of brick terraced houses once stood. A bare, barren expanse of land faced him, weeds growing through the mountains of rubble, heaps of bricks piled high alongside. Nothing left but the architectural elegance of the surrounding houses of Sir Thomas Herbert's and Lady Peckitts mansions.

Patrick caught up with a stooped, elderly man, walking slowly, relying heavily on his walking stick and asked him for information on the people who once lived here and if they had been rehoused.

"Not all were rehoused, young 'un. I wasn't. I had to find lodgings for a while. There was a site built a few years ago but some of us missed out.

"You lived here then?" This was a stroke of luck, Patrick thought, his spirits lifting.

"Only the last few years before they pulled 'em down. Moved in to look after my brother."

"Do you remember anyone who lived in Peckitts Yard?"

"I knew a few by sight but I didn't mix much. Some from that row went to Walmgate. Who are you searching for, mister?"

"I'm looking for a Molly Turner. She was my next-door neighbour a long time ago."

"Ah, I can see your problem." He nodded his head, understanding. "Well, you've got a fair old task on your hands but I think Walmgate 'll be your best bet. Good luck, young 'un." With that, he waved goodbye and tottered steadily away.

"Thank you. That's a big help."

Knowing the area well, he made his way through the narrow streets but, once again the hopelessness of finding an old lady who might, or might not, still be alive was enormous.

These streets were relatively quiet just before midday and he was wishing he'd packed a sandwich as he settled on a bench to think. While sat staring at the ground, a pair of scruffy, hob-nailed boots, tied with string, came into his vision. Slowly raising his head, a mass of matted, curly brown hair confronted him. But underneath this unruly mass of curls, was a young girl with a pair of the widest round eyes he had ever seen and she was studying him seriously.

She spoke in a very matter of fact way. "Need any help, mister, 'cos we can help?"

Patrick studied her closer. Her dress was no better than rags, her green woollen cardigan hung almost to her knees. Her face, or the bit he could see through the tangle of hair, was pale and smudged with dirt but those big, brown eyes held his with a confidence he would have been proud to possess.

Eventually, he said, "No, I don't think so, young lady." But, if nothing else, the girl was persistent and when she spoke again, Patrick began to have second thoughts.

"There isn't just me you know. Me two brothers are just round the corner. We live here. We can take you to wherever you want to go."

Patrick remembered the homeless kids from his market days. Most were streetwise and knew every trick going. A smile broke across his face. "You live here, do you?"

"Well, pretty close anyway."

"You know the area?"

"Yep. Every inch, mister."

I bet you do, he thought. "Well, I believe you know the area but what about the people who live here?"

"I know most of 'em."

"Do you know if a Molly Turner lives here? She moved here before Lady Peckitts Yard was demolished."

"Might do."

"What's your name?"

"Libby."

"What will it cost me to find out, Libby?"

"A shilling." This one certainly knew the ropes.

Patrick fished in his pocket and produced a shilling, glad he hadn't spent it on his dinner. "This is yours when you tell me where Molly lives. If you know, that is?"

Libby's eyes lit up and made a grab for it but Patrick was quicker.

"Not so fast young lady. Payment on delivery."

Annoyed that Patrick had beaten her, she put a couple of fingers to her lips and a piercing whistle rang out. Within seconds a couple of boys, maybe ten or eleven years old, or thereabouts, it was bad to tell, came to stand with the girl.

"Promise not to move, mister," she pointed a finger at him, "'cos we have to go to work see and we don't like working for nuffink."

"I promise I'll sit right here while you carry out your investigation."

"I don't know what that word means, but we're not doing anything else for you, just find out where she lives."

Patrick laughed out loud. "I understand, Libby."

Libby instantly ordered the two boys on which houses to go to and they ran off, 'hobnailed boots clattering out along the cobbled street, with Libby shouting over her shoulder. "Don't you dare move, mister. We won't be long."

Chapter 7

Patrick stuck to his word, never moving from the bench, although the cold began to eat into his bones. Twenty minutes passed before the clatter of feet returned. Red-faced and panting, but faces beaming through the grime, Libby spoke first. "Got yer' her address and she's still alive. Pete remembered a girl calling there. She was on horseback, wasn't she, Pete?"

"Yeh. Lovely horse. I found a stable for her and she let me hold the horse for a while, an' I remember her name as well as the name of the old lady she was looking for." Pete was top dog at present.

"Clever lad, our Pete. That's why it didn't take us long, see."

They were all proud as punch at a job well done. Libby held her hand out. "Can I have the shilling now? You promised."

"You certainly can, you've earned it but first, you'll have to show me the way. Will you do that?"

"'Course we will. Come on." Pete, now the leader of this unlikely set of juvenile detectives, led the way.

"Why are you kids not at school during the week?" Patrick asked as they urged him to hurry up as they had other fings to do.

Pete laughed. "You must be joking, mister. School's not for the likes of us, we makes our own way."

"Did you say you remember the girl's name who came to visit Molly Turner,

Pete?"

"Sure I do." Pete shot a quick glance at Libby.

Libby held her hand out. "The shilling, mister."

These kids had learnt their trade well, Patrick could see they were not backward in their dealings and handed the money over. They were now outside number two, Walmgate.

"Tell him, Pete."

"It were Ruth Brennan. She was nice, a real knockout to look at." He rolled his eyes and smiled at the memory. Also, he was one up on his siblings, if they were siblings.

The name hit Patrick like a kick in the stomach. He hung onto Libby to stop himself falling and they all helped him sit down on a garden wall, his face a ghastly white. Libby knelt in front of him peering up with a worried face at him. "You okay, mister? You're not gonna die on us, are ye'?"

"No, I'm not going to die, Libby. It was just a shock when I heard her name mentioned.

"Whose? Moll or Ruth Brennan?" Pete was asking now.

"Ruth Brennan." He paused and lifted his gaze to the youngsters. "You see, Ruth Brennan is my daughter." Their mouths dropped open and all three gaped at him in astonishment.

Pete was first to speak. "You're having us on, mister. Tell us you're joking."

"It's no joke, kids. My name is Patrick Brennan and I haven't seen my daughter since she was your age. This is why I am searching for Molly Turner, to find out where my daughter is living. I want to see her again so much." Then the tears came. Libby held his hand and Pete pulled a rag from his pocket and placed it gently in Patrick's other hand.

"Why haven't you seen her, Mr Brennan?" And while crouched and sat around him on that garden wall, Patrick Brennan told these three children, strangers before today, his heart-breaking story and by the time he'd finished, all three had tears in their eyes. In fact, Pete was sobbing so much, he asked Patrick for his bit of rag back.

They sat in silence for a few minutes, Pete eventually speaking up. "You know, Mr Brennan, Ruth, your daughter, she is nice, really nice. I don't mean just a good looker. I mean, you know, a really nice person. When she talked to me. I could tell." He nodded sagely as if he was a very good judge of people's character. Maybe he was. Libby offered Patrick his shilling back. He declined.

"No, you have more than earned it, kids. Now, have you all got parents to go home to or do you live at the orphanage.

"No, we're mostly in the workhouse, we don't know where our parents are." It was Libby, wide eyed again and inquisitive as ever. "D'you think our parents might be looking for us, Mr Brennan, like you're searching for Ruth?"

"I think there is every chance, Libby, because parents never stop loving their children but, sometimes things happen to upset life's dreams. So, remember, you must never give up hope and never stop believing." Patrick raised himself from the wall. "Now, I may never meet up with you three again but I want you to know you have given me new hope and, without you, I may have wandered these streets for ever in search of information about my daughter."

With the colour back in his cheeks and three grubby but smiling faces in front of him, Patrick shook their hands one by one before saying. "Now, I have taken up too much of your time, I think you should all go and find others who will also benefit from your local knowledge and, who knows, maybe even earn more money. Goodbye all of you."

"Bye, Mr Brennan." He watched as they disappeared from view. Suddenly, the door opened behind him but it was not Molly Turner, as he expected.

He stared at the old lady, a total stranger. There was also no recognition on her part. Plump, hair in curlers, wrap around pinny and still in carpet slippers, she stood on the doorstep, returning his stare. When she spoke her voice was harsh, making it clear she did not want anyone hanging around her front door. "What are you doin' mister? I've been watching you for the last couple of hours. And those kids? What are they up to? Nothin' worth pinching round here, you know."

"No, we're not pinching, the kids were helping me find someone, a Molly Turner. I used to know her a long time ago, when she lived at her old home but I heard they were demolished."

"That's right. Nothing left." Her voice was softening, not quite as defensive. "Y'know Molly, eh? What's your name?" Still cautious, making sure, before admitting anything to this stranger stood on her doorstep.

"Brennan. Patrick Brennan." Patrick eyed her carefully, well knowing what the reaction would be. He was right. The round face paled, a hand shooting to her mouth, barely in time to stifle the gasp of shock. "Oh my God." Taken completely off guard, Dot suddenly looked frightened but then, at the end of the street, she spied the unmistakable figure of Moll Turner walking steadily in their direction.

Patrick, unsurprised by Dot's reaction, followed her gaze and recognized Molly as she shuffled nearer. "So, she does live here then and, no doubt, you know what happened."

Dot could only nod her head and greatly relieved when Moll finally arrived. "You pop inside Dot, I'll take over from here." Dot gladly disappeared inside and Moll seated herself on the low garden wall. With Patrick offering no conversation, it fell upon Moll to break the ice.

"How long have you been out, Patrick?"

"A long time now, Molly. St Catherine's took me in and gave me shelter until I could find work. It was impossible with my prison record, no one was prepared to take a chance on me. So, I went to war."

Molly's eyes widened. "You've bin through the war, Patrick. Oh, dear God. How did you ever survive? So many dead. Some so badly injured it would've bin better if the good Lord had taken 'em."

"To be honest, Moll, I had it easy, assigned to the kitchens. Only went near the front line when the officers complained and gave orders to set up camp closer to the action." Patrick's head dropped and his voice lowered as he remembered. "What those men suffered is indescribable."

There was silence between them for a while, each lost in their own thoughts before Molly returned to the present.

"I heard they had a shelter there quite some time ago. You see, Patrick, I try to go to the graveyard every couple o' weeks."

Patrick stayed silent.

Moll gave him a questioning look. "You're not going to ask me what I'm doin' there, or whose grave I'm visiting?" She kept her gaze upon him, waiting for a reaction. Patrick's head stayed down, unable to meet her eyes. Molly gave Patrick enough time to answer. He remained quiet.

"Well, if you think I'm going to sit here and make small talk all day, you're mistaken." She began to raise herself off the low wall but Patrick took her arm and asked her to stay.

He finally found words, whether they were the right ones or not, he wasn't sure. But he was talking. Ready to talk about the dreadful past.

"Yes, I want to know, Molly." He paused, his voice shaking slightly. "But I already know the answer. It is Sarah's grave, isn't it?"

"Yes, and it's only right you should know. Have you visited her grave since you've been out?"

"No, this is the first knowledge I've had of where she was laid to rest."

"It's strange but I had a feeling we might meet again at some point. I've been expecting a knock at the door for a while now, Patrick. How did you find me?"

"The kids are helpful round these parts, Moll. You should know that."

"I do. They're not a bad lot really, you know but they just don't stand a chance. No sort of a start for 'em, is it?" She looked directly into those dark sharp eyes and saw the hurt there.

"You mean when parents like me destroy their lives with violence."

"I'm sorry, Patrick but it's true. It messes everyone's life up."

"I thought after the long, painful years in prison, I knew I would never be free of the awful burden of guilt but I did hope that it might ease." A deep sigh escaped his lip. "Not so, I realize it will be with me until the day I die, Moll. My conscience will never allow me to forget."

"No, you'll not forget and those close to you will never forget. What happened will never ever be put right by a jail sentence, or anything else. It is something that you can only learn to live with and try and make things better for the future."

"I suppose that is why I'm here, Moll. You see, my thoughts were that you might know where Ruth is. I'm not sure it's the right thing to do but I've made the decision to try and find her."

"You think finding Ruth will help?"

"I'm not sure, Moll but it may give me a chance to find some sort of peace and come to terms with what I did."

Moll stayed silent for a while before easing her limbs up off the wall before she stiffened up altogether. "I know where Ruth is, Patrick." She chose her next words carefully, not sure how much information to give him. Eventually, feeling those, dark, inquisitive eyes upon her, she said, "Ruth is alive and well but I am not prepared to tell you where without first asking her permission." She paused, closing her eyes in thought, then said, "now, this is what I'll do. I'll write to Ruth, tell her you've been in touch and you would like to meet. I will ask for a reply and then bring you the letter. How does that sound?"

"Thank you, Moll. That sounds very good and fair. You know where I lay my head on a night. I'm never far away from the church."

After bidding goodbye to Patrick, Molly watched the retreating figure until out of sight. With a big sigh, she returned inside to a cup of tea waiting on the small table beside her favourite chair. Dot poured a cup for herself and, once settled, wanted to know everything about the meeting.

Molly told her everything, that she would write to Ruth, wait for her reply, then take it straight to Patrick. That way, it was entirely Ruth's decision.

Once Molly had finished, Dot sat quietly, brow furrowed, deep in thought before answering, as if weighing things up in her own mind, then the usual jovial attitude from Dot broke through. "Well, I think you are doing right, Moll It has to be Ruth's decision."

"I'm pleased you think so, Dot?" Molly looked relieved to have back up from such a close friend. "I didn't think it right to let on where she was living. You know, that girl has grown into a fine young woman." She shook her head as she remembered the screaming child being carried away by the policeman. "It just goes to show, Dot, that however bad things are, if you work at it there is always a ray of hope. Ruth is living proof of that."

"She seems a determined character, let's hope she makes the right decision." The smile was back on Dot's face. "It's quite exciting, really, Moll. What do you think she'll do?"

"Well, as you say, she's determined and she did tell me there was nothing in her heart for Patrick, but if they do not meet, I don't think Ruth could live with the knowledge of never knowing what happened in Patrick's life after gaining his freedom." Moll finished her tea. "Now, neither of us can decide for her, can we? So, I must settle myself down and write a letter."

Chapter 8

The Reverent Jacob Thrall returned from his church service in subdued mood, a frown creasing his brow. He was worried. The congregation were dwindling. Could it be the weather? Himself maybe? Had he stayed too long and lost touch? Maybe time for new blood? It could be any number of things. He realized age was not on his side but there were many preachers much older still going strong.

With the fire already laid, the flames took hold easily and he sat quietly in front of the flickering glow, remembering the prophetic words uttered to him by Ruth when Josh stormed out. "Love does not die, Jacob. It only lies dormant for a while." Those words proved to be true, Josh finally making his dramatic return home in time to be best man at Ruth and Jim's wedding. As he had promised.

Injured but alive, he, and others like him, had experienced suffering that no human being should ever be witness to, scenes that would haunt him for the rest of his life. His decision to sign up and fight stemmed from learning Freda, his first love, was Jacob's daughter, Jacob finally admitting to an affair with Freda's mother. Initially devastated by the news, Josh decided to break free from the daily grind of hard work and poverty, to experience adventure and excitement in his life before it was too late. Well, he'd certainly achieved that but had never found another love like Freda.

As the mining industry at Roston continued its decline, so too did Gallows

Howe as trade fell, but new business ventures were creating more job opportunities, especially at Castle Moor. Stone on the high moor was found to be of a much harder quality and, once crushed, produced silica and was soon in big demand for furnaces, mouldings, iron and much more. It was not building quality, far too hard for that. The alteration to the old building close to the railway were already under way and work on the construction of the incline plunging down the moor side was clear and visible for miles around. Josh, living in a small rented cottage at the base of the village with a couple of workmates were in full time work there and, for the first time in his life, the jingle of money in his pocket put a smile on his face.

This appeared to be the final nail hammered into the heart of what used to be Gallows Howe, its former glory now just a ghost of a past age. Why, only a matter of a few years ago, a breed of lively youngsters were coming and going at all times of the day and night and when things were busy, there young coltish enthusiasm inspired him and those around him. But those days were gone, along with the horse trade, which was almost non-existent. Pal and Danny were still stabled there but that was it, as usually, Ruth needed the little Cob for work.

But Toby never missed a day exercising Pal, usually early mornings as he was in full time work. When Jacob had last seen his friend, Len Bailes, a retired farmer from Castle Moor, he'd answered, "I'm getting too old for work now, Jacob. I can't even manage a walk up to the old buildings. Sad, isn't it?" Jacob had to agree with him. He realized the lifeblood of the hamlet had disappeared. So taken up with his church and the aftermath of the war, the years had rolled by without him noticing. He realized he must be approaching his eightieth birthday. Surely that couldn't be right. He checked his maths again. Yes, it was right. He shook his head in disbelief and suddenly felt old. Morose and brooding with the eerie quietness creeping in around him, he retired to bed early, with not even enough enthusiasm to read.

The very next day he spent at the church, arriving back later than intended. A letter lay on the doormat, the one he was expecting from the diocese. Stooping, he picked it up, wandered over to the fireplace and kicked his shoes off. Settling in his chair, he removed his collar for comfort and started to read. Skimming over the first part, the last few lines hit him hard.

I can confirm that the building of the new church will go ahead on the chosen site at Castle Moor. Oh, and by the way, have you thought of retirement?

Well, no, he hadn't. But he was seriously thinking about it now. Did he have the energy needed to take over a new church at his age? Could he face the upheaval of a move to the village? Gallows Howe was his home. Too many ties and memories floated around the old place. The thought of leaving filled him with dread. But things were changing, even the sturdy oak and stone-built gallows had finally reached the end of the road, destroyed in the last storm. Only the stone foundations remained, reaching out of the ground as a reminder but no longer sending a sombre message across the moor to wrong doers. Also, very soon, the bell from the tower would peel for the very last time across the dale.

Tears misted his vision as he glanced towards the old timepiece on the shelf. Only seven o clock. Too soon for bed. Picking up a book, he began to read. After only a few minutes the words blurred into each other. He blinked and wiped his eyes, trying to clear his vision without success, so closed his eyes, hoping the rest would help clear them.

When the book dropped from his lap with a thud, it startled him awake. The fire had long since burnt out. Cold and stiff, he could not believe he'd dropped to sleep but, thankfully, the nap had cleared his vision. It was only tiredness. Rising steadily from the chair, he washed the few pots in the sink and decided on a sandwich before bed. Age was definitely catching up with him but it shocked him just how quick. Why, it seemed no time at all since Ruth arrived here as a young girl? Now she is grown up, married, and moved out.

Jacob understood everyone's time comes eventually; he preached it every Sunday. Even Methuselah, who had a good run, had to admit he was mortal and finally succumbed.

Jacob smiled at the thought, throwing another log on the fire creating a shower of sparks, before sitting down to eat his sandwich.

Chapter 9

The large brass bell rang loud and clear across the school playground, heralding the start of the school day and, for once, the children were relieved to be inside, cheeks cherry red from the early morning frost. The warmth hit them on entry, as Freda had lit the pot-bellied stove earlier. Once the children hung their coats up, Mr Haigh rattled through registration and, with no absentees, he addressed the pupils.

"Children, we have a very important visitor calling today. A Mr Jocylyn Dymock." Addressing both classes Mr Haigh strode between the lines of pupils with great authority, befitting his position as Headmaster. "He will explain the ongoing work at the new stone quarry at Castle Moor, which, I must say, is a very exciting project." He watched for a reaction but they appeared to be in their own small world, his words met with a few sniffles, a gormless stare into space, or utter silence.

He sighed inwardly. He did not expect hand clapping, or cheering but he had, at least expected a little more enthusiasm than this. If it had been someone from the realms of football or cricket, no doubt they would be jumping for joy and cheering from the rafters. Work issues did not ignite any sort of spark in them at all. He ploughed on regardless, but also realised a careful choice of words was necessary as many had suffered great personal losses due to the war.

"Now, this project is a fantastic opportunity for our community and Mr

Dymock will arrive and explain the advantages for this area." He studied the lines of bored faces. "Any questions?"

A hand shot up. Johnny Miller, from Castle Moor; twelve years old, with a shock of ginger hair and freckles to match, asked, "Will it mean more work for everyone, sir?"

"Not quite everyone, Johnny, but there will be opportunities for some and, possibly long-term employment for others. Why do you ask?"

"Well, I aim o' leaving school in a year's time and there might be a job going for me."

Mr Haigh sighed again. It was not the response he was expecting but, at least it was a response. "Yes, I like your positive attitude, Johnny, but you must understand, education must come first, then employment is easier to find."

"If you say so, sir."

"I do say so. Any more questions?"

"Yes, sir."

"Yes, Dennis."

"Will there be a job for me dad, sir?"

"Is he injured, Dennis?"

"Yes sir, his leg was blown off just above the knee." Dennis held his leg out to demonstrate the extent of his father's injury. He screwed his face up. "*Ugh*, I saw it when he took the bandages off. It looks a real mess, all blood and..."

"That's enough explanation, Dennis. Yes, I am sure it does. There are many who have suffered life affecting injuries but it is possible there could be office work of some kind."

Dennis shook his head vigorously from side to side. "I don't think so, sir."

"Why do you say that, Dennis?"

"Well, he can't read or write, sir." The class giggled.

Mr Haigh was stumped for an answer to the young boy but Ruth spoke up.

"Would you allow me to answer this one, sir?"

Relieved, Mr Haigh stepped back. "Of course, Ruth."

Ruth walked to the front of the class. "When I was a young girl, Dennis, I was very lucky and had good teachers who taught me to read and write. My English teacher told me to learn a good command of the English language and this will help you through life. So, I listened and learnt all I could. Later, at the orphanage, I met a boy who never had that chance but, over the years, with hard work, he learnt and now runs his own business." Ruth had their attention now. "It is never too late to learn, that is true, but it is much easier when young." She then spoke directly to Dennis. "If your father is willing to learn, I am sure I could help."

"You mean you'd do that for him, miss?"

"I would, Dennis."

"I'll tell him. Thank you, miss."

Mr Haigh took over. "Next question."

Olive stood up. "Were you really in an orphanage, miss?"

"Yes, Olive and the teaching was very bad."

"Will you tell us about it, miss?"

"One day, I will, Olive, I promise."

"Thank you, miss."

Another hand was raised.

"Yes, Harold?" Mr Haigh answered. Harold lived at Millberry Hall. A grand sounding name, conjuring up visions of a great mansion set within its own landscaped gardens. Not so, it was a ramshackle, rubble-built cottage, two up, two down, surrounded by a couple of fields above Park Wood, a forest where the Kings of the past once hunted deer. It was a good mile walk for Harold, come rain or shine, across the moor to school.

"Who will be taking us for English today, sir?"

Ruth stood alongside Mr Haigh. "It will be Miss Styles today, Harold."

A cheer went up from her class. As they filed out, Mr Haigh smiled at her. "I don't know how you do it, Ruth but you certainly relate well to the children."

She answered and her smile was bright. "Thank you, sir. But my learning has come from yourself these last few years. Also, the children are very keen to learn which is a big plus." With a scraping of chairs and chatter, the children took their seats in the next room. Ruth had her hand on the doorknob ready to enter and quieten them when she turned, grabbing the chance to question Mr Haigh about the visitor. "Sir, when Mr Dymock calls today, how should I address him. You see, I've only ever met one titled person, that was Judge John Durville, who helped me in my younger days. Never having met gentry before, I don't want to embarrass myself, or let you down."

"Ruth, you will not let anyone down. If you address him as Sir, or Mr Dymock, that will be adequate. Now, it is time for you to keep those rowdy youngsters in check."

"Thank you, sir. I will."

Mr Haigh hesitated, waiting as she entered her classroom. The chatter died instantly with never a word uttered. He shook his head, as he now had the task of bringing his classroom to order. The morning flew by and at the sound of the dinner bell, the children filed into where the wooden forms and dinner tables were set. Dinner was eaten quickly, as always, and Ruth was about to usher the children outside for playtime when a commotion outside caught her attention. A quick look out of the window revealed a gleaming motor, chauffer driven, just easing away from the school gates and a smartly dressed gentleman striding swiftly across the playground. "Oh, no, what a time to arrive. The children will not be happy at this."

"Please sit still a moment, children. We have a visitor."

"But it's break time, miss."

"I know it is but this is a very important visitor." Groans and mumbling all round.

A knock at the door and Mr Haigh answered. "Come in, Mr Dymock." They shook hands. "We were expecting you. The children are very much looking forward to meeting you." They walked through to where Mr Haigh's class were seated.

Opening the dividing door between the classrooms, Ruth brought the two classes together. Once all were settled, Mr Haigh did the introductions. "This is my assistant teacher, Mrs Ruth Styles."

"Hello, Mr Dymock."

"Hello, Mrs Styles. His eyes immediately locked on hers, holding them a moment longer than Ruth deemed necessary. Her heart suddenly missed a beat, Mr Haigh saving the day by introducing Jocylyn to the children.

"Children, I would like you to meet, Mr Dymock."

"Good afternoon, sir. "All in unison. Mr Haigh beamed. What a splendid start. Clearing his throat, he carried on. "Mr Dymock will explain his new quarry project and what it will mean to the community. Please remain quiet while he is talking."

"Thank you, Mr Haigh." Jocylyn launched into a well-rehearsed speech, his voice clear and articulate, and while he talked, Ruth tried to focus on what he was saying but her thoughts began to stray. The word handsome did not do him justice. He had removed his hat on entrance to reveal long dark hair swept neatly back behind his ears. He stood tall and erect, dwarfing Mr Haigh by several inches and not an ounce of spare flesh on his body. Jawline was strong and those dark eyes, and voice, were now holding the children spellbound, as it did Ruth. The well-tailored suit, dark in colour, gold cufflinks sparkling at his wrists and an immaculate cravat at his throat finished the image perfectly. Suddenly, Ruth realized, he'd stopped talking and was staring at her. She had missed something. Colouring slightly, she apologised.

He spoke, his voice cultured but easy to listen to. "No need to apologise, Mrs Styles. I was saying," a smile playing about his lips, "that you have a very well-behaved class here. A credit to you both. It is not easy to keep a child's mind occupied but they have behaved impeccably. Thank you so much for allowing me this time with them."

Mr Haigh said. "Well, I must admit they have been on their best behaviour but your talk was very intriguing. Thank you for your time, Mr Dymock."

Shaking hands, Jocylyn said, "I really am impressed with your educational skills, Mr Haigh. I hope to see you again in the future, possibly for good, reliable workers in the coming weeks." With that, he sauntered over to where Ruth sat. She rose and he raised her hand and brushed it against his lips. A shiver of excitement swept through her. "Mrs Styles, I have to say this was a most pleasurable afternoon for me and I am sure our paths will cross again," pausing slightly, then adding, "before too long, I hope." The dark eyes bewitched her once again. He bowed low, then left the room, the car already waiting for him.

The children brought her back to reality. "Can we go outside, Miss?"

Gaining her composure, she said, "of course you can. Mr Haigh, is it possible to let the children have a longer break than normal? They were very good, weren't they?"

Mr Haigh breathed a sigh of relief. "Exceptionally good, Ruth, they did us proud. Also thank you for your help with Mr Dymock. I believe he took a shine to you. He is a real charmer, isn't he? You see, I have always said that is what a good education can do for a person, Ruth."

"Yes, education does help, Mr Haigh, but the silver spoon in the mouth is quite a big step up the ladder, don't you think?"

He allowed himself a smile. "You are a very perceptive person, Ruth. You also have a way with words." Pulling his pocket watch from his waistcoat pocket, he studied it, then said, "come along Ruth, we just have time for a quick cup of tea before the children come back in."

Chapter 10

W hat with schoolwork, the farm, and trying to keep Jacob's house in order, Ruth felt a sense of guilt at neglecting Dan Parkes and decided to call and explain her predicament. Riding home from school she descended the rough track to the cottage and caught Dan feeding Dulcie. As soon as she dismounted, Nip ran to her, tongue hanging out, ready to be stroked and Dan's face lit up. "Hey, Ruth, where have you been lately. I was beginning to wonder if you were ill, or something."

"Oh, nothing like that, Dan. I've been wanting to explain for a while but I wasn't sure how to tell you."

"Tell me what, Ruth?" Dan thought it must be serious.

"That I haven't the time to do your housekeeping as I should, Dan. I really am sorry. How will you manage?"

Dan held her by the shoulders. "Is that all." The smile returned. "Still the same old Ruth. Always thinking of others, aren't you? I hope you never change, though." He kissed her forehead. "No need to worry on that score, I move out in a couple of weeks. Come inside, I'll tell you all about it." Nip ran before him and opened the sneck on the gate. Ruth gave the dog a cuddle then patted her head. "Still the clever dog, aren't you, Nip." As if to show her another trick, Nip jumped for the latch on the cottage door and it swung open, then sat waiting for more praise from Ruth. "You really just get better, Nip." Only then, did she notice the young lady lounging on the settle by the fire. "Oh, Dan, I'm sorry. I didn't realize you had company. I'll call back some other time."

"No need, Ruth. I'd like you to meet Abigail. Abigail Ventriss. Abby, this is Ruth Brennan." He paused, smiling. "Sorry, Ruth, not used to your married name yet." He corrected himself. "Ruth Styles now. Used to live at Gallows Howe, now married and living at Roston."

Abigail somehow uncoiled in one languid movement from the comfort of her seat. A tall girl, more feline than female, Ruth thought, with a head of long, auburn hair that shone, even in the dim light of the room and her high sharp cheekbones accentuated the dark luminous eyes. The jodhpurs fitted like a second skin and not even the loose-fitting jumper could hide an exceptional figure. "Hello, Ruth. I am pleased to make your acquaintance. Dan has told me so much about you, all good, I hasten to add." Abigail held out a well-manicured hand and Ruth noted the firm friendly grip and relaxed.

"I'm pleased to meet you too, Abigail. I must admit, I was surprised. I don't know why, it was just so unexpected that I was lost for words."

Dan stood in front of the fire, confident, pleased to catch up with Ruth again. "You've timed your call just right, Ruth. As I said, I'm moving out Pickering way as Abby and I are thinking of getting married."

Ruth smiled at him. "About time too, Dan Parkes. Congratulations to the pair of you."

"Kettle's boiled, we are in for the night now. It would be nice if you could stay, Ruth." And Ruth knew they both meant it.

"Honestly, I would love to, especially with that news but I have a load of work for school tomorrow. Tell you what, we'll arrange a night out, all of us, before you go. How does that sound?"

"Brilliant, Ruth. You think Jim'll be up for it."

"'Course he will. He's not seen much of you since our wedding. Oh, I can't wait to tell him." Ruth knelt to the dog's level and gave Nip one last cuddle. "Right, must be going. Lovely to meet you, Abigail."

Dan put a hand on Ruth's arm. "Before you dash off, Ruth, the other thing is, I'm about to ask you a big favour."

"Go on."

"We have nowhere to stable Dulcie for at least a year, when we move. I thought if you have a spare stable, she might be useful for work?"

Ruth put a hand to her mouth. "Could we? Definitely. Dulcie would be a big help, as we've had to retire Pippen."

Dan's face showed his relief. "That would be good, Ruth. I'm not sure how long it will be for but if we keep in touch, I can let you know."

"When do you move?"

"The wagon comes next week, Ruth. So," Dan spread his arms, "it's goodbye to all this."

"I'll certainly miss you Dan but let's look to the future and the best of luck you two. Bye."

Ruth walked outside, a place which had been her salvation and she had a tear in her eye as she would never forget stumbling into the cottage with Dan on her shoulder. But with the beautiful starry night and the moon casting an eerie yellow stillness across the open moorland, it soon dispelled any misgivings. In the distance, the weird screech of an owl reached her ears as the little Cob broke into a gallop, its hooves clattering out a message along the hard metalled road, before drifting away in the slight breeze. Ruth wished the ride could last forever. That is if she hadn't been in such a rush to tell Jim the news.

Jim was already waiting for her, tea on the table and the fire lit. "Oh, Jim, that's a lovely surprise. You must have finished early, did you?

"I did. Jed joined me and helped with the new fence down to the river. That'll stop the beast getting wrong. It looks good now."

They kissed and sat down for tea. Ruth couldn't wait. "Guess what, Jim?"

"Oh, let me think." He wrinkled his brow. "Well, you look radiant, have you met a new fella?" He brightened. "I know, you must be pregnant."

She threw her head back, giggling at the suggestion. "No, nothing like that."

Jim had a satisfied smirk on his face. "Well, it's possible."

"I know it is. No, I called to see Dan Parkes tonight and he's gone and got himself a girlfriend and they are to be married. She is a real beauty, Jim."

Ruth looked questioningly at him. "Did you know?"

"No, hadn't a clue, I've only seen Dan a couple of times since our wedding. Best thing that could happen to him. I wonder where he met her?"

"She is quite upper class. I'm thinking someone from the shooting parties that he often mixes with."

"Ah, well, if she's from breeding, she'll soon straighten Dan out." Jim couldn't suppress a chuckle. "God, it'll be funny if she tries ordering him about in front of his mates. He could be in for a rough time."

"Also, he asked if we could take Dulcie in as they are moving to Pickering and have no stable for her. I said that would be okay as old Pippen can take things a bit easier."

"Yeh, it'll help us out."

On the mention of breeding earlier, Ruth remembered Jocylyn Dymock. "Well, as it happens, I did meet a new fella today. At school and he wasn't at all snooty. In fact, he was the perfect gentleman."

Jim couldn't help but notice the admiration in her voice. A sudden pang of jealousy caught Jim unawares. His eyes lighted on her. "Was he now and what might he be after then?"

"Apparently, he's the one backing the new project, the quarrying of silica at Castle Moor. To start with, there'll be employment leading stone for the incline and it'll need men with a good team of horses and wagons. I think that is where we might benefit." She held her head on one side and smiled at him. "If we have Dulcie, we might fit the bill?"

Jim relaxed back in his chair. "You're right, Ruth, it could work. Any idea how we might contact him?"

"He is calling back at the school to ask Mr Haigh's advice."

"Wow, if this comes off, it could be a good fill-in before work starts on the church." Jim reached out for her, the flash of doubt that Ruth would be swept off her feet by smooth talk, vanishing as he held her close.

Chapter 11

A warm spring was promised and Jim and Dave McCloud had become firm friends after their first meeting in the Tavern many years ago. Jim smiled at the memory as he rode Pippen towards Spaunton moor to help Dave with the lambing. It was tough going as he knew nothing about sheep but he supposed it was a job that must be learnt.

Asking Jim to separate the flock, they worked steadily away until dinnertime, then settled down behind the moor wall, sheltered from the cool breeze blowing up the valley and ate their sandwich's.

Dave explained his worry about the sheep rustling just lately. "All of 'em that's gone missing have all bin local and it's getting worse."

"Any ideas, Dave?"

"Not a clue, I don't know how to tackle it. The police 'll never catch 'em." He grinned to himself. "Can you imagine, Sergeant Wright chasing after a gang of 'em on his pushbike. Especially over this moor."

Laughing at the thought, Jim said, "no, I don't think that'll happen, Dave, but I have an idea." Dave listened. "I'm thinking of buying a dozen sheep or so, as we have a stray with the farm. Now, I think it's someone who knows the area and someone who picks up on local knowledge, maybe gossip in pubs. Now, when Ruth and I were youngsters running ragged around York, we got caught pickpocketing."

Dave replied, "Yeh, I heard about that at Josh's trial."

"Well, all thieves get cocky. I know how they think, Dave, 'cos I was just the same. It all seems so easy. What you don't realize is that the clever ones are watching you, setting you up. That's what we'll be, Dave. We'll be the clever ones and set 'em up." He looked at Dave. "What do you think?"

Dave was interested. "Go on."

"If we let it be known that I've bought a flock of say, ten or twenty, and keeping 'em in that rough bit o' land fenced off close to the Roston, Lastingham moor path. That way, we can keep an eye on it ourselves. It would be an easy pick-up place, and if it is someone local, they'll know it as a quick load up and away. It also means there is only one way back to the path. To the left of the gate is the old quarry face down onto rocks, and straight on, they are faced with a boggy morass of moor."

Dave thought for a minute, then scratched his head. "By God, there's more in that noddle 'o yours than meets the eye. It sounds good, Jim but it 'll be to man every night. I'm not sure two of us can manage that." He glanced across at Jim. "I can just imagine what Ruth 'll say about it, you just newly married, like."

"What d'you mean? I've been married ages." Jim's face crinkled into a grin, "Well, five months anyway."

"Yeh, you are looking a bit pale. A night or two away might put a spring back in your step, eh?"

"Nah, Ruth's good for me, Dave, she really is. Also, you have Jenny to think about."

"Yeh, s'pose so but we're not married yet. Next year, mebbe." Dave was quiet for a while. It was a well-known fact Dave didn't think and talk at the same time. Eventually, he broke the silence. "No, it needs more than just us two, Jim. We'll have to find another couple of lookouts. I could ask Jack, or Wally?"

Jim disagreed. "No, go with me on this, Dave. Best if we keep this plan to ourselves for now." He paused before adding, "if you let it be known that I'm keeping a few sheep up in the garth, give it a few days and then get ready for some long nights." His face brightened. "Hey, that old timber stable in the corner 'll come in handy for a shelter for us." Jim had a satisfied look on his face. "You've got to admit it, Dave, I'm brilliant sometimes, aren't I?" Jim's enthusiasm bubbled over with his plan, a broad grin spreading across his features.

"Aye, modest with it as well, eh? Who have you in mind to help us, Jim?"

"Josh, Barney and maybe Toby, or Pete." He thought, then shook his head. "No, not Pete. Keeps getting black outs and dizzy spells. By, the bloody war has a lot to answer for, Dave. I know Pete would do it if I asked but he'll not be quick enough if they make a run for it. I'm sure the others will be up for it, though."

"It sounds good, Jim. Also, rather than buying sheep, why not take a dozen o' these, use a different marker, put 'em up in the garth, then let it be known you're into shepherding. We can do it now once we finish here. You know, there's a lot to be said for having a pickpocket for a mate."

"I don't mean to brag, Dave but I used to be pretty good at one time."

"Ha, you mebbe were, but nobody could tek anything o' mine without me knowing."

Jim looked at him. "You think not?"

Confident, Dave replied, "I know so."

"Well, you mebbe don't want this photo back. Jenny's a good looker, isn't she? It was in your inside pocket. You should keep it in a safer place."

Dave's hand shot to his jacket pocket. It was empty and he'd never felt a thing.

"Good God, man, when did you do that?"

"Remember when we sat down for sandwiches?" He looked at Dave, who just nodded. "It was then."

"D'you know, Jim, I'd never have thought that possible." He returned it to his inside pocket and said, "Yeh, Jenny is a beauty, isn't she?"

"She sure is. Hang onto her, Dave, she'll keep you right."

Once done, Dave sorted the sheep out and with a good dog driving them they were soon in the top garth, freshly marked and nobody any the wiser.

"You know, Jim, I can see this plan 'o yours working."

"It'll work, Dave. I just hope it doesn't take too long." Jim mounted up. "Right, you put the word out in the Tavern, I'll get the lads sorted. Any problems, I'll let you know." Jim waved and headed home while Dave tidied up, excited with their plan.

Jim rode the last couple of miles in darkness. With just the occasional cloud scudding across the face of the moon and the stars piercing the midnight blue of the heavens it was enough to light the moorland path. The warm glow of lamplight from the kitchen window was a welcome sight, knowing Ruth was back inside and maybe already done the yard work. After stabling the horse, he went inside, Ruth instantly rushing over and planted a kiss on his lips. After releasing him, he said, "now that's what I call a real welcome home."

"Well, you're worth it, Jim."

"You might not think so after I tell you what Dave and I have sorted out."

Ruth looked worried. "Should I sit down?"

Jim chuckled as she scowled at him. "No, nothing serious, Ruth," and Jim related his plan.

"It sounds dangerous, Jim?"

"No, there'll be no need to confront them. Whoever's on watch just need to keep a check on who it is and how many turn up."

"You will inform Sergeant Wright of what you are doing?"

Jim smiled at her. "Not just at present, Ruth. I don't think he would let it happen. First off, if Josh, Barney, and Toby are willing to stand one night a week at the garth, we'll see what happens."

"I don't like it, not one little bit, Jim. It's asking for trouble. They could be armed."

Jim was amused. "Nah, you've been reading too many novels, Ruth. There 'll be no problem and the thieves will get put away for a while." Ruth noted the smile on his face and the dark eyes flashing. "It could be good fun as well."

Ruth shook her head in disbelief. "I will never understand you men."

Chapter 12

T he warmer weather appeared to usher in a new lease of life for Albert. Twitching the curtains aside just a little, so the brightness didn't wake Martha, he gazed out on to the valley below to see a brilliant blue sky, with just a few bulbous clouds floating high above the horizon. Dressing quietly, he let Martha sleep on and wandered downstairs and out into the garden. He breathed in deeply, the fresh morning air filling his lungs. For how much longer, he was unsure. Jacob had advised him to give the pipe up, which he had found difficult but felt much better for it. He was hopeful the better weather would also improve his health.

He felt in good spirits this morning. The best for a long time. Early mornings remained chill, but as the sun continued its climb, Albert appreciated the warmth penetrating through his clothing, brightening him all the while. The snowdrops still formed a quilt of white along the front border of the garden, also the soft cushion of lush grass on the lawn felt good, adding a lightness to his step. He fingered the new buds on the fruit trees, sticky to the touch and glistening in the sunlight like precious jewels. Purple and white crocuses were flourishing and splashes of yellow were beginning to burst forth from their long green chutes of the daffodils as they searched for warmth. For the first time this winter, as nature brought fresh life into the world, Albert felt a real pulse of energy back in his body.

Martha, up and about now was busy in the kitchen, making sandwiches.

He walked in and put his arm around her shoulders. "You spoil me," he said with affection.

"Ah, no, these are mine, Albert." She frowned at him. "Did you think they were yours?"

"Aye, I did, actually." Despondent, he reached for the knife to cut some more bread, when Martha stopped him, a twinkle in her eyes. "Yes, these are mine. Those are yours, Albert." She nodded to a package on the draining board. "Did you think I'd forgotten you?"

"I knew you were joking all the while. I just thought it best to play along with you for a while." They cuddled. "I'll be back mid-afternoon, love."

"Don't be doing too much, Albert."

"I won't. I'll ride up on Honey, it'll give her some much-needed exercise."

On reaching the field gate, Honey spotted Albert, her head rising in recognition and immediately trotted down from the top corner of the paddock toward him. He rubbed her neck affectionately. "You pleased to see me, eh?"

The horse threw her head back and snorted. Albert laughed. "I thought so. Come on, let's get you some exercise. I've neglected you lately, Honey." He felt the smoothness of her coat and saw the sharpness in her eyes, the horse as keen for the ride as much as Albert. Once tacked up they tackled the steep bank to the farm steadily, not wanting to overdo it. It was the first proper ride for quite a while. On arrival, Ruth had left for school and Jim was just letting the beast out for the first time since winter.

"Now then, stranger," Jim shouted, and walked over as Albert dismounted. "You're looking in good fettle, Albert. This bit o' sun brought you out, eh?"

Albert was smiling. "Yeh, it does you good, doesn't it? You know what, I never thought I would say this but, I think I've bin a bit down in the dumps, Jim. For the first time in me life, I found it a long winter. What are you on with today?"

"I'm putting sheep pens in the end building, Albert. I thought now was as good a time as any to try it out."

"Ha, I was right." Albert pushed his cap back and scratched his head. "I knew you wouldn't settle until you'd given it a go," he said, a smug smile on his face. "But you do right, Jim." Albert gathered his tools together and began work on the pens. "Mind you, watch out for this sheep rustling."

"Hmm, it all seems a bit strange to me, Albert, only a few going missing at a time." Jim shook his head. "Makes me think it's just young lads. Who else would take a risk like that for a few woolly jumpers? He paused. "But we've hatched a plan, Albert."

"Have you now?" Albert appeared serious. As they worked away, Jim explained. When finished, Albert nodded in silent agreement. After giving it some thought, he said, "it could work, Jim. I could do a night or two for you, up there, you know. That would help spell you off."

Jim cast an incredulous look in Albert's direction. "You'll do no such thing. Martha would skin me alive if anything went wrong. Just keep it under your hat for now. I'll let you know what happens."

"Okay, will do," and they worked on until late afternoon and Albert checked his watch. He'd found a spare after giving his other to Jim, thinking he wouldn't miss it. But he did. "Hey, Jim, I better be getting Honey back home. This weather has done us both a power of good." As he rode off, he shouted back over his shoulder. "Keep me informed, Jim, won't you?"

"Will do." Jim watched him go, a sense of relief sweeping through him at Albert's improved health. I suppose it is possible he'd got a bit down, he thought to himself. Whatever, it's good to see him back out.

But now it was down to business. Just as he finished the yard work, Ruth, astride Danny, galloped up, face flushed from the ride home. "Sorry I'm a bit late, Jim. I needed a word with Mr Haigh before I left. I'll just sort this little fella out, then we'll have tea."

"You'll have to eat on your own tonight, Ruth, I want to catch Toby and Josh before they head home. You can leave the horse, I'll ride back to Gallows Howe on him."

Ruth frowned at him. "You're going ahead with your plan then, eh?"

"I am, Ruth." He walked across and gave her a hug. "Somebody has to, or else it'll escalate into big trouble for someone."

"Does it have to be you?"

"'Fraid so, Ruth. Won't be long." He turned and mounted at the gallop.

Damn, I must learn to mount like that, she thought, watching the dust rise from Danny's hooves.

Sighing, she went indoors, allowing herself a slow smile. On the table, places were set and sandwiches already on the plate for them both. It looks like Jim didn't expect his business taking long. When eating on her own she took her plate over to the fire, then got her schoolwork out. Lighting the lamp, the time passed quickly and she didn't even notice the night closing in before a flurry of hoofbeats heralded Jim's return.

After stabling Danny, Jim entered the now cosy room, a wide gap-tooth smile on his features, dark eyes sparkling with excitement.

"Well, it's on, Ruth. The lads are up for it but we'll give it this week for word to get about, then a couple of us will take a night each through the week. We figured with two, we'll always have back up." He added as he saw her frowning, "that's just in case things go wrong, but they won't, I promise. Josh and Dave will take first watch, Toby and I next, then Dan and Barney." He went over and kissed her as if that would make it right. Ruth knew it was pointless trying to persuade him otherwise when in this frame of mind.

Dave McCloud was in cheery mood as he wandered down into Roston for a pint. After all, it was Saturday. The pub was busier than usual. Not surprisingly, business had picked up since Nancy Lawson had taken to working weekends as she added a real touch of glamour behind the bar. With her red hair flowing loose around her shoulders and not a semblance of make up on those full red lips, she was dressed quite conservative for her. The black dress fitted perfectly, with just a small amount of cleavage showing, making sure admiring glances were thrown her way. A small simple silver necklace completed the picture. Certainly, a much more confident figure now than in the past. Not quite as flirty as in the past, which made her even more attractive. Tony couldn't believe his luck when she asked if he wanted help serving on.

Although her parents, Robert and Esther, were not regulars in the Tavern, they quite often called in, accepting that Nancy enjoyed the extra money and, also, was very good with the clientele. Robert and Esther had called in

60

with friends and a few visitors were seated around a table in the far corner. But, in the main, it was farmers, either catching up on gossip, spreading it, or making it. It didn't really matter which to Tony Henton. It was all good for business. Once Dave had a pint in his hand, he headed towards Jed Elcock. No sooner was he seated, when Wally walked through the door. Dave looked up. "Good to see you, Wally, this weather given you a thirst, has it?"

"Yep, it has that. Mine's a pint if you're buying, Dave."

"Good God, Wally, don't they pay you up at that place o' yours?" He raised himself and went to the bar glad of an excuse for a chat to Nancy. Finally gathering Wally's pint up, he plonked it on the table in front of him. Wally made himself comfortable, draping his coat over the back of his chair before swiftly taking a quick drink. "You bin busy then, Dave?" he asked casually.

"Sure have. Good weather for getting on, isn't it?

"Was that you working up near Ana Cross last week? It was too far off for me to recognize who it was."

"Yeh. I was just telling Jed; Jim and I fenced that top garth off for his sheep. A real sound job if I say so meself."

Dave left it at that and asked Jed if he'd had any winners lately, knowing he enjoyed the occasional flutter when he could afford.

"Not a sniff lately, Dave." He pushed his cap back showing a thatch of white hair above a wrinkled brow as he hung on to his trusty shepherd's crook. "I think I'd have more luck putting money on you winning the next election and ousting that useless mob o' Lloyd George's in London."

Dave grinned. "Nah, I'm too honest for that job. But, I've told you before, Jed, there's only one winner on the old nags and that's the bookie."

Dave noticed Wally was trying to steer the conversation back to the sheep, while trying to appear he wasn't really bothered. Eventually, after skirting round the edges, he couldn't resist asking the question. "How many is he intending setting off with then, Dave?"

"Who you on about, Wally?"

"Jim. Jim Styles. You said he was getting a few sheep?

"Oh, only about twenty I think but all prime stock by the look of 'em."

Jed butted in. "Those two seem to me mekking a real go of it up there," He stopped for a drink of his beer, then added, "I bin up to see him a couple o' times. He has the stock in the best of fettle. And, Ruth, she never stops working and all she wants to do if she gets time off is ride. Mind you, she is good with horses. I wouldn't be surprised if she lends a hand with the sheep."

After another couple of beers, Dave decided to leave as the dreaded domino board appeared and the gathering fug of smoke was beginning to sting his eyes, changing the atmosphere in the room. Jed shuffled across to his seat in the corner, a couple of the Clemmit family from a smallholding near Copton village sat down after collecting their drinks and the scene was set.

Well, Dave had done as Jim asked. It was out in the open, the hook thrown. Would it work? He had no idea. What he did know for sure was that he had let himself in for some long uncomfortable nights in a tumble-down hut, staring out across the bleak, bare moor just waiting for trouble.

I must be mad, he thought to himself, but a smile creased his face as he walked away from the flickering lights of the village and headed up the well-trodden track towards home.

Chapter 13

Ruth, later away from school than usual, dashed outside, mounted Danny and eased him gently into a canter on reaching the moor top. Arriving home, a letter awaited her in the centre of the table. Jim must have placed it there so she didn't miss it. Instantly recognising the scrawly handwriting, she drew a chair up to the table and sat down, her limbs unsteady, her heart beating a little faster. Why? She was not expecting bad news. Whatever, Ruth decided to read it before Jim returned, in the hope that it was good news. Slowly she undid the envelope and read.

Dear, Ruth.

I hope this finds you well and truly married. I am looking forward to seeing you both and meeting up with your husband, Jim. Now, the real point I am writing is to inform you that your father, Patrick, turned up on my doorstep inquiring on your whereabouts and he would like to see you. Well, I spoke the truth and told him I knew where you were living, but that I would have to write to you, asking if you were willing to meet up.

Please, give yourself time to think, Ruth and reply when you know what you want to do.

All in all, your father looks in good health after what he has suffered. After all, he signed up and went through the war years when he couldn't find work and is back living and helping at St Catherine's.

Thinking of you, Ruth. Remember, it has got to be your choice and whatever you decide, I'm sure it will be the right decision.

Loving you always, dear girl. xxx

Aunty Moll.

Ruth sat staring into space. This was a bombshell. She'd always known it was possible but this letter really brought it home. Whenever Ruth found herself in a state of confusion, she did what she always did, she quickly changed into her work clothes and immediately began the yard work. The animals were simple, easy to look after and never any bother. Most of the beast were all a bit less work at this time of year, as they were out most of the day, but one of the sows had just had a litter of seven and they were to bed up. The hens and geese were all to feed and, one of her favourite jobs, gathering the eggs.

The old wood henhouse was nestled among the apple trees at the far side of the orchard. It had seen better days but was doing its job at present. Ruth always found the simplicity of hens comforting. Some would still be scratching around outside, clucking contentedly, others would be in their nest boxes, where she had to slip her hand underneath for the eggs. There was no noisy squawking from any of them. Such simple animals living a simple life. How we humans could learn from them. Looking up to the rafters, she noticed there was those who liked an early night as they were already roosting.

Before finishing, Farmer spied her and trotted up the field. Jim must be out on Pippen as she was nowhere to be seen. Ruth gave Farmer a sweet and talked to him for a while, her arm hung around his broad muscular neck, drawing strength from the big horse. Returning inside she was now ready for a late tea.

Jim arrived moments later. "Sorry I'm late, Ruth but I just rode up to the garth to feed the sheep. It's Dave and Josh tonight, so I needed the sheep to be well settled." He noticed the concern on Ruth's face. "Aw, don't worry, Ruth," he said throwing an arm around her and pulling her close, "the lads know what they're doing."

"It's not that, Jim. I had a letter from Aunty Moll this morning."

"Ah, I thought that was who it was from." He paused. "And?" An enquiring glance, followed by a frown as he studied Ruth. "Not bad news, is it?"

"No, it's not bad news, Jim. It's news that I have expected for some time now."

Jim pulled a chair out and sat close to her. "Is it about your father?"

"Yes. Patrick found Molly's address and he called asking if she knew where I was living. That's why she has written to me. I have to make a decision whether I want to meet him, or not." Her voice broke and the tears began to trickle down her face. Jim held her close until her sobbing eased. Again, she found solace and strength in Jim's arms. Always had done, ever since they met.

This was the soft side of Jim that very few saw, or even knew existed. Tender, understanding and loving. "Now, dry those eyes, Ruth, and let's do what we normally do when faced with a problem. Let's talk it through, eh?"

Ruth rubbed her eyes dry but still held him tight, as if her life depended on it. "I'm frightened, Jim. Frightened that it will plunge us back into those dreadful, terrifying years that I thought were in the past. Afraid that something will tear our happiness apart. I am not prepared to go down that road again. I would not be strong enough to face it again.

"Shh, Ruth. That's not going to happen. Listen to me and look at it logically. This is a big shock for you, I know, I've been there. But you are in charge now. That little, nervous nine-year old girl that cried in my arms in the orphanage has disappeared with the past. She is now a married woman, twenty-three years old and a schoolteacher. We have our own farm and run our own business. How come you still feel all these old insecurities that should be dead and buried? There are only two people who can destroy our happiness. That's you and me." The gap-toothed smile lit the room, Ruth's mood brightened. She smiled and hugged him tighter.

Later that night, sat close on the old settle close to the fire, Ruth spoke in not much more than a whisper. "Jim?"

"Mmm, what is it?"

"I've been thinking about what you said."

"And?"

"I do need to meet my father once again, because it feels the right thing to do. If not, I will always wonder what might have been. Does that make sense?"

"Perfect sense. I know I gave Edith a hard time when we met but it did help me realize why I held so much bitterness within me. You see, we both carry quite a bit of baggage on our shoulders, through no fault of our own but we are now beginning to understand why."

"You think it's the right thing to do, then?"

"Definitely," he said with a finality that did not warrant a rebuke. He gave her a few minutes, before adding, "well, are you going to write the letter, or not?"

She took his hand, leading him upstairs, a twinkle back in those clear blue eyes.

"I am. First thing in the morning will be soon enough. We have more important things to do tonight."

Chapter 14

The night was as black as pitch as thick cloud drew a veil over the face of the moon and any star in the heavens, as Dave and Josh arrived for their night shift at the garth. Everything was eerily silent. On the stroke of midnight, Josh threw his bag into the corner of the ramshackle shelter and an ear-piercing screech shattered the still night. A cacophony of noise followed from other nightlife creatures. With thumping hearts, it took them a while to realise they had just disturbed the owl's resting perch. When Josh finally grabbed Dave's coat to halt his run for freedom, they both collapsed with relief and laughter until tears rolled down their cheeks.

Once serious again, Dave said. "Well, that proved I'm not the bravest bloke on the planet, Josh. If they do happen to come tonight, it's going to have to be you that confronts them, as I shall be legging it back to Roston." Dave could still feel the drumming beat of his heart in his chest.

Josh smiled in the darkness. "Yeh, it was so unexpected and sounded like someone been stabbed. I don't suppose anything 'll happen tonight, I think we'll have frightened anyone away with all the noise we made."

Once calm was restored, Dave asked Josh if, in his four years of conflict, did he ever think the worst, that he may never return home.

"Yes, every day when on the front line, Dave. The only time I felt safe was when I was injured and in hospital." Josh hesitated, recalling the fear of those days, crawling up his back once again. He carried on. "Well, it wasn't really a hospital. It was just a load of tents, but we were well clear of the shelling there. Even now, I still wake up with nightmares of what I saw."

As Dave kept a watchful eye on the moor, Josh's voice dropped to a whisper as he began explaining the terrifying moment when creeping up to the trench. He reached the point where the German pulled the trigger which almost blew his head off, when a loud, rasping cough echoed close to the shed. It sounded human. Jumping out of their cover, they were just in time to see the white rump of a young deer scurry away through the branches, even more startled than them.

Dave was first to find his voice. "Damn it all, Josh, that's enough horror stories tonight. Let's just see if we can get through this last couple of hours in silence, eh?"

"Sure thing, Dave. I'll get my head down and leave the watching to you." Josh lay full length on the straw bed in the corner and promptly dropped to sleep.

Dave kept a close eye on the distant skyline until the dull shards of crimson begin to cast a glow along the moor top, thankful that his first stint on watch was over. Gently, he shook Josh awake. "Come on, Josh. We've done our bit. Let's head home and report all quiet. Easing their stiff aching limbs into motion they took the steady descent deep into the wood, skirting the steep rock face of the abandoned quarry. The horses stood waiting patiently for the two men, tossing their heads in recognition as they approached. Once mounted, they enjoyed the early morning sun break above the thin mist in the valley and were soon back in Roston.

"I'll call and see Jim, tell him it was a quiet night, apart from the owl," said Josh laughing. "Although it would be funnier if I didn't say anything, but he might not see the funny side."

Jim was out in the stable when Josh called to relate the news. "Hope you have better luck, Jim," and rode off to Castle Moor.

At midnight the next evening, Jim and Toby cantered up into the wood, fastening the horses up well clear of the garth and walking the rest of the way. On entering they made sure the owl was nowhere about before Jim said, "Well, I reckon we have about six hours of watch to do, Toby. Do you want to take first stint?"

"Yep, will do." Toby smiled. "I have a day off tomorrow, so you get some sleep. I'll let you know if anything happens."

"You lucky sod. You must have a good boss at that quarry?"

"Mmm, reasonable, Jim. And it's good money. More than I can make elsewhere but he knows I'm pretty good with horses and said if anything crops up, he'll keep me in mind."

"Sensible man, Toby. Right, wake me if I snore. I don't want to frighten these rustlers off."

"Will do."

Toby sat a little way back in the shelter so as not to be spotted but still had a good view of the horizon right round. Anything moving he would quickly see and he well knew the only access was from the Roston, Lastingham road. There was no way in from the disused quarries, or through the soft peat bog to the west. The night was clear and only the sounds of the night creatures could be heard. Toby had lived all his life in the country and, even in the still of the night, there was part of him that was entranced by the silence.

After checking his watch, he then studied the skyline once more. Movement. He was sure there was movement. He forced himself to wait a minute, make sure it wasn't just a trick of the night sky before waking Jim. No. They were coming closer. He nudged Jim awake, speaking in no more than a whisper. "Come on, Jim. Action stations." Jim rose steadily and peered through their spyhole. "You're right, Toby. It's on. You ready?"

"Sure am." Toby's eyes were alive with excitement, body, and mind fully alert. "Jim, listen how quiet that old cart is on the rough road, they must be on rubber tyres."

"Must be, Toby. Right, I'll climb over the back wall and head for the gate, that way I'll be ready for 'em if they make a dash for it. Let them back up to the gate, gather a few sheep, then catch 'em red-handed."

"Okay. You get going."

Jim ducked out of the shed, keeping low. The silhouettes of the two men in the cart stood out stark in the moonlight. Jim stayed low behind the wall, watching, waiting, the minutes ticking by as the cart trundled nearer and nearer. So close now, he heard the driver say, "Steady, boy," as he swung the cart into the gateway. "Back up, now." Someone jumped out, opened the gate and Toby watched as the flash of a black and white dog crept silently forward on its belly, urging the sheep nearer to the trailer. "Okay, Luke, quickly now." The driver was nervous. Suddenly the dog ran to the shed, barking wildly, teeth bared, and hackles raised. "What is it, Meg?" Luke thought it must be a rat or a rabbit and walked over to the shed, jumping backwards as Toby suddenly emerged from the shadows.

"Got you, lads. Stay where you are. There's four of us, you haven't a chance."

"Run for it, Dick. They'll not catch us." Luke leapt the wall and began running for a break in the trees as Dick whipped the horse and cart into a gallop, heading straight for the peat bog.

Jim heard the frightened whinny from the horse as it lunged, belly deep, into the morass but he hadn't time to stop as Luke hurtled for a break in the trees. "STOP," Jim screamed as Luke headed for the sheer drop to the quarry. He would be smashed to bits on the rocks. Jim gave chase, finally bringing him down in a rugby tackle at the very edge of the cliff face and grasped hold of his legs. The briars and nettles, clawed and scratched at any exposed flesh, quickly drawing blood. Jim hung tightly onto Lukes legs but not tight enough. He squirmed a heavy hobnailed boot free from Jim's grasp and landed it squarely on Jim's forehead with a crack but he didn't let go. "Stop it damn you. Stop it, young 'un," he shouted. Panting heavily, and with the blood running into his eyes, Jim was glad when Luke finally gave up the struggle but still he kept tight hold just in case.

The shrill whinny of fear from the horse in the distance was still ringing out across the moor from the floundering horse, but it began to quieten, even though up to its belly in the bog. "Come on, you, if you want to save your horse." Running to see if they could help, Toby, calm and collected, stood waist deep in the bog, talking to the horse, breathing on its nostrils. "Steady there, you beauty. Steady. We've got you." He stroked its neck as he spoke. Turning to Jim. "Jim, can you unhitch the cart. Once that's off his back, I'm sure he'll lead out."

"Will do." Jim waded into the bog and there was a clatter of chains as the shafts dropped free of the horse. Luke stumbled in with a halter and Toby placed it gently around the horse's neck. With Luke on solid ground and Toby leading, urging Luke to be gentle, they eventually had the horse out onto the dry moor.

"Hell, Toby, I always knew you were good with animals, but you were brilliant in there. How did you know what to do to keep him calm?" Although they were all sodden through up to the waist and caked with stinking mud, they sat among the heather and regained their breath, as Toby explained his teacher was exceptional.

"And who might that be, Toby?"

"You know very well, Jim. It was Ruth."

Jim grinned in the dark. "Yep, she is good, isn't she?" He sat up abruptly, already thinking on what to do next. "Now, what do you think we should do with this young tearaway, Toby?"

"Well," Toby dropped into serious mode, "I think we should hand him over to the law. Don't you?"

"I'm not sure, Tobe." Jim scratched his head as if thinking. "After all, he did help us rescue the horse."

"Yeh, but don't forget it was his horse."

Jim nodded. "True, and he was stealing our sheep." Deep in thought, Jim said, "what do you think if I take him back home and tell his father to keep a better eye on him."

Luke butted in. "That won't do no good. It was him that told us to go sheep stealing, else there would be no grub on the table."

Jim cast Luke a sideways glance in the dark. Barely a teenager. A lump rose in Jim's throat as he cast his mind back to his own early days in York. A person there had given Jim a second chance. Should he also give Luke a chance.

"What did your mother say to that?"

"We lost mam when I was a kid."

"I'm sorry to hear that, Luke." Jim's mind was made up. "Toby, while we

71

pull the cart out, will you bring Farmer up from the wood and I'll take this lad home. You ride home and get changed." He winked at Toby. "Our plan worked a treat, Toby and no one hurt." He rubbed his forehead. "Apart from me," he said, grinning.

Toby walked off, water sloshing loudly in his boots and soon returned with Farmer. Tying him to the back of the cart, Luke and Jim jumped on the seat but there was no sign of Dick or their dog, Meg. Shivering in the cool night air, Jim asked "where do you live, Luke?"

"A small farm just outside Copton village, just afore you go over a humpback bridge."

"I think I know it. Turn off to the right up a rough farm track."

"That's the one." Luke settled into silence, staring straight ahead.

"You worried, Luke?"

"A bit."

"About what your father will say, or what Dick 'll say?"

"Oh, I'll cop it from the pair of 'em, he said resignedly. Both barrels."

"What if I have a word with your father, Luke?"

"That'll do no good. He doesn't listen to anybody, let alone a stranger. He'll just give me a harder whacking." The boy sniffed as he tried hard to keep the tears at bay. Jim knew exactly how he felt, and a lump formed in his own throat. "I know exactly what you're going through, Luke."

"How do you know what I'm going through? You have your own farm and sheep and married. You don't know what it's like having nothing. Going to school in rags. Hunger gnawing away in your belly. No money, a father that doesn't care and wallops you for no reason." He blew his nose noisily. "And no mam."

Jim thought it time Luke knew a few home truths about life in general and began to relate his own story on the long ride back to Copton village. He told Luke of his own troubled background and his early years at York before finding a new way of life at Roston as a young lad and turning his life around. He left nothing out. The beatings, the stealing, the fighting, and hunger and most of all, no parents. Luke sat open mouthed staring at this stranger sat next to him.

"Did that really happen, Jim. You're not just mekking it up are you, just to make *me* feel better?"

"No, I've made nothing up, Luke. Both Ruth and I had it rough early on but I listened to the advice from a good man at York, who told me to leave the stealing behind, or, the way I was going I would end up in prison and never see Ruth again."

"Was she your sweetheart, Jim?"

Yes, she was." He smiled to himself, remembering their early days together.

Luke's tears had dried, and he smiled across at this stranger. "D'you love her, Jim?"

"Yes, very much, Luke."

They were close to Luke's home now as they turned into the rough road leading up to the farmhouse. "I'm frightened, Jim."

"Don't be. You go straight in when your father opens the door and go to your bedroom. I guarantee he will never touch you or beat you again."

The house was shrouded in the darkness just before dawn, a grey mist creeping down from the hills. Climbing down from the cart they stepped up to the front door and Jim knocked loudly, the sound echoing along the inner passage. That must wake anyone in the house, however sound they slept, Jim thought.

Eventually, a flickering light emerged at one of the windows, a face scowling out above it.

Jim kept his voice quiet and even, not wanting to frighten Luke further. "Do as I say, Luke. Walk straight in and go to your room. Let me handle it."

The door eventually creaked open and what could only be described as a caricature of a man's features appeared. He was big and burly, unkempt, and instantly aggressive, as if expecting trouble, his braces down by his side as if he'd just thrown his clothes on. "What's this? What are you doing here with my lad this time o' morning?" The man went to grab Luke by the scruff of his neck, but Jim was much quicker and held the man's wrist in a vice like grip.

"In you go, Luke." Luke darted inside and disappeared. Still holding the man's wrist, Jim carried on, his voice no more than a whisper. "It's time we had a talk, Mr Clemmit, don't you think?"

"Who the hell d'you think you are, you young upstart." He went to pull his hand away from Jim's grip but Jim gave him no slack. Clemmit immediately went to put the candle down to leave a free hand, but Jim grabbed him by the filthy red neckerchief fastened around his neck and pushed him back against the wall until the big man was gasping for breath.

"Don't you even think about striking me, Clemmit, or I'll knock you into the middle of next week." His voice was full of menace, his dark eyes flashing dangerously. In fact, he was hoping Clemmit would lash out so he would have the pleasure of inflicting a beating on him. Make him suffer like the two lads had suffered over the years. But Clemmit was nothing more than a bully and he realized he was up against a stronger individual than his young sons and backed down.

Jim eased the pressure on the man's neck, allowing him to talk. Rubbing his throat and wheezing for breath, he spluttered out, "Okay, okay. No need for violence. What have they done this time?"

"You know what they've done. You put them up to it. Your cart, your horse, your orders. I should have gone straight to the police, but I think the lads are worth a second chance at getting their lives in order. If I hear of any more beatings coming from you, not one finger laid on them, you understand, I shall personally come back up here and thrash you to within an inch of your life. Do I make myself clear?" These words were hissed very close to Clemmit's ear.

Clemmit was trembling with fear and Jim, adrenalin coursing through him was also struggling to keep control as his anger boiled to the surface again as it had opened so many wounds and old memories from way back for comfort.

"I understand," said Clemmit. "Now, get out of my house."

"I'm on my way." He turned before closing the door. "By the way, you have a horse out here to wash down and stable up before you go back to bed." With that, Jim walked away and mounted Farmer to return home. At that very moment the sun broke over the distant horizon heralding a new day and a satisfied smile broke out on Jim's face.

Chapter 14

On his arrival, Ruth had already done the yard work and was busy changing for school. Expecting Toby to be with him, she waited until he dismounted and looked at the state of him, the dried blood a dark stain on the side of his face. "Jim, whatever happened? You're injured and where the devil is Toby?"

Although in a stinking horrible mess, Jim was beaming. "It's all done, Ruth. Toby rode home earlier, and I had to take one of the Clemmit's home. That's why I'm late. But my plan worked, and nobody got hurt, Mrs Styles." He rubbed a finger over his forehead and winced. "Apart from me." He dismounted. "It worked, just like I said." He strode forward and went to put his arms around her, but Ruth backed off. "Not in that state, Jim Styles. I'm late for school as it is and I have a letter to post. If you can spare time from your thief catching, could you square the kitchen up for me, please? See you at teatime." She blew a kiss over her shoulder, adding, "and please, please get a bath before I get back."

Jim ran into the kitchen, quickly picking up some dry clothes up then headed for the stable, stripped off his wet clothes and jumped straight into the horse trough in the corner. The water was bitterly cold, but it helped revive him. After washing the blood and dirt from him, he noticed an old towel hung on the corner of the wood stall. He was just about to leap out of the trough when the stable door opened.

"My God, is this how you get a bath up here when you think there's no one about?" It was Nancy Lawson. Jim quickly shrunk down in the bath again, hands cupping his groin area. "Ahh, I can explain, Nancy. But first, could you pass me the towel hung on that nail there?"He nodded in the general direction.

"Have I to avert my eyes, Jim Styles?"

"Aw, please, Nancy. This is embarrassing, just pass the towel. Please." He was begging, hoping no one came in to the stable.

A mischievous smile played around those full red lips. "Well, It 'll certainly cause amusement when they hear about this in the pub."

She took the towel and walked slowly across to the water tub, holding it between thumb and forefinger, teasing Jim to reach out for it. He made a grab for it and missed.

"Don't worry. I'm not here to cause trouble for you, but trouble does seem to seek you out, Jim Styles. News travels quick. I spotted Toby on his way back this morning and he told me that you caught the culprits."

"Ahh, I forgot Toby would come this way. You must have been out and about early, Nancy?" Shivering, he said, "come on, Nancy, please pass me the towel."

She did as he bid, turning away as he got dried and dressed into his fresh clothes. More comfortable now, he relaxed.

"Yes, I usually rise early. Toby said it worked well." Nancy sat down on the old bench near the stable door. "I would never have thought of Wally been the bad guy, Jim. I knew the Clemmit kids had a reputation and it was only a matter of time, but…" She rose from the bench and went to finger his brow. He shied away.

"Better not touch it, Nancy. Still a bit painful."

"Harder punch than you expected, was it?" she said with a grin.

"No, it was a kick from Luke's hobnailed boot."

"You think that'll be the end of it, Jim?"

"Yeh, for sure." He smiled at her. "Fancy coming in for a cup o' tea?"

"Course I will. I just have time before getting back to the village."

"Just on the off chance, d'you mind not mentioning catching me in the bath to Ruth. You know, it can get embarrassing, like, you know… if she thought…"

Amused at his predicament, she said, "your secret is safe with me, Jim. Now are we going to have a cup of tea, or not?"

While the kettle boiled, Nancy listened intently as Jim related their achievement of the previous night. "He almost went over the edge into the quarry, Nancy. Another few yards he could o' been a goner, or badly injured." Jim closed his eyes at the thought. "Toby was brilliant, though, saving the horse on his own. Calmed it down and stopped it sinking and maybe dying from a heart attack in the bog."

"He is good, especially with horses. The word is he's been offered a job at Jocylyn Dymock's stud farm, near Malton."

"Well, I hope you're right, Nancy, as I'm sure Toby will be able to teach em a thing or two about handling horses."

Chapter 15

1921

The summer of '21 saw Jocylyn spending more time at Castle Moor as his business demanded it and Nancy was proved right, Toby duly moving to Malton to live in a tied cottage on the grounds of the stud farm. On his first sight of Greythorpe Manor, the spectacular grounds and surroundings took his breath away. The huge stone pillars at the entrance supported large wrought iron gates that swung open for access to a long, winding drive leading to the Manor house itself. Once past the house and sweeping off to the left, a cobbled road disappeared under a colourful avenue of lime trees in full bloom and there, for some reason, in the distance stood a charred, tumble-down relic of a building that appeared to have been destroyed by fire. Not sure if it belonged to his employers, or not, Toby dismissed it from his thoughts.

He was much more interested with his own residence, a small, brick-built cottage positioned just inside the entrance. Although apprehensive, Toby held an inner belief that he would cope with the job. A chance of a lifetime, son, his parents had said. He knew he would miss them but once settled, he could easily make the ride home occasionally.

Jocylyn was there on his arrival and introduced him to Victoria, his younger sister, Toby's immediate boss. Victoria was not much older than

Toby but years ahead in confidence.

"Pleased to meet you, Toby." Toby took the proffered hand, her hand feeling very smooth in his but with a strong grip. Victoria spoke directly to Jocylyn. "Right, you can leave Toby to me, Jocylyn, I'll show him around the estate, the stables and exercise yard and what his jobs are." Then she spoke directly to Toby. "I'll also open the cottage for you, Toby, to see if your living quarters are suitable. How does that sound?" A broad smile broke on her tanned face and the dark eyes surveyed Toby as, holding her head on one side, she waited for an answer.

Toby finally found his voice. "That sounds good, thank you."

"Bye, Jocylyn." Victoria waved as she walked off. Toby ran to catch up. Victoria's dark hair was pulled tightly back into a ponytail, and she was dressed in polished riding boots, black jodhpurs that fitted like a second skin, with navy jumper, and white shirt. She cut a striking figure and her energy was obvious.

"Right, we'll just take a bit at a time, Toby. Don't want to frighten you off at the very beginning, do we?"

"You'll not do that, miss. I'm looking forward to the challenge. This is what I want to do."

"Well, for a start, you can call me Vicky, or Victoria. I answer to both. I do not like too much formality. Joss is my elder brother and is spending more and more time on his new business venture which you will have heard about. This leaves more work at my door."

They approached a long line of stables. Some were occupied, some empty.

"Don't look so worried, Toby. It won't all be left to you. We have stable hands to come and help but I want you to look after the health of the horses, their training and exercise routine and see to any problems that arise. Is that okay with you?"

"That's fine, Victoria. I do have one question, though?"

Victoria stood, hands on hips. "Yes, which is?"

"Will there be a spare stable for my horse, Pal, 'cos we've been together since he was born."

She smiled that warm smile of hers. "Of course. Come this way," and they headed back to the cottage. "Jocylyn told me about Pal. I'm looking forward to seeing him." On turning the corner, there stood a white painted building directly behind Toby's cottage. Above the double door, a sign stood out in black lettering. PAL.

Toby was astounded. "I can't believe you've done all this for me and Pal, Victoria."

"You better believe it, Toby. But, you understand, there is a lot of hard work involved. It's not all beer and skittles, you know, even though it appears idyllic. We are often calm on the surface but paddling like hell beneath the water."

They both smiled, the tension easing away with Victoria's relaxed attitude, even if she was paddling furiously.

"Now, we must see about getting transport for Pal."

Chapter 16

J im and Ruth had gathered Dulcie up from Dan but were still in desperate need of an extra mount with Pal and Toby gone. Although Jacob had cut down on his workload, he needed the little Cob for his own transport. As the months slipped by, Jocylyn called at the school to ask advice on suitable men for the ongoing quarry work, Ruth put Jim's name forward but also mentioned they were looking for a suitable horse. "You see, up until now, my ride to school gave Pal the exercise he needed, but with Toby's move to Malton, that's all changed." She paused, serious. "By the way, how is he doing?"

"Absolutely fine. He is an amazing young man with animals, adamant that he learnt everything from a young woman at Gallows Howe." He sneaked a sideways glance at Ruth, a smile on his face, the dark eyes studying her keenly. She felt the colour rise in her cheeks. "Now, who could that be, do you think?"

"Ahh," she shook her head. "Toby possessed a certain talent with animals from a very young age, they are in his blood. One day, when we have time, I'll tell you about how he stayed with Pal and saved his life."

"I shall look forward to that, Mrs Styles. But, be that as it may, he attributes it all to his good teacher." He paused before speaking his thoughts to Ruth. "In fact, I think given a few years, Toby will progress to much higher ranks than us in the future." He turned to face her. "Now, about your ride to work.

I think you might be in luck. We have a mount that retired from jump racing a year ago that I think could be perfect. For a thoroughbred, it is extremely well behaved in traffic but lively and fast when given free rein. I assume you do quite a lot of riding?"

"I do. Every chance I get. It is a big part of my life and nothing more exciting than riding this open moorland when I have time."

"Well, I guarantee the horse is sound and the price will be right, Mrs Styles. The horse's name is Dunella. In fact, on my next visit, I will ride her over and you and your husband can run your eyes over her and see what you think."

"That's very kind of you, Mr Dymock. It would certainly solve my problem."

"No, it is the least I can do after taking away your ride to school."

Comfortable in his company, Ruth wandered out into the school yard to keep an eye on the children in their break time. Jocylyn followed, each taking a seat at the table close to the railings. Jocylyn spoke first, his eyes fixing on Ruth again. "You may have heard I have just purchased Oak Tree Farm at Castle Moor and will be living there a few days a week until the builders finish the main house." Ruth was surprised. She had no idea Jocylyn Dymock was interested. But why wouldn't he be? An ambitious man with ambitious plans, she thought, and obviously, money was no problem. He carried on. "For personal reasons, I have cut my workload at Malton and am now living at Oak Tree." A rueful grin crossed his features. "Although, I can hardly call it luxurious as yet." He paused, then said, "ah, I almost forgot. I have also agreed with Mr Haigh for the school to begin a vegetable garden close to the orchard."

Ruth's face lit up. "That is very generous of you. The children will love it, especially the ones frightened of missing something outside." A smile played about her lips, as she thought of the children gardening.

Again, his eyes locked onto hers for a split second longer than was comfortable. Her heart missed a beat. Damn her heartbeat. Why did he affect her like this. She smiled and looked away.

"You should smile more often, Mrs Styles, it suits you," but then quickly changed the subject. "So, in the future, I'll see you when chaperoning the children in the garden." He lifted his hat and turned to go.

Ruth shook her head. "Oh, I think Mr Haigh will take charge of that."

"Not so, Mrs Styles. He told me that your experience on the farm makes you perfect for the job."

Happy with the news, she said, "well, if that is the case, I must brush up on my gardening techniques, Mr Dymock."

As Jocylyn ploughed more time, money, and effort into his project at Castle Moor, the hard work and commitment needed, prevented his mind returning to the grim nightmares of the past. Oak Tree Farm was now his home and saved time on travelling and proved a handy retreat for him. Built in the mid 1800's, when the railway's first steamed through these dales, its remote position suited Jocylyn and could only be reached by a steep track descending to the base of the dale. The preceding years had not been kind to the property, neglect and poverty once again leaving its mark. A large forest of trees sheltered the rear of the building and the double bay window frontage and stone flagged steps leading to the entrance, added a majestic appearance. The dull grey of the Westmorland slate roof made the red pan-tiled roofs of the buildings stand out in stark contrast and the panoramic view of the lush green valley and rising moorland in the distance gave the house a freedom all its own.

Jocylyn, at present, was living in the servant's quarters, a huge difference from his normal lifestyle. It was rough. Only two rooms, one a small bedroom and the other his living room. This still had the cast iron tub in the corner with a grate underneath for boiling clothes on wash days. The lathe and plaster ceiling had become crumbly, causing dust to settle everywhere. The damp had also affected the walls and his only water supply was what he carried in from the stone trough outside. No inside toilet, here, just a small double earth closet built away from the house.

This would be his home for the foreseeable future, until the builders renovated the more spacious rooms of the main house.

But Jocylyn was enjoying the challenge, the isolation and silence. Wandering outside on an evening, as dusk crept in, the nightlife took over. The shriek from a peacock that had taken up residence in the wooded area, the shrill call of a screech owl in the distance, and then the silence and tremendous speedy twists of the bats flight as they flitted in and out of his view. He could enjoy the wonders of nature in his new home.

The hard work helped alleviate the dark cloud of depression that was ever present but after a few tough days, the room was habitable. Once the fire was lit and roaring away under the cast iron tub, he lifted a lamp down from the shelf, put a match to the wick and settled down in an old, comfortable chair. This was as near to contentment as he would get for a while, so, opening a bottle of wine, he allowed his mind to stray to a certain Ruth Styles.

The very next day he returned to the stud farm and picked Dunella up, keen to hear what Ruth and Jim thought. He was pleased to hear Victoria and Toby were managing very well without him, but before leaving for Oak Tree, Victoria took him to one side, her concern for him evident. "Jocylyn, are you okay, or are you doing too much? You look tired."

"No, please do not worry about me, Vicky, I think we both know this is my lifeline, what keeps me sane. You'll see, dear girl, this project will be my saviour."

"I do hope you're right, brother."

They hugged before Jocylyn mounted the beautiful chestnut mare and rode off into the distance, Vicky watching him until out of sight. Jocylyn enjoyed the solitude of the ride back and returned to the quarry on the Monday to oversee the plant being installed. The self-acting trucks were mobile now and the shed for the explosives for blasting the stone was built high on the moor for safety.

Blasting was already taking place on the very brow of the rising moor. Plumes of smoke rising from the earth like giant mushrooms into the clear blue sky. With work on the new church held up for funds, Jim had taken on leading stone to the trucks, a much safer and easier task than the church job. Just keep the horses clear of the noise, move in and load up with the other men and lead to the incline. The demand for silica sand was constant and growing, for glass making and furnace moulds at Guisborough, Whitby and beyond. After the long hard years of war, there was work in the dales and, more importantly, a living wage on offer.

It was a brave venture and Jocylyn was sinking every penny he had into it. With only himself to think about, his decisions would decide if it ended in success, or bankruptcy. He knew one thing; if it went down, it would not be from lack of effort on his part.

Chapter 17

Ruth missed Jacob's horse, Danny, terribly, but Jacob, having no need for an extra horse had sold him on. As she flung a saddle onto Farmer, she spotted the postman weaving his way along the rough track on his bicycle and decided to wait for him. "Morning, Mr Linus. You're early this morning. I must be running late."

A tall, pleasant man, with thinning grey hair and tanned features and once off his bike, his arms and legs flopped loosely like a puppet devoid of strings. She smiled at the thought. Pushing his peaked cap back, he wiped the sweat from his brow and, once his breathing eased, said, "no, you're not late, Mrs Styles. They've taken on more staff." He handed a couple of letters over. "There you go. That's all for you today." Wheeling his bike around, he mounted and wobbled unsteadily along the track to finish his rounds.

"Thank you, Mr Linus," she shouted after him. Taking a hand of the handlebars to wave, he almost fell into the gorse bushes lining the side of the track, Ruth unable to suppress a chuckle at his antics. Studying the letters, she recognised Moll's handwriting and, although keen to read it, it would have to wait until later and placed them on the mantelpiece.

Farmer was a more sedate ride than Danny, or Pal, but on a beautiful warm morning such as this, the birds in full voice and the hedgerows vibrant with the smell of honeysuckle and colour, what could be better. The brilliant white blossom of the blackthorn was just beginning to fade and fall like snowflakes, and the smell of newly mown hay swept the valley. Once on the high moor, Ruth pulled Farmer to a halt and gazed on the village from above, the fields alive with horses and men making the most of this good spell of weather. Further up on the snaking climb from Roston, Ruth watched Mr Linus push up the final fierce climb to deliver to the few houses left lining the railway.

On arriving at school, Ruth dismounted just as Freda was finishing. Catching sight of Ruth, she rushed across. "Hey, Ruth, I have some exciting news for you." Freda looked around to make sure no one was listening. "I've just heard Mr Haigh and Mr Dymock discussing the new garden at Oak Tree Farm, and guess what?" She paused, waiting for a response, but Ruth remained non-committal. "You'll be taken 'em for their lessons."

Ruth put what she hoped was a surprise expression on her face, not having the heart to tell Freda she already knew. "Wow, Freda, everything seems to be happening at present, doesn't it? What with the quarry and a new church in the future, it's all change." She studied Freda a little while, before asking, "Is there anything else you want to tell me?"

Freda leant closer to Ruth, her voice dropping to a whisper. "Well yes, there is, but please keep it a secret for now. Michael has asked me to marry him."

"Well, that's marvellous news, Freda. And you've accepted?"

A frown, followed by a shadow of doubt crept across Freda's face. "Hmm, not yet. I'll have to break it to mother first before I do anything."

Ruth couldn't believe what she was hearing and was running out of patience with this grown woman who, in her mind, was still acting like someone of school age. "Freda, I'm afraid these words will sound harsh, but you really must take charge of your life and break those family bonds that are stifling you. I mean, for goodness' sake, what age are you now?"

"Er, well, I'm thirty-one."

"Well, there you go. You cannot go through life pleasing everyone. If you are hesitating because of facing your mother, then, I'm sorry, I don't think you care enough about the man." She put a hand on Freda's shoulder. "The decision is yours. It would not be right to keep him guessing."

"Oh, but I do care for him, Ruth. He's been very good to me and you're right, I know I must decide soon."

Ruth's expression softened, realizing Freda's upbringing. She smiled, placing an arm around Freda's shoulders while leading Farmer to the nearby garth to let him loose for the day. "Y' know, Freda, I bet when you tell your mother the news, she will be delighted."

Freda looked shocked. "You really think so, Ruth?"

"I do. You'll be surprised, because Winnie has plenty to occupy herself and keep busy. She also needs a life of her own as well as looking after you, you know."

Freda pursed her lips, deep in thought. "Hmm, I'd never thought of it like that." Brightening, she lifted her head and smiled at Ruth. "Thanks, Ruth. You may have solved a big problem for me."

"No, you are making a problem when there isn't one there."

Freda hugged Ruth before leaving, appearing to have gained a newfound confidence from this conversation and would maybe move forward now. But Freda hadn't finished.

"Oh, another thing, I've just heard Barney Stopes is to meet the young French girl who nursed him back to health during the war."

"When did you hear this, Freda?"

"Earlier today when Josh called to see Mr Dymock."

"You seem to have all the good news this morning, Freda."

Ruth watched Freda disappear down the main street, shaking her head at the difference in their lives, experiences and upbringings and realised that everyone has their infallibilities and weaknesses whatever their background. Now, pull yourself together, Ruth, as you have a full day of work before you arrive back home to read the letter.

Albert was almost done when Ruth rode into the yard, Jim was still leading stone and would be back later. "Sam has got all the field work done and I've got the beast fed and the yard work finished, Ruth, only the pigs and hens to feed. Oh, there might be a few eggs to gather as they've started laying again" Albert said.

Sam was the mine worker who had stayed on in the village and continued to help two days a week. "Thanks, Albert. I don't know how we'd manage without you." He came and put his arm around her shoulders. "You and Jim 'll always manage, Ruth. Look at the difference in the old place now. Things are thriving. Make the most of it while prices are good and remember to save a bit as you go." With that, he mounted Honey to make his way home. Jim arrived a few minutes later.

Ruth had the table set by the time Jim entered and his eyes lighted on the letter behind the clock on the mantelpiece. "That this morning's post, Ruth? I seem to recognise the writing. Is it the one you're expecting from York?"

"Yes, it's from Aunty Moll. I've been wanting to read it all day. Now it's time, I'm nervous."

Once tea was finished, he moved closer to her. "Whatever it says, we can face it, Ruth, like everything else we've done. Now, settle down and read it. Do not dwell on it." Typical Jim. Face it head-on and go from there. Ruth reached up for the letter and Jim handed her a knife from the drawer to slice it open. With shaking hands, she withdrew the note and began to read, slowly, taking in every word. Jim sat patiently hoping for a positive response.

Once finished, her gaze lifted to Jim, saying, "Patrick would like to meet with me if possible."

Jim smiled. "Well, that's good news, Ruth." He paused, a frown on his face. "Isn't it?"

She smiled back, tears in her eyes, a tremor in her hands. "Yes, it is. I wasn't sure how he would reply when he knew I was willing to meet. Again, that awful fear of rejection hit me in the pit of my stomach. What if he decided against seeing me after I'd made the commitment?"

"That was unlikely, Ruth. Remember, Patrick wanted to find you. Now you can go ahead and arrange a meeting."

Excitement shone in her eyes, her earlier nervousness disappearing as the news hit home. "Could you make the journey with me, Jim?" This said hopefully.

"Would you like me to?"

"Definitely. I'm not sure I could face the meeting alone."

Jim reached out and held her close. "Yes, you could, Ruth. I've never known a woman as strong as you. Just think, how long is it since that fateful day?"

"Eighteen years since they carried me away screaming. But, since visiting my mother's grave, I can talk about it calmly. I can even picture the scene without any fear of nightmares returning. I believe I grew up an awful lot on that trip, Jim."

Night was closing in. Jim stood and reached up to light the lamp. A soft glow spread across the room when a sudden knock on the door startled them both. It was late for visitors. A quick glance at the clock showed almost 10 pm. Jim strode to answer the door and was surprised to see Luke Clemmit stood on the threshold.

"Luke, come in, come in." Jim greeted the young boy, placing an arm around his shoulders, ushering him into the light. Luke gave a brief nod in Ruth's direction, cap twisting nervously in his hands. Jim tried to put Luke at ease but knew in his heart this meant trouble. "What's happened, Luke? What on earth are you doing wandering around at this time of night. A lad your age should be tucked up in bed getting ready for school in the morning."

"It's Dad, Mr Styles."

Jim turned serious. "And?"

"I think he's dead."

This was a shock. Jim was expecting trouble but not this serious. "Sit down, Luke and tell me what's happened." Ruth was already on her way to the kitchen to bring the boy a drink.

"I went in after feeding up and him and Dick were arguing again. He slung a blow at Dick, but Dick was much quicker and grabbed the twelve-bore stood in the corner of the room.

"Oh, my God!" An exclamation from Ruth as she entered the room.

Luke glanced at her. "No, it wasn't loaded, Mrs Styles, he just swung it and smashed Dad on the side of the head. He dropped like a stone. Never moved a muscle. Dick grabbed me by the collar and warned me not to tell anyone, then ran off. I don't know where he's gone. I wasn't sure what to do so I thought you might be able to help me."

"Wasn't there anyone in Copton who could have helped, Luke?"

He shot a look of incredulity at Ruth. "What, a family like ours asking for help? Nobody gives us the time of day, let alone helping with this mess."

Jim turned to Ruth. "Right, I'll saddle up and ride over there." He was already slinging a jacket on. "We can't leave the man laid there all night. He might still be alive."

"I doubt it," said Luke. "It was a hell of a blow."

"Well, it's worth a chance." Turning to Ruth, he said, "I know Ned Willis who lives there, Ruth. He'll help me."

Ruth looked hopeful. "Is he a doctor, Jim?"

"No, he's a vet but he'll have more idea than me on what to do."

"Sounds about right," Luke said without any emotion in his voice. "He's more animal than human, anyhow."

Jim and Ruth looked at each other, sadness in their eyes. "I'll make the spare bed up for Luke. He'll be all right here for the night, Jim."

"Thanks. I'll be as quick as I can." With that he rushed out of the door.

"I'm having a bite to eat, Luke. Would you like something?"

"Yeh, I am hungry, Mrs Styles." He appeared to be in a man's frame but he still looked to be a little boy lost, struggling to understand this cruel world. And none of it his own doing. Ruth returned and handed him a sandwich. "Thank you." Silence for a while, Ruth letting him take his time until he felt ready to talk. "I didn't love him, you know. Not like most kids love their parents." He was speaking more to himself than Ruth. She let him carry on. "He's a cruel man, Mrs Styles. He used to beat all of us, mam as well, before she died. We were all frightened of him." Silence. "I'm not sorry, you know. I should be, but I'm not."

Lifting his head, he studied Ruth, a questioning look in those young baleful eyes of his. "Why is it that some people can't help being cruel, and others are kind. I can't understand that."

"I wish I could answer your question, Luke but it needs someone much wiser than myself to make sense of it." She went and sat in the chair next to him and took his hand. "But what I can tell you is that your safe here for as

91

long as you want, and you will be well fed." He raised a smile. Ruth, assured by the smile, continued, "And I promise you there will be no beatings in this household."

After clearing the plates away, Ruth said, "Right, let me show you to your room and where things are, then you must try and get a good night's sleep."

They walked upstairs and Ruth lit the lamp, giving Luke time to adjust to his new surroundings.

"This room all mine, Mrs Styles?"

"It is. You have water, towel and a bowl on the washstand, and a hairbrush and mirror to make sure your handsome for breakfast."

He gave an embarrassed laugh. We are making headway, thought Ruth.

"I'm not handsome, Mrs Styles."

"Oh, but you are and when you wake up in the morning and brushed your teeth and combed your hair, you'll be a right catch for any young girl."

Another laugh as he sat down on the bed and bounced up and down a couple of times. "Wow, this feels great. My bed was a couple of horse blankets spread on the floor and my brother snoring above me in the single bed."

Ruth's heart ached for this lonely and badly treated boy. What chance had he and, more importantly, where would he go from here if her and Jim didn't handle it right. She chose her next words carefully. "Well, I'm sure you will be comfortable and when you rise early in the morning, Jim will have news from home."

He looked pleadingly up at her. "I'm not sure I want to hear it, Mrs Styles."

Chapter 18

J im expected a long night lay ahead of him. Not only had he to find Ned Willis's house, the veterinary surgeon, he also had the thankless task of rousing him from his bed to ask for help on treating, or pronouncing dead, a certain Mr Clemmit. Jim was not sure of the man's first name, only heard of him referred to as Red.

Fortunately, Ned was quite used to being woken at odd hours of the night. It went with the job. Farmers put the welfare of their animals first, the vet a very distant second. Once dressed, Ned gathered his equipment together and in good humour, considering the task, they mounted and were soon riding up the rough track, the moon often flitting behind the heavy clouds but not a glimmer of light showing at any of the windows. Dismounting, Jim was first to the door and was about to knock but found it unlatched. Taking a deep breath, he felt his way along the dark passage. Ned struck a match behind him, casting eery dancing shadows along the walls.

Jim pushed the door open into what he thought would be the living room. Suddenly, Ned cursed, "damn it," quickly dropping the match. The room became as black as the hobs of hell once again. Jim hesitated waiting for more light before entering the room. Hardly daring to breathe, he tried to stay calm.

"Sorry, burnt me fingers, Jim. I have another here."

The rasping strike of a match sounded loud in the deathly silence, but it allowed Jim enough light to see what was before him.

"Don't come any further, I have a gun here!" The gravelly voice sounded deadly serious, coming from the far side of the room. Jim and Ned froze in shock. They'd expected an unconscious, or dead body but Red Clemmit was nowhere near departing from this world. Holding a blood-stained rag to his head with one hand and a twelve-bore shotgun in the other, he suddenly recognised Ned Willis, as Ned lit a candle on the table.

"Ned. Ned Willis?" Clemmit screwed his eyes up for a better look. "What the hell are you doing creeping in here in the middle of the night?"

"We've come to help you, Red. We heard you were injured."

"I am bloody injured. That fool son o' mine belted me with the gun and then ran off." He leant forward for a better look, then suddenly recognised Jim. "I might o' known you'd be involved, Styles. Get out o' my house" He let the bloodied rag drop from his head and raised the gun.

The tension in the room was almost unbearable. Christ, Jim had expected a confrontation but nothing as serious as a gun aimed directly at his chest. Although frightened, he was not about to show it, not even a hint and answered Red calmly. "I'll go as soon as Ned here treats your injury. He's brought everything with him." Jim stared into the grizzled blood-stained face, hoping to God the man came to his senses. After a full minute of staring death in the face, Red finally lowered the gun.

Ned blew out his cheeks in relief. "That's more like it, Red. Let's be sensible and calm down before anyone else gets hurt." Ned lit a couple more candles, already opening his bag ready to set to work.

Red was not for calming, still aggressive. "I shoulda given you a thrashing the first time I saw you, Styles. That would have stopped you interfering with this family."

"You're not a family, Clemmit. You rule those boys by fear. Well, you got what you deserve."

"Why, you… but before he could reach for the gun, Ned bravely stepped in to examine the wound.

"Good God, Red. You're a lucky man. I think you may keep your sight in this eye."

Red cut him off. "What the hell d'you mean lucky. I have two useless clods for sons, one who does nothing but whinge and the other takes to beating me with a gun and then runs off."

Jim could not take it any longer. "I would say you're lucky he used the butt of the gun. If it had been me, I would have used it the other way round and you would be plummeting down to where you belong, Red Clemmit." Before the man could answer, Ned butted in again. "Keep still, Red, damn it. Let me work on this wound or you'll bleed to death for God's sake." The urgency in Ned's voice stilled the big man.

Jim turned and said, "I'll see you outside when you've finished with him, Ned, and, if I were you, I wouldn't bother being too gentle."

Jim was relieved to be out in the open air, the realization hitting him on just how close he had come to meeting the grim reaper. His whole body began to tremble, his chest tight as he struggled to breathe, the shock of what he faced coming to the surface.

Sat outside on the cold stone flags of the garden path, the shaking diminished and his breathing returned to normal. Eventually, the pink, red glow of dawn slowly eased the blackness of night away, along with the morbid thoughts of what might have happened when facing the loaded gun.

Jim was glad Ned was taking some time to stitch the man together, it allowed him the space to get his thoughts in order now the shock had subsided. Jim studied the surroundings in the early light. There appeared to be a good range of buildings, pig styes, cow byre and stables but the red pantile roofs were in a sorry state, almost in a state of collapse. Rotting cart bodies, broken cartwheels and axles were left scattered, apparently where they were last used, some in the yard, others in the corner of the orchard and a timber shed had already given up the fight with gravity and collapsed completely. He stared up at the farmhouse itself. The windows were rotten, sashes hanging loose and where panes of glass had broken, they were just boarded up. God, poverty was a cruel taskmaster. Deep in thought, Jim didn't know how many acres were with the farm but in his eyes, it looked a good farm going to waste.

There were footsteps behind him. Ned had finished.

"Thank God for that," he said with a sigh of relief. "All done. He's out for the count now, Jim."

"I hope you gave him an injection that would stun an elephant. Did you?"

Ned grinned. "No, I didn't need to. He still had plenty of alcohol in his system to put him to sleep for the night. I'll let the doctor know when I return home and he can take over." They sat in silence for a while.

"You realise you were quite lucky in there, Jim."

"Maybe I was born lucky, Ned," he said with a grin. "Honestly though, I realize anything could have happened, 'cos when I came outside, I began shaking like a leaf." He turned and grinned at Ned. "Thanks for helping me out, Ned. It's not that I'll lose any sleep over Red but I do think the lads deserve better than this."

"They do, Jim, but Red's well-known for a violent temper. This has been festering for a while now. Well, since their mother died, anyway."

"Right, come on, Ned, let's head home. It's been a long day." Mounting easily, the sun had lifted clear of the horizon with the promise of a glorious day ahead. Reaching the end of the farm track, they reined their horses to a stop where Jim would branch off and head back to Roston.

"Well, it was an odd way to meet up with you, Jim Styles, but I am glad to have made your acquaintance."

"Same here. Next time, let's hope it's in less scary circumstances. Thanks again, Ned." And they went their separate ways.

Jim arrived back as Ruth and Luke were finishing feeding up. Ruth ran over to him, then noticed the gap-toothed smile on his face. "What's the news?" she asked eagerly. Jim hesitated, as Luke stayed where he was but watching them both intently.

Jim called him over. "Luke, come on, you need to know what happened." The boy wandered over, a worried look on his face. "You can stop worrying, Luke. Your father is alive and well." Luke's eyes widened, the relief showing on his young features. Wiping away the tears, he said, "I always knew he was a tough old sod but I didn't think he could survive that smack." Luke sat on the mounting steps. "So, Dick won't be done for murder then?" he asked.

"Definitely not. But there is one thing, Luke?"

"What's that, Mr Styles?"

"The vet did a damned good job with the stitches to your fathers head, but it 'll spoil his good looks for a while." Laughing, they all walked back into the kitchen where Jim's breakfast was on the table. "Oh, thanks, Ruth. I just have time for a bite before I go to the quarry. Luke, I have a favour to ask. D'you think you can look after things here for us until I get back?"

"That is already sorted, Jim." Ruth said. "By the way, I've written the letter to Aunty Moll. I'll post it as I go to work. See you tonight."

Chapter 19

J im was sure that, given a week or two, Luke would return home. Or, if he was intent on being independent, to make enquiries at Castle Moor, or the brickworks who were taking men on. But as days shortened, Luke showed no sign of moving on, or indeed, wanting to. Jim was pleased with his decision to give Luke a chance. For once in his short life, the boy appeared to be happy and, Jim realized, if Luke did leave, he would be sorely missed, as most of the farm work would fall to Albert and Sam, as Jim continued the contracting work at the quarry.

Jim and Luke were raking up and tidying the stackyard and shutting the hens up when a clatter of hooves halted their work and Jocylyn Dymock arrived in a cloud of dust mounted on a beautiful chestnut horse. "Good evening to you both." Beneath the broad brimmed hat his face was tanned, eyes bright from the ride. Dismounting, he shook hands with the pair of them.

"Good evening, Jocylyn. Good to see you." Jim cast his eyes over the horse. "I take it this is Dunella." Both Jim and Luke stood, admiration clear in their eyes, at this fine specimen of a horse, only a blaze of white on its forehead breaking the shining coat of chestnut. Even after the long ride, the ears were up, nostrils flared as if ready to go once more.

"What a magnificent animal, Jocylyn." Jim's face showed his disappointment as he said, "but I'm afraid this horse will be out of our price range."

"I don't think so, Jim. Wait until you hear the full story." Jocylyn was eager to tell them the good news. "Dunella's owner is a good friend of our family. He is getting on in years now and when he retired the horse, he has continued to pay for the stabling, exercise, and its upkeep. He is now faced with a situation where he must cut down on time and expense involved. So, he wants Dunella moved to a good home where it will be exercised, well looked after, and can enjoy its retirement. I spoke with him and told him what I had in mind and he agreed this was a marvellous solution for us all."

"You mean you have to find this beautiful animal a home?" Jim asked, making sure he understood the man.

"That is exactly what I mean, Jim." At that moment, Ruth ventured out to see who the visitor was and heard everything. Jocylyn turned and acknowledged Ruth, before carrying on, "and all he asks is that he can visit every now and then."

Ruth smiled across to Jocylyn, excitement clear in her eyes, then spoke to Jim. "Well, Jim, this must be our lucky day. The bargain of the year." She went over to Dunella and stroked her neck and mane. The taut skin flickered under her touch, the eyes, ever intelligent, turned towards Ruth and gave a soft whinny, as if in recognition. At that moment, Ruth fell in love with the animal and threw her arms around Jim, then Luke.

"What about me?" Jocylyn stood with open arms, a smile on his face, expectant.

Ruth dashed over and gave Jocylyn a quick hug, her heart fluttering at the closeness. "Thank you so much for thinking of us, Jocylyn. Because we were willing to pay. This really means the world to us." She paused before adding, "and the previous owner is welcome to visit us, and Dunella, as often as he wants. We would love to make his acquaintance."

"That's settled then. It will take a few days to get used to her." Jocylyn was talking directly to Ruth. "I believe it will be yourself who rides her the most, so be ready as she can be a bit flighty at times but nothing you won't be able to handle. And when you let her go, she is an exciting ride." He smiled at the pleasure on their faces.

"Please, won't you come in and let us thank you properly before you leave?"

"I'd love to but I have someone waiting at the end of the track. But, I am staying at Oak Tree for a few days, if any of you have the time to visit and I will show you around the old place." Waving goodbye, he strode towards the figure waiting in the distance.

The three of them disappeared inside. "I cannot believe our luck, Jim. Just out of the blue like that." Ruth shook her head in disbelief.

Luke was incredulous, finally finding his voice. "Wow, what a gift from the man. This'll make things a lot easier for us, won't it?"

Ruth replied. "A lot easier, Luke. This leaves the other two work horses free for you and Jim."

On entering the kitchen, a frown creased Ruth's brow. "You know what, you two? We need to sit down and discuss Luke's future." Ruth studied the young boy. "And there's no better time than right now." There was a long silence before Ruth spoke again. "You see, we can't move forward, Luke, until we know what your intentions are. If you intend moving back home, or if you want to stay here, or move on to pastures new. What do you want to do, Luke because we must let your father know?"

Luke appeared worried. They were now seated around the table.

"The thing is," Luke said eventually, "I don't want to be the cause of any bother. You know what my father's like. He's a violent man. If I have the choice I'd like to stay here but it may not be possible. I'm up to most of the jobs that Albert and Sam set me." He looked balefully from one to the other, like a soul lost in the wilderness, unsure of what the future did hold for him.

After a while, Jim spoke. "What about if I go see your father and explain the situation, Luke. He might see it makes sense. There's no doubt Ruth and I need the extra help here."

"What if he doesn't see sense, Jim. He could be dangerous. You well know that." Luke was still frightened of his violent father.

"Well, I suppose he'll have the law on his side, you only been fifteen." Jim grinned." But look at it this way, with you gone it's one less mouth to feed."

Ruth butted in. Yes, we can do all this, and if Luke does decide to stay, it is with one condition."

They both chimed in. "And what's that?"

"That Luke spends time learning in the evenings. He must not miss out on education, Jim." They looked at Ruth. "Agreed?" she asked.

Jim grinned as he studied the expression on Luke's face. "Agreed," Jim replied.

After Luke had retired to bed, Jim and Ruth sat talking.

"So, you think Dunella will be a decent mount to get you to and from school earlier, eh?"

Ruth's face broke into a grin. "She certainly will."

"If you ride Dunella every day, the trip to York with the Cob and trap will seem quite sedate to you."

"It will, Jim but it will be nice to have a break from work. It will put my mind to rest over meeting Patrick. I have told Moll I'm prepared to meet my father and I think that will be best for both of us. After all it has been a long time." Ruth carried on, the serious face disappearing. "Also, if the meeting does go well, hopefully we'll have time to call and see John and Edith and maybe Aunty Moll as well." There was a faraway look in her eyes as she said this.

"It'll go well, Ruth. Believe me, I speak from experience." He held her close. "Just be ready for the change in your father. He will have suffered through the war years, as many others have. And don't forget, he 'll certainly be as worried as you about meeting up. It's a big step after such a tragic parting." Jim was desperately trying to reassure her, searching her face to see if it was striking home. He wasn't totally sure but he did not want Ruth returning to the nightmares of her past.

"Oh, I know you mean well, Jim and I also realize you have been through it, but we can never be sure. All I can say for certain is the past is dead and buried, no longer a burden for me and I will not be returning there." She kissed him, and added, "my life is here, on the farm, with you in this beautiful part of the world. It also just happens to be my playground as well." A smile crossed her face. "When I have the time, that is."

Chapter 20

It wasn't much of a place, nothing like as clean as the small room he'd occupied at St Catherine's but he did have more privacy. It came about when a friend of Emmy's called at the refuge asking if she knew of anyone willing to help on his market stall three days a week. Emmy introduced him to Patrick, who gladly accepted the job.

Tapping the side of his nose, the man said, "Also, if you keep your head down, Patrick, there is also a property close by the market, habitable, but it's due for demolition sometime in the future. Could be useful until that day comes."

Patrick, craving to be clear of charity, thought it worth the risk. The accommodation consisted of two rooms, one up, one down and an outside toilet at the end of the alley. Once cleaned up, the living kitchen area was adequate and, luckily, the former occupants had left two chairs, one which proved comfortable, even though the horsehair stuffing was bursting from the seams. The black leaded range heated the room and proved essential for cooking his meals and the low-slung ceiling joists made the room feel smaller, but it warmed quickly in the cold weather.

Almost a year had passed since Patrick first contacted Molly and his hopes of a letter from Ruth were fading. Knowing Moll visited Sarah's grave quite regularly, he hoped a note may have appeared at the shelter but no such luck. If Ruth was not prepared to tell of her whereabouts, then he could do no more.

Settling down as darkness fell, Patrick heard a light tap at the door. Startled by the knock, as he didn't think anyone knew he was here, he answered the door cautiously and who should be stood there but young Pete.

"Gor, you took some finding, Mister." He stood there in the fading light, dishevelled, one bootlace undone and socks round his ankles. "I've bin round these houses twice now, looking for ye. I didn't even know these were still lived in. Must o' missed ye every time."

"Well, it's good to see you, Pete. I take it you have some news for me, or have you just called to inquire about my health."

"Don't know what you're on about. I've come to give you this." He handed the envelope across. "Molly gave it me a week since, said it was important." He swiped a sleeve across his runny nose. "Bet it's from your daughter?"

"Come in, Pete." Pete followed Patrick inside and watched as he lit the lamp on the mantelpiece. The warm glow soon illuminated the small room and Patrick fished into his pockets and handed Pete a few coppers for his time. As he ran off, Pete shouted over his shoulder, "hope it's good news, mister, but ye better keep your head down, as the police 'll throw ye in a cell." Patrick drew a chair up, close to the light of the lamp. For some reason his hands were shaking and his mind was racing. It must be from Ruth. With thumping heart, he sliced the letter open and as he read, he thought he would faint.

July, 1921

Dear father.

I received a letter from Aunty Moll explaining your situation. I have talked this through with Jim, and I do feel the way forward is to meet again. Many years have passed since that fateful day, and I believe life will have changed us both.

I will be in touch with Moll and inform her when I will be visiting York again.

Regards

Ruth Styles.

Relief flooded through his body, and he sank back in the chair. She was willing to meet up. Ruth gave no idea when, or no address to get in touch. It would be her choice when, and how, this would happen. He couldn't believe it. A chance to meet her after all these years. Many thoughts raced through his brain. When would she reply? Would he recognise her? The only image strong in his mind was of a hysterical nine-year-old girl, his daughter, been bundled outside by a police officer into Aunty Moll's arms while he was hauled away in handcuffs.

Patrick, no longer able to hold his emotions in check, wept openly, tears of relief staining his cheeks until sleep gradually afforded him peace of mind.

Chapter 21

B ack in Castle Moor, Josh, late finishing work at the quarry, intended visiting Jacob but spotted Barney entering the Buck. He checked his pocket watch, maybe just time for a quick one, he thought. Not having seen Barney lately, he was keen to hear the news on Maria's visit, as it was her grandparent's bravery that saved his and Barney's lives when badly injured.

The Buck had become a well-known drinking house, a three-storey stone building at the end of a low terrace of stone cottages and set back from the steeply rising main road. As dusk closed in, a dim glow from a carriage lamp tried vainly to display the peeling, painted sign hanging from a wooden post, the only evidence that it was a pub. Swinging the gate open in the small picket fence surrounding the garden, Josh strode up the stone flagged path to the entrance.

He was no stranger here, as he and Pete had spent many a night at the bar, putting the world to rights in the difficult times. But nowadays, Josh was loath to hand his hard-earned cash over the bar to Harry, the landlord. He was unsure of what the future held, but for once, money rattled in his pocket due to regular work at the quarry, and it was a nice feeling.

Entering the dimly lit room was like walking into the living room of any house in Castle Moor, apart from this one had a bar. Not surprising really, as its original purpose was for a domestic dwelling but as Castle Moor became busier, the call for a public house could not be ignored. The landlord, Harry Ennis, a single man and not one to miss a way to make money, applied for a licence. Once legal and his own furniture moved upstairs, the old pantry became the bar and the beer was served straight from the barrels. Along with new decoration, hunting pictures were hung from the high picture rails and the special silver tankards saved for his regulars, sparkled in the lamplight behind the bar. The room was quite small, but three round tables were squeezed in, along with a dozen chairs.

The Buck also held a reputation for its prime position in the village and its panoramic views over the river Esk and the moors beyond. At present the moor bore the scars of the quarrying and the new incline plunging down to the crushing shed. The prized window seats for customers lucky enough to find them free were rewarded with a view of the stunning sunsets, especially during the summer months.

"Evening, Josh. Long time, no see. The usual?" Harry, as welcoming and jovial as ever, liked to keep tabs on his customers and was pleased to see Josh walk through the door.

"Evening, Harry. Yes, thanks. I see you are entertaining the best of company tonight." Josh surveyed the small room, a smile breaking across his face. He nodded politely to a couple of strangers he didn't know, before Pete and Barney waved him to their table. Pulling a chair out for him, Josh gathered his pint up and joined them.

"Come on, have a seat, Josh. We haven't seen you for ages. Where have you bin hiding?" Barney asked.

Josh settled back easily in his chair. "Heck, I've not been hiding, lads. Now there's work about, it's good to be earning decent money after always been skint." Josh studied Pete, then asked, "How are you doing, Pete? Healthwise, I mean."

Josh could see his friend had failed, lost weight and was gaunt in the face. Even his smile was strained. "I'm getting by, old mate, but the doc told me I'll never be fit enough to work again and it's unlikely to get any easier, I'll have to live with it the best I can." He tried to brighten up. "So, you'll be glad to know there'll be no more shepherding for us. But hey, I'm still here and we have a lot to look forward to and catch up on. Barney has some great news. Tell him, Barney."

"Well, you'll have heard Maria is coming to England at the end of the year with her grandparents and she wants to meet up again."

"That's brilliant, Barney. I take it you've kept in touch then?"

"Yeh, 'course I have."

Josh smiled at the thought of Barney sat writing a love letter. "You must realize now it's not only your body she's after, she must also be swooning over your literary skills on how to write a love letter." Pete and Josh rocked back in their chairs with laughter at this sarcasm. "I hope your spellings were all correct, or you might never hear from her again."

"Aw, come off it, you two, give it a rest. Mind you, if you want a good laugh, our war hero Josh was nearly frightened to death by an old owl up on the moors." Wiping the tears from their eyes after imagining Josh running away from the owl, Barney put on his serious face. "You know that little farm we stumbled on where she looked after us, Josh?"

"Course I do. Could I ever forget it. They saved our lives that day."

Barney went on. "Well, Maria told me after her parents were killed in the war, her grandparents travelled to France to look after her. They risked everything for their family. You see, Maria's father was their son,"

"And?" Josh was all ears.

"They're from England, really. Own property and land in a little village just outside York. I hadn't heard of it. You know, we wondered how they had learnt to speak such perfect English, Josh?" Barney carried on before Josh could answer. "That's why, because they're from this country. In her last letter, Maria told me there are too many painful memories in France, so she will try and settle here if possible."

"That's good news, Barney, I bet you can't wait to hear from them?"

"All being well, there should be a letter this next couple of weeks." Barney relaxed back in his chair and took a sip of his beer.

"Roll on the next few months eh, Barney?" A few more had gathered and the noise level was rising. "What about you, Josh?" Pete asked. "New job must be going well. I've heard he's a man of breeding. Is that right?"

"I don't see much of him, I've only met him a couple of times, but Jim and Ruth say he's straight enough. Ruth's riding one of his horses to work and it looks a proper thoroughbred to me." Josh pulled his pocket watch out. "Cripes, look at the time. See, that's what happens when I get with you lot. Got to go, catch up with you soon." Josh pushed his chair back and rose to leave.

"It must have been his round, Barney," Pete said. "He can't get out quick enough. See you, Josh," they shouted after the departing figure.

Chapter 22

A lbert waited expectantly at the farm gate to help with the last wagonload of sheaves before calling it a day. Luckily, the weather had stayed settled throughout harvest, the sun a constant shimmering disc in a brilliant blue sky most days, bathing the whole valley in a golden light. Albert smiled at the scene before him, as it dipped low towards the horizon, stretching the shadows across the fields. The rows of stooks stood military fashion in the fields, the horses moving steadily from stook to stook. Soon, all would be safely gathered in, just as the hymn says, thought Albert.

The cart trundled into the yard, Ruth handling the two horses, Jim alongside and Luke on top of the load. Albert had a drink ready for them all and they took a breather before Albert climbed the ladder to finish 'topping out' as he put it.

Jim wiped the sweat from his brow. "That's the last load for today. Another day leading tomorrow should finish it if the weather stays like this," Jim stood back and surveyed the craftsmanship of the stacker. "Y'know, Albert, I've seen many other corn stacks and never seen any to match the tidiness that you manage to do."

Albert was quite proud of his technique. "That is praise indeed. Now, I'm heading home before that honeyed tongue of yours finds more work for me."

"No, don't worry, Albert, nothing else will be done tonight. But we'll need you tomorrow. Can you manage another day, d'you think?" He looked questioningly at Albert.

"Course I can, Jim," he said in disgust, as if they should ever doubt him. Mounting Honey, he waved goodnight as they disappeared into the farmhouse.

Albert arrived to find Martha sat with a cup of tea and red-rimmed eyes. She'd been crying. He rushed over to her and grabbed her hands.

"Whatever's the matter, Martha. Have you happened something? What's upset you?"

Martha pointed to the open letter on the table. Reaching for his reading specs from the mantelpiece, he sat down to read.

> *John and Edith Durville*
> *10, Darwin Court,*
> *York*
> *Sep. 20th, 1922*

> *Dear Albert and Martha.*
>
> *I hope this letter finds you both well.*
>
> *The good news first is that John and I recently tied the knot last year at the Register Office in York. Just a small ceremony with a few close friends and witnesses and we are truly happy. John asked me if I would write this letter to inform you of the death of his only surviving family member, his son, Henry just last week.*
>
> *It has hit him very hard, but I'm sure he will fight back. I will be with him every step of the way, as he was for me. We look forward to visiting in the near future, as your part of the world means such a lot to us both. Will be in touch when appropriate.*
>
> *Yours sincerely*
> *Edith Durville*

Albert reread the letter, shaking his head at the bad news. "That will take some getting over for a man of his age, Martha. You mark my words."

"Well, at least he's with a good woman, Albert. Edith 'll see him through it."

Retiring to bed, Albert had a restless night, unable to put the young man's death out of his mind as Martha snored peacefully at his side. No one was immortal, he well knew that. But maybe it was a blessing, as Henry would never have been considered safe for release from hospital.

Up at daybreak, Albert pulled the corner of the curtains aside an inch or two, not wanting to wake Martha and then paddled downstairs. He knew a hard day faced him but the pleasure he derived from working with 'the young 'uns,' made it worthwhile. He arrived just before the first load. Only Jim and Luke today, Ruth must be at work, so he decided to tell them all later. When the last load arrived it just topped the second stack off nicely as Ruth rode up on Dunella, instantly admiring Albert's fine work.

"You are a very talented man, Albert Styles," she said, before planting the customary kiss on top of Albert's head as he'd removed his cap.

He smiled and put an arm over her shoulders, basking in the praise from Ruth. "You always seem to say the right thing, at the right time, Ruth. I don't know how you do it?"

"It's all my teaching, Albert," chirped in Jim.

Now Ruth had arrived, Albert decided the time was right to tell them about the letter. "Martha and I received bad news yesterday morning, from York. Henry Durville died last week and John's taken it quite badly. Edith hopes that, given time, John will accept that it was a blessing for everyone really, as Henry could not be allowed to live in a civilised society."

Ruth said, "That is tragic news, Albert. As you know, I had no use for Henry, but I do feel for John and Edith."

"But Edith did finish with good news," Albert added. "They tied the knot just a few weeks ago in a quiet little wedding ceremony at York with just a few close friends and will try to visit these parts when John is up to it." This final news lifted their spirits and Albert wandered over to Honey. "Right, I'm off for my tea. I can't make it tomorrow, as Martha needs a few jobs doing at home, so I'll see you all next week. Cheerio."

Waving goodbye, Ruth rushed in to rustle up tea, as Jim stabled the horses and watered the beast. Luke wandered around to the orchard and checked that all the hens were in and roosting and safe from any prowling foxes.

Chapter 23

O ver in Malton, Toby was out at the crack of dawn just as the sun broke above the horizon, casting an eerie light across the yard. Organisation was the key. With twenty thoroughbreds to feed and train they were long days but after Vicky told Jocylyn, in no uncertain terms, they just couldn't cope with the workload, he hired more staff to help and as Toby opened the stables, the two young girls arrived.

He smiled a greeting. "Morning girls. No late nights for you two, starting at this time of the morning, eh?"

The elder girl replied. "If you want to work with horses, you cannot burn the candle at both ends. You well know that, Toby."

He grinned at her. "Very true. Now, Victoria informs me we have a very important guest arriving from London today. Lady Florence, a good friend of Jocylyn, and the family, occasionally travels up for a ride on Maximillian. Apparently, she also likes to keep a check on how we are looking after him. With Jocylyn and Victoria busy, this puts you in the hot seat, Lucy. Think you can handle a fully-fledged Lady from the big city."

He studied the girls. Lucy was the more experienced, in her early twenties and, surprisingly, still unattached. Tall, athletic, dark hair tied up in a bun and always quite relaxed, especially with the opposite sex. Sophia, younger and quite shy, was relatively inexperienced and, Toby felt, very much in the older girl's shadow. But she was learning steadily and would always tackle any job Toby asked her to do.

Lucy answered with such self-confidence, Toby wondered why he had ever doubted her. "Of course, Toby. Just one thing though, how do I address her?"

"Hmm." Toby frowned in thought. "Good question. I've never met a titled person before. How does, m'lady sound? And maybe a small bow of the head."

"Sounds good to me. If it's wrong, no doubt she will not be frightened in correcting me."

Toby admired her no-nonsense reaction to any problems. Much like himself, he thought. "Not sure what time Lady Florence will arrive, so you better start on Max straight away."

"Will do."

Toby added, "just a word of warning. Keep your eye on the weather this morning, there could be a storm brewing. Wear your waterproofs, or have them with you and I'll take care of your job's here while you're gone."

As Jocylyn spent more time and money on his business venture, the two girls proved a great help.

"After I sort Max out, we'll take the two new ones for some gentle exercise, Toby, then return for m'lady. That sound okay?"

"That 'd be good. But remember, girls, the horses are your friends. Never be afraid to talk to them, because they do understand."

Lucy smiled and made a mock salute. "Understood."

Toby watched the girls ride off, then his mind returned to home. More than a year had passed and the workload over that period had been intense for both him and Victoria. These last few weeks, he realized a break would be good. While saddling up a relatively new mare that had just arrived, Victoria walked in, as optimistic as ever.

"Okay this morning, Toby?" she asked. "Happy in taking this new one out. Get her used to your unique style of handling horses."

"Course I am, Victoria. But the weather looks threatening," he said, lifting his head. The clouds had blackened, blotting the earlier sunlight out and the quickening wind rustled through the very top of the trees. "The girls are already out there. I did warn them to keep an eye on the weather, though."

"You did right." She glanced at the sky. "I know Jocylyn has every faith in Sophia but she still lacks experience." She waited a second, then asked, "Which way are you thinking of going?"

"I'm heading on past the old mansion to the river and then onto the forest path." Then he added, "but I'll give the girls a bit more time, as they were only out for a short ride."

Five minutes later, they returned and had just finished grooming, when an immaculate Rolls Royce purred into the yard and drew to a halt. The chauffer quickly stepped out to open the door. This must be Lady Florence.

There was certainly an aura of grace and grandeur surrounding the lady as she stepped from the car and surveyed the yard and stables, before her eyes finally alighted on Toby. Dressed in her riding habit, she looked every inch the lady. Black hard hat and gloves held in her hand, hacking jacket to match, buttoned at the waist. Blond hair pulled tightly back with orange cravat at her long slender neck. Her black skirt hiding the top of the knee length leather riding boots which shone like mirrors.

Toby's mouth had suddenly gone dry as she haughtily stood and scrutinised him, but he bravely took the bull by the horns to break the silence. "Good morning, m'lady." The girls followed his lead. Lady Florence acknowledged them all with a slight nod of the head.

Turning to the chauffer, she said, "Leave my travel case in the tack room, Bailey, as I might need a change of clothes if it is muddy, then call back for me in about four hours. That gives me sufficient time out on Max."

"Thank you, m'lady." He bowed low, then swiftly swung the Rolls around and left the yard. Hardly a sound from the motor, just a scuff of tyres on the gravel.

Lady Florence turned her full attention on Toby. "Am I right in thinking you are Mr Toby Smith?"

"That is correct, m'lady." Toby was not used to bowing and scraping in front of gentry, but this was his job, so it had to be done.

"Jocylyn has spoken very highly of you in the past. Will you be joining me today?"

"No, I'm sorry, m'lady, but I have another horse coming in that I must see to. Lucy will be riding out with you today."

Lady Florence's nose lifted slightly and her sharp green eyes found his. "Hmm, you have a more important customer than myself, you think?"

Toby bristled but answered evenly enough. "No, all customers are important to us, as are their horses. But a promise is a promise and I did say I would be here for him."

Looking straight ahead now, she said. "Your loyalty is to be admired, Mr Smith."

"I learnt it from my parents at a very early age, m'lady."

She shot him a sidelong glance, not quite sure if this was a dig at her breeding or just downright sarcasm but she was not about to let it drop.

"You are from over the moors, I gather?"

"Yes, that is right, m'lady."

"Well, I hope you are up to looking after thoroughbreds and not just plough horses as there is a huge difference in the handling of such animals."

"I agree, but it is very similar to handling people, m'lady. Treat them with respect and they'll respond." Lucy turned away as Lady Florence strode up to Toby. Her eyes flashed in anger at being spoken to by a stable hand. "Don't you dare speak to me like that. You realize, I could have you sacked?"

"I don't think so, m'lady. Not without Mr Dymock's say so." When there was no hint of a backward step from Toby, she flounced off as, by this time, Lucy had Max already tacked up for her ladyship. A magnificent animal, standing at about sixteen hands with four white socks and a coat shining like silk even in this dull light. Lucy had chosen a grey mare of a similar height to join Lady Florence for company on her ride.

Lucy led the two horses to the mounting steps. Once mounted, Toby asked her to confirm the ride they would be taking.

"We'll head for the path along the river Derwent, bypass Castle Howard and the great lake then hit the rough, narrow road that takes us through Prestwick wood."

"That sounds good, Lucy. Keep note of the weather, won't you?"

"Will do. This mare is pretty good in all weathers. Like all females.

Unflappable." The grin said it all as m'lady studied the pair of them.

A couple of hours later, Toby poked his head out of the tack room and noticed the temperature had dropped dramatically and the clouds hung low and threatening. Concerned, he grabbed Pal's bridle and saddle just as Victoria came out of her office.

"Any problems, Toby?" Vicky also looked concerned.

"No, not as yet but I thought I would ride out to meet the girls as I reckon m'lady's mount could be a bit of a handful in this storm that's coming."

"Mind if I come with you?"

"I'd love you to. A ride is always better with company."

Quickly getting into her waterproofs, Vicky was soon up and mounted, catching Toby as he neared the burnt-out dwelling. She saw him studying it as he past. The red brick masonry still stood, although still smeared black by smoke. Part of the roof timbers, black and charred silhouettes against the darkening sky a reminder of a disaster years ago.

"You've been here more than a year now, Toby and never asked about this wreck of a house. Why?"

"Well, I wasn't sure if it belonged to your family or not. So, I reckoned it was none of my business."

Victoria's face tightened and said, "This house, this mansion, holds too many horrific memories for Jocylyn. This burnt-out building is why he moved to Castle Moor. To try and forget by sinking everything he has into the start of a new venture."

Toby listened but his eyes lifted to the storm. The underbelly of sky sunk lower, the trees bending like mere stalks as the first severe wind hit them. Leaves and twigs brushed past them. In the distance, a wall of rain came into view and a cacophony of sound from the unsettled birds.

Toby shouted against the wind. "I think we better catch up with the girls. This storm looks as though it could be dangerous, Vicky. Can we short cut into the wood?"

"Yes, follow me." Vicky at once lay flat on the stallion's neck, kicking it into a gallop as she did so. Toby had all on to stay with her as they raced across the rough grassland. Whoever taught her to ride had done a good job. On entrance to the wood, branches cracked and were beginning to fall such was the force of the gale.

Both were out of breath and Toby had to shout to make himself heard. "We must be ahead of them now, or we would have seen them come out of the wood. Let's ride to meet them." Riding into the wind proved tough and the ground was covered in pools and rivulets of water. The rain stung the exposed skin on their faces and the horses lowered their heads to face it. A flash of lightning lit up the trees, instantly followed by a crack of thunder. The horses shied but both Vicky and Toby were experienced enough to calm them. A few hundred yards more, they reached a turn in the track and there, ahead of them, saw the two girls cowering under a fallen tree. Both were hanging onto the reins of their mounts but looked bedraggled and muddy. Lady Florence was pale with shock and covered in mud from head to toe.

Lucy was first to speak. "Thank God you're here. We didn't know what to do. The lightning struck the tree and it crashed down right in front of us with no warning. Max shied, throwing Lady Florence backwards, which saved her life. But a branch slashed Max's leg and I don't know how badly injured he is." Lucy was frightened, but handling it well. "I thought it best to wait as I knew you'd come looking for us."

Toby and Victoria dismounted. "You've done really well, both of you." Toby told them. Gingerly, he fingered the injured leg. "Yep, we're in luck. It's a nasty gash but nothing broken. I'll just check for any other injuries, then we can all ride back together. We'll take the short cut."

"I am not riding back." This was Lady Florence being difficult. Defiant at an awkward time as the wind and rain slashed at their exposed faces.

Toby went across to her and talked quietly to her. "Are you sure you are not injured, m'lady?"

"No, I'm not injured. Do I look injured? But I'm not mounting that horse again in this storm." Toby was sure she was going to stamp her foot like the spoiled brat that she was. But she just stood with her back to the storm looking more bedraggled by the minute.

He smiled at her. "I must disagree with you, m'lady. I'm giving the orders now, so please listen carefully. I am going to place you back in the saddle and walk alongside until your confidence returns. And, trust me, it will return."

Toby hoisted her off the ground as she screamed, "don't you dare handle me like this. Put me down at once!" He carried on as if he'd never heard her, and gently lowered her onto the saddle as if she was a featherweight. Once seated, her protests stopped. Toby did as he said and walked by her side. Still clutching his hand, he could feel the fear trembling through her body. At that moment, he felt a sympathy towards this woman. So, holding the reins with his free hand as the thunder and lightning crashed around them, he continued talking to the horse and Florence above the sound of the storm. Vicky and Lucy followed, amazed at Toby's unruffled nature in times of a crisis. Once out of the wood, Toby mounted, but still held onto Max, as m'lady's confidence slowly returned. As he said it would.

Once back and the horses seen to, Toby told Victoria that he was pretty sure they didn't need to call a vet, he could treat the wound. Once the Rolls had left the yard, Toby set to work on the injured Max. His remedy was a concoction that he'd used on Pal after an injury while out riding as a boy. It had come from Winnie at Castle Moor.

When Toby finally settled in for the night, his thoughts drifted to home once more, deciding to ask Victoria if she could spare him for a couple of days away. It was while sat reading in his cottage that he thought he heard a knock at the door and who should be there but Victoria.

"Hello once again, Toby."

"Hiya, Vicky. This is a surprise." Toby looked worried. "Nothing wrong, is there?"

"No," she laughed. "There doesn't have to be a catastrophe for me to call and see you, does there?"

"No, 'course not. Here, I'm forgetting my manners. Come in and have a seat, please." He fluffed the cushion up in the other chair and Victoria settled herself. "Can I get you a drink?"

"No, thanks, Toby. I just called to say what a wonderful job you did in the storm with handling the horses, and the girls." Then she added, "and also with Max, Florence's horse."

Toby relaxed down into the chair opposite. "Hmm, it was a challenge, wasn't it? A grin broke across his face as he thought back. "It was a fantastic ride in those conditions but also exciting, I love that." With admiration in his voice, he asked, "Who taught you to ride like that, Vicky? Was it Jocylyn?"

"Yes, mostly. We grew up together and rivalry is often strong between siblings, but I love him to bits, really." She caught Toby by surprise with her next question. "Enough about me, where did you learn your equine skills, young man? Jocylyn informed me much of it stemmed from a certain Ruth Brennan."

"That's true, Vicky. It is strange, really, Ruth was originally a city girl from York, but was cruelly treated. Stumbling on Gallows How, she settled there. The first place to show her kindness she told me. An amazing girl, never taught anything about horses but soon had them doing exactly as she wanted." Vicky listened intently, head tilted to one side, as Toby continued. "It was as if they understood she was a friend, trusting her completely, understanding she would never hurt them." In serious mood, Toby said, "I knew then that is how I wanted to be, especially with horses."

Victoria listened quietly before saying, "She must be a good teacher, Toby?"

"She is. I picked a bit up from farmers but their treatment of animals didn't suit me. Ruth was gentler."

"That's a lovely story, I would love to meet her someday. I think we would have a lot in common."

Toby smiled. "I'm sure you would."

There was silence for a while before Toby plucked up courage to ask a favour. "Vicky, while you're here, would it be possible for me to have a couple of days off before long, I'm missing home a bit." He screwed his face up into a grin. "It's okay if I can't, I'll get over it but I'd like to catch up with me mates, tell 'em about this job and such."

"Well, that's one of the other things I've called to see you about, Toby. With the two girls on hand, the workload is less and I understand why you and Pal enjoy those moorland rides so much. I have a friend from my university days in that area and I keep in touch with her and go walking there." She paused. "Thinking ahead, next weekend would be good for me. How would that be?"

Toby's face lit up. "That'd be brilliant. My parents told me to turn up when I could. To be honest, I was a bit nervous about asking you."

"Goodness me, I'm not such an ogre of a boss, am I?" She laughed at her words but there was concern on her face, hoping he didn't see her that way.

"Lord, no. You couldn't have treated me better. I just didn't want to let you down."

"You'll not do that." Back in work mode, Vicky said, "that's settled then. Just leave the girls plenty of work for when you're away and look forward to your trip home." Rising from her chair, she gave him a quick hug before leaving. "Cheerio, Toby. See you first thing in the morning." And with that she was gone.

As his thoughts returned to home, he realized he still didn't know the story of the burnt-out building. Come the weekend, he grabbed a quick bite to eat, threw a change of clothes into the saddlebag before tacking Pal up for the ride. He decided to leave Friday night, allowing him a full two days at home. Nights were drawing in but an hour's ride before dark should see them make good time.

The fresh countryside thrilled him and a shiver of excitement ran up his spine as the narrow, twisting tracks followed the high banks of the river Rye. A well-lit sign, The Sun Inn, almost brought him to a halt for a break but as night settled softly over his shoulders like a cloak, Pal caught a scent of the moor air and his stride quickened, as if he sensed what lay ahead. Hitting the rising road out of Hutton, the moon, hidden behind swollen black clouds of night, finally broke through, lighting the snaking track over the highest point towards home.

Once descending from the high moor, the ride eased and were soon on the high street of Castle Moor where his parents lived. Patting Pal on the neck, Toby dismounted, led him to a timber shed stable for the night, brushed him down and fed him. With a sliver of light escaping onto the street, Toby knew they had not retired to bed. A tap on the door and his mother answered, peering at the figure stood on the doorstep.

"Don't you recognize me, mother?"

His mother opened her mouth but no words came out. She just flung her arms around his neck and hugged him so tight he could hardly breathe. Finally, finding her voice, she shouted for Stan, her husband. "Stan. It's Toby come to see us. Come in son. Come in. You've had a long ride."

Toby strode in and put his arms around Stan. "By, it's good to see you both looking so well. I've put Pal in the shed for the night, Dad. Is that okay?"

"Course it is, son. Come on, sit down and tell us how it's going." When all were settled and a pot of tea in front of them, Toby related what Jocylyn and Victoria had done for him.

"My goodness, I always knew you'd be good with hosses, Toby. They sound good to work for?"

"Yeh, they really are. I've dropped in lucky there." Toby paused before asking how Ruth and Jim were doing.

"They're doing pretty good. They've taken a young lad on from Copton on and Sam's still working there. Ruth has her teaching and Jim's leading stone for the project that your boss is financing."

After much talk on local news and gossip, Toby retired to bed, relieved to see his elderly parents keeping so well. First thing in the morning, his aim was to see as many friends as he could before returning to work. It was nice to be back home but, as he dozed, he knew his life had moved on and was now with the horses at Malton.

"You're spoiling me, mother," Toby said next morning as he sat down to a cooked breakfast. "More grub like this and Pal 'll be tired out on the ride back."

"Now get it down you. It 'll do you good." While clearing away, she remarked, "try and see Jacob, if you can, Toby. He's not in the best of health. Lost a bit o' fight since hearing the church is closing."

"Yeh, he'll be gutted. It was his life, wasn't it?" Rising from his chair, he grabbed a hat. "Right, I'm away, ma. I'll call on Jacob first, then catch up with everyone else."

"Don't you ever stop, young man. Mark my words, life 'll pass you by if you aren't careful."

He turned back at the door and answered. "It 'll have to be quick to pass me, ma. See you later."

A bitter cold wind swept across the high moor and the valley of Roston appeared desolate and bare, houses standing empty and the railway line unused. Nothing stays the same, mused Toby. In the distance a rider came into view, scrabbling out of the rough climb from the village. With such an easy style of riding that appeared effortless, they negotiated the rough trackway towards him. There was only one person he knew that could sit a horse like this. He waited atop the moor as Ruth Styles cantered up to him on Dunella. "Hiya, Ruth. I'm sure you were put on this earth to ride horses." There was no mistaking the admiration in his eyes, as he added, "you're looking well. Jim must be treating you right."

They dismounted and Ruth threw her arms around him, her face flushed from the ride, hair tousled and loose around her face. She was wearing a long, black skirt, white blouse and hacking jacket which Albert had acquired for her from Honey's owner. "Toby, it's brilliant to see you. Where are you heading?"

Toby held her at arm's length and shook his head. "You are even more beautiful than I remember, Ruth." They hugged again. "I was coming to see you and let you know how things are at Jocylyn's place."

"Well, can we catch up on the ride to Jacob's. I must call and see him. He's not well."

Mounting, Toby said, "that's not good news, Ruth but he must be a big age now."

"Yes, well into his seventies at a guess." She frowned. "Strange, he's always a bit secretive about his age. I don't know why."

"Mebbe didn't want the church to know so that he could go on preaching." They smiled at the thought. "How do you like Dunella?"

"I've never ridden such a fine animal." She thought a minute before saying. "Well, maybe I have. The one your mounted on."

Dismounting, they walked over to where Jacob was out and about feeding the little Cob. Delighted to see them both, he asked if they had time for a cup of tea. "I'm sorry, Jacob. It's just a quick call this time. Next visit, I'll have more time."

"I'll have one with you, Jacob," Ruth said, "I'll pop the kettle on." Waving goodbye, Toby continued to the new quarry workings where he caught Josh, who promised to meet him in the Buck later. Toby knew that could be a mistake but he readily agreed.

He was right. Next morning, he rose, head thumping, vowing never to get drunk again but after saddling Pal and tackling some of his favourite moorland rides, his head cleared. With a pack of sandwiches for his dinner, he bid a tearful farewell to his parents and made a late start back. But this was no problem, he could enjoy the solitude of the ride. He was also ready to be back at work, doing the job he loved and eager to see how Winnie's remedy had worked on Max's injured leg.

Chapter 24

W ith rarely a spare hour for themselves, the year had flown by and the day of Ruth's reunion with her father had arrived. Ruth called out to Jim in the yard. "Come on, Jim. We're running late, we need to be away in fifteen minutes and you need a change of clothes yet." At that minute, Luke walked past, smiling, and said, "My, you look a real picture this morning, Mrs Styles. I hope your couple of days away go well." He turned and walked towards the buildings, shouting back over his shoulder. "Don't worry, I'll send him straight in, 'cos I can finish what's left."

"Bless you, Luke. Jim never seems to notice the time."

Ruth frowned on opening the wardrobe. Ruth was travelling in her favourite white blouse, a long dark skirt and jacket, but packing a change of clothes proved difficult as there was not much choice in her wardrobe. Once packed, she thought of the ride ahead, finding a warm bonnet that covered her ears and pushed her hair up underneath. A few minutes later, Jim dashed in, was washed, and changed within fifteen minutes. Ruth smiled at him. "What a transformation. Why can't you do this more often?"

"Well, I don't get the chance very often, Ruth. I'll just pack a few spare clothes and then we're ready for off." Once packed, he studied Ruth. "You're right, we should do this more often. You really are a beautiful woman, Ruth Styles."

Ruth was flattered and smiled at him. "My goodness, what an old romantic you're getting to be, Jim. But it is nice to be told, occasionally."

Once outside, Luke had Dunella ready and waiting. "Thanks, Luke," Jim said. "Look after things, won't you?"

"Will do."

Mounting two up on Dunella they rode off, Jim shouting back as an afterthought, "and don't let Albert do too much, Luke."

Ruth had already arranged to borrow the Cob and trap, and Jacob, as good as his word had everything ready for their journey to York.

"Right, you two get away, I'll stable Dunella for you."

"Thanks, Jacob." With cases loaded, they were soon on their way. A light westerly wind brushed across the moor top but as the sun rose, so did the temperature and the blue of the sky held the promise of a fine day. Taking the reins, Jim, with a click of the tongue, eased the Cob into a trot. As he did so, he cast a quick glance at his wife. The last couple of days had seen her withdrawn and quiet, lost in her own thoughts of the forthcoming meeting with Patrick at her mother's grave. Afterwards, they were to call at 10, Darwin Court where accommodation awaited with Edith and John.

An early layer of cloud obscured their vision of the valleys either side and the usually busy wayside Inn was very quiet. Trying to take Ruth's mind off, what could be, an emotional meeting, Jim talked of Jocylyn's workload and the quarry at Castle Moor.

"You know, Ruth, Jocylyn Dymock is a brave man. At present, he's sinking everything into this business venture. I hope he does succeed as it's bringing work into these dales."

"He is certainly not afraid of hard work either, the way he's tackling the improvements at Oak Tree Farm." Ruth turned to Jim, her face brighter now. "You know what I'm looking forward to, Jim?" Before he could answer, she said, "taking the school children down to the garden."

Jim smiled at her. "You just enjoy being outdoors, Ruth." Placing an arm around her waist, he pulled her close. "I'm glad about that as well," he said, planting a kiss on her cheek.

On reaching the flat land, the cloud had lifted and the warmth was back in the sun. Ruth showed him the bridge where she rested and where she'd left the boat under the shelter of the small coppice of trees on her first journey.

"What a journey, Ruth. And at that age. I couldn't have done it. I wouldn't have been brave enough. Sleeping rough, nothing to eat. God, I wouldn't even do it now."

"I had no option, Jim. I had to do it and that makes the difference." Her serious face was back on. "And now I'm going to meet the man who caused all this heartache."

Jim could see tears were close as she turned away but not before her lips begin to tremble. "That is all behind us now." Jim tried to lighten the mood. "Once the meeting is over, we have a full weekend to ourselves with Edith and John and your Aunty Moll." He paused, the gap-toothed smile on his face. "That's if we have time."

This had the desired effect, bringing Ruth out of her morose mood, feeling compelled to return the smile. As they approached, the outline of the city began to take shape, the factories and buildings lining the river. Motor cars were more dominant but the little Cob was well-behaved, a pure gem. Another horse touched by the genius of young Toby, Ruth thought.

Reaching into his pocket, Jim checked the time. "We have an hour to spare, Ruth. What if we pull in here and have a bite to eat. Did you pack anything?"

A hand shot to her mouth. "Oh, sorry, I forgot, Jim."

"Ah, God. I'm starving. That means we'll have to spend some money."

Ruth broke into a laugh, easing the tension. I suppose these will have to do then." And she brought a pack of sandwiches out and a bottle of tea."

"Sometimes, I just don't get your sense of humour, Ruth."

"That's because when hunger strikes, you only think of your stomach."

With the Cob hitched to the nearby fence they took the chance to stretch their legs with a walk alongside the fast-flowing river, Jim thinking of Ruth's brave journey in a little boat.

"Was the river flowing as fast as this when you escaped, Ruth?" he asked.

"I think so, Jim. I remember, as I untied the boat, the current almost whipped it out of my hands and I had to hold on tight and scramble into the back so I wouldn't be seen. I was so frightened I hid under a stinking old sheet."

"Your early life was a thrill a minute."

"Can you understand now why I suffered nightmares for years?"

"I certainly can." Smiling, he said, "and then it got worse. You married me."

Laughing, they turned and headed back to the trap and were soon approached their destination, Ruth gathering up the posy of wild flowers brought from home. The graveyard of St Catherine's was quiet, just an elderly man placing flowers on a freshly dug grave and a workman gathering litter and removing dead flowers into a bin. Jim took her hand and Ruth tightened her grip as she saw a man sat opposite Sarah's grave. Her heartbeat quickened on drawing closer, but her confidence grew, knowing she could hold it together with Jim by her side. As they neared the man rose slowly from the bench, Ruth recognizing Patrick instantly. Oh, he'd aged. Understandable after all these years of guilt, a prison sentence and then the horrors of war.

Still a tall, imposing figure, no stoop. The once black hair that she remembered was now well-flecked with grey at the temples but the dark eyes still penetrated and had lost none of their fire. Dressed sombrely in a dark suit, shaved and respectable, Ruth was shocked. No, shocked was not the right word. Surprised. Surprised that the years had treated him kindly.

She realized she must say something to break the ice. Her mouth was dry but finally she forced a smile and said, "Good afternoon, Patrick. I must say you look very well." It sounded so stupid, even to her own ears, but it was all she could get spluttered out. Patrick held out his hand and Ruth took it. The strong grip and the warmth of his hand brought back memories instantly.

"You were always a beautiful child, to be sure, Ruth. Now you are even more beautiful as a woman." His eyes studied her. "I wouldn't have recognized you if I hadn't been expecting you. I take it this is your husband?"

"Yes." Turning to Jim, she said, "Jim, this is my father, Patrick." They shook hands. "Hello, Patrick. Pleased to meet you." Proceedings were polite but strained. There was a certain tension simmering beneath the surface. Jim could sense it in Ruth.

"Ruth, if you hand me the flowers, I'll put them on the grave. This will allow you and Patrick time to talk. I'll be here, or at the trap, if you want me. Okay?"

"Thanks, Jim. That would be good."

On grasping the flowers, their hands touched and their eyes met. That was all Ruth needed. Jim turned away and wandered over to the graveside to leave father and daughter together. The grave was tidy. Moll, or Patrick, must be tending the grave regularly. Jim knelt and placed the flowers on the grave, then studied the headstone, paid for by a kindly doctor, Ruth thought. He shook his head at such a tragic loss of life that had affected so many. After a minute or two, Jim looked about him but Ruth and Patrick had disappeared, so Jim raised himself and walked back to the trap. Ruth knew where to find him.

Walking as far as the rough stone wall at the perimeter of the church's land, Ruth was first to break the wall of silence. "Are you going to tell me about your life, father, or do I have to prise it out of you. If you're not going talk, I'll tell you how I coped, shall I?" There was a touch of steel in her voice now the pleasantries were over with. It was time for the truth. "You never saw me bundled away by a policeman, did you? You were handcuffed by the police and led away from the scene." Ruth spoke with a faraway look in her eyes, as if reliving the scene once again.

"I was taken in by Aunty Moll but there was no way she could afford to feed me, so my home became the orphanage which was run by cruel, sadistic people. It was there I met Jim." She paused slightly before carrying on. "He gave me the strength to see it through. I was also thrown in prison but a kindly judge took me on as housemaid."

Looking expectantly up at her father, she said, "Do you want me to carry on, father, or have you heard enough?"

"Please, carry on, Ruth. It hurts but I need to know."

"After his son attacked me, I fled to the coast hoping to find work and this was where my luck changed. By accident I stumbled upon kind people out in the country who cared about what happened to me. After suffering nightmares for years, I finally found peace of mind after visiting my mother's grave and I could grieve properly." She paused, a silence falling between them. Finally, she said, "I've said my piece. Now, if you have nothing more to say, I shall return to Jim because we have a long travel." A hardness had swept across the usually caring features.

Patrick reached for her hand again. "Please, Ruth. Be patient with me. I never thought you would agree to see me. When I received the letter, I wept with joy. I couldn't believe it." Patrick had let the flood gates open and Ruth knew instantly these words were straight from the heart. "All that kept me going through the prison years was the thought of meeting you. Unable to find work, I was left with no option but St Catherine's." His head hung low, unable to meet Ruth's gaze, but he carried on. "When the war broke out, I signed up and it took me off the street. After the war, I returned here and the ladies looked after me and found me work. In fact, it was one of the ladies who told me to get off my arse and try and find you. So, I took her advice and here we are." He looked away as emotion took over.

Ruth gripped his hand tighter. "Please, look at me, Dad." There, she had said the word that had stuck in her throat for years. It had always been Father, or Patrick, never Dad. This meant a closeness never felt, until now. She asked again because it sounded so good. "Please, Dad?"

Slowly turning towards her, ashamed, cheeks wet with tears, Patrick reached out for her and Ruth couldn't help herself as she led him by the hand to a nearby seat and they held each other tight.

Ruth spoke quietly, in a faltering voice full of emotion. "God, how I yearned for the comfort of these arms around me as I suffered the long, lonely nights at the orphanage." She sniffed and dried her eyes but still held his hand. "But those times in early life, I realize, has made me stronger. I also found the love of my life in Jim. He was a ragamuffin, like me, and together we became strong enough to stand on our own two feet."

Patrick was amazed, and proud, at the strength of mind his daughter had shown over the years. Composing himself, he asked if they had time for a coffee in the wooden building that had been his home.

"I 'll go find Jim. I'm sure he won't mind." With a spring in her step, she returned to the church gate and waved Jim over. Once back with Patrick, he led the way to the café.

He was surprised at how busy it was for the time of day, but some were just leaving. Ushering Ruth and Jim to a quiet corner, Jenny was first to their table, Ruth noting the smile she greeted Patrick with, before quickly taking their order.

Patrick related how it was Jenny and Phyllis's unstinting kindness, that guided him through the most difficult times when all seemed lost. At that minute, the door swung open and who should stride in and join the other ladies but Emmy and a deep conversation followed between them all.

Patrick spoke. "I believe you are about to meet the woman who convinced me to find you if it was the last thing I ever did. Don't be surprised, as she can be quite forthright."

Jenny brought their coffee's to the table. "Nice to see you have company with you, Patrick. Are you going to introduce me?"

"Of course I will, Jenny." Rising from his chair, he said, "this is my daughter, Ruth and her husband, Jim. They have travelled all the way from the North Yorks moors to meet up with me after many difficult years apart."

A hand shot to Jenny's mouth. "Oh, my goodness, Ruth, this is marvellous. Patrick has told me such a lot about you, I feel I know you already." She bent and hugged Ruth, then did the same to Jim. "My, what a handsome man you've got there, Ruth."

Jim's face broke into the gap-tooth smile. "Keep talking, Jenny, you're saying all the right things to make me a very happy man."

"Ah, don't let it go to your head, Jim, she says that to everyone," remarked Patrick.

As Jenny fussed over them, she said. "Would you mind if I bring Phyllis and Emmy over to meet you all?"

Not waiting for an answer, Jenny waved the ladies over, Emmy leading the way, tall and erect, Phyllis with a steady left to right sway, just behind. Emmy, direct as ever, not waiting to be introduced, asked, "So this is your daughter, Patrick Brennan. And her husband. You must have taken my advice. Good for you." A smile lit her bony features. She bent and hugged Ruth. "Am I allowed to hug your man, Ruth."

"Of course, Emmy."

Jim rose from his chair and Emmy clasped him in her skinny arms and whispered in his ear, "you are looking after her, aren't you?"

Jim whispered back, "course I am, Emmy. Always will."

After more pleasantries, the ladies left, as three customers patiently waited to be served. Jim checked his watch. Time to make a move, as night was closing in. They still had to get to John and Edith's before dark but the streets were well lit. After thanking the ladies for their hospitality and saying their last goodbyes, Jim walked straight to the trap, allowing Ruth and Patrick time to arrange for another meeting, or say their final farewell.

Patrick reached out for one final hug with Ruth before she left, and said, "If there is anything I can do, or help you with in the future, promise you will write to me, won't you?"

"I promise, Dad."

"You have made today one of the best days of my life, Ruth Styles." He took a piece of scrap paper out of his pocket and scribbled his address down and handed it to her.

As Jim walked away, he now knew in his heart they would meet again in the future but, when only a few yards away from the trap, a figure stood, gently stroking the Cob's head.

"Like horses, d'you?"

The figure spun round, ready to run. "Don't think of running off, young un, I'm much faster than you. If you haven't pinched anything, there's no need to run."

"I've not pinched anything, mister. I was jus' bin friendly with the horse."

"That's okay, then. He likes a lot o' petting. What's your name then?" Before Pete could utter his name, Ruth arrived. "Good evening, Pete. My, how you've grown. Hope you've kept out of trouble since we last met?" she asked.

"Cor, miss. Never thought I would see you again. I hang about 'round here, and run errands for people but I don't cause trouble. Excitement shone in his eyes as he remembered. "Hey, it was me who found your dad for Moll and gave him the letter. Have you seen him, cos, for sixpence, I know where he lives," he said proudly.

"Oh, thank you, Pete but that's where we've been. To meet my father after all these years. And to think, if it hadn't been for you, I might never have found him."

Pete beamed. "I know he wanted to see you more than anything in the world. He told me that himself." He wiped his nose with his sleeve, then looked at Jim. "Is this your husband, miss?" Jim listened in amusement at the conversation.

"That's right, Pete. Jim, meet Pete. This is the boy who helped me so much first time we met, didn't you?"

"Yeh, I'm always helping people."

"You sound very good at your job, Pete. Just look how happy you've made Ruth and her father. Now, for sixpence, are you going to jump up on the trap and show us the way to Darwin Court?"

"You mean I get a ride on the trap with you both? And get paid as well?" Pete couldn't believe his luck. "Cor, wait 'til I tell the others."

He jumped on board before they had chance to change their minds. "I hope you know the way, Pete?"

"'Course, I do. I could shut me eyes and get you there in no time."

I bet you could, thought Jim, as he cast a sly wink at Ruth, who was struggling to hide her laughter.

Threading their way through the maze of dimly lit streets that they knew so well, but didn't let on to Pete, their trusted navigator.

"Turn right here, Jim and you see that long curve of houses," he pointed ahead at the brightly painted crescent of buildings. "That's Darwin Court. But, be careful, they're a snooty lot up here. They've run me off the street a few times."

Jim fished in his pocket for sixpence and gave it to Pete. "Thank you, Pete. We could never have managed without your help. Can you find your way back?"

Jumping nimbly into the street, he said, "No problem. Bye." And he disappeared back into the darkened streets.

"Oh, Jim, thank you for being so good with him." As they trotted around to number ten, Ruth cuddled close. "Did he remind you of anyone, Jim?"

"Yeh, he did. He brought back memories of two other youngsters roaming the streets, getting up to no good. You and me."

"God, I do love you, Jim Styles."

Chapter 25

On arrival, both were nervous but Jim had only one thing on his mind. He well remembered the dressing down the judge gave him the day he called to see where Ruth was. Although only a boy, the words hurt and he vowed, one day, he would walk up to this mansion with his head held high. And, by God, those thoughts were just about to come true. The frontage was as he remembered. The steep stone steps rising from the street, the brightly painted door and brass number plate, still highly polished. Gripping Ruth's hand, he pressed the bell, heartbeat quickening as he did so. A quick glance at Ruth and she tried a smile, but it only betrayed her nerves. Jim realized they were out of their depth in such company but knew they would have to cope somehow as it was too late to change things now.

As if waiting for them, Edith answered the door herself. "Please come in both of you." Edith greeted them with a quick hug, while John immediately called for one of the staff to stable the horse for the night. Ushered into the drawing room, Edith asked if they would like a drink before sitting down to eat.

"A beer would be nice, Edith. If you have one?"

"Of course we have, Jim. And Ruth?"

"A red wine please, Edith."

A clinking of glasses as Edith prepared the drinks and brought them over as John walked in.

"The horse and trap are all taken care of, so the night is ours. Now, as it is Edith's birthday, and you have had such a long travel we both thought you may enjoy a meal."

Jim's nervousness began to disappear as he settled into the sumptuous chair. "Well, John, we did have sandwiches at the graveyard, but a meal would be great."

As John and Edith carried the conversation with ease, Edith asked how things had gone at St Catherine's.

"I was very unsure to start with, Edith, but after the initial shock of seeing him again, I relaxed and we talked mainly about the future. We didn't go back too much over old ground. I always think it best to look forward."

"Well done, my girl, and I take it he met Jim.?"

"He did and we had a coffee in the little shelter and the ladies who work there were all very nice. They knew of our past and that this was our first meeting, so they made a big fuss of us."

John listened intently and with sincerity in those black pearly eyes of his, said, "I am so pleased for you both. You don't realize just how much Edith and I admire your determination." He paused studying them both. "We always have." He paused, before saying, "in fact, it was your tenacity and strength of spirit that changed my life."

Ruth coloured slightly at the praise from this man. "Thank you, but we've only done what we had to do to survive."

"Well, it appears to be working and I see no reason why it should not continue." John raised himself from the chair. "Now, if you take your drinks, we'll retire to the dining room." John smiled at Ruth. "I shall ask you to lead the way, Ruth, as I think you will remember."

"Of course I do. Oh, John, this is bringing back happy memories of my days here." Wistfully, she said, "for a while, I thought this would be my home before everything happened."

"I thought so, too, Ruth. But it was not to be."

On entering the room, Jim had never seen luxury such as this. A solid oak table, already set for four and when all were seated, a maid entered with the food. Jim wasn't sure which of the cutlery to use first but keeping an eye on John, he managed quite well and didn't show himself up. With the meal over, they returned to the comfort of the drawing room and relaxed by the open fire. With conversation flowing on John's favourite subject, the orphanage, and on Ruth's teaching and the farm, the evening flew by.

As the clock struck eleven, Ruth's head shot up. "Oh, I'm sorry, Edith. Look at the time, Jim. We are keeping these two good people from their beds."

"Not at all," Edith said, "we are so glad of your company. It really was an enjoyable night." This was said from the heart. "After all, we have a lot of catching up to do. Now, I'll show you to your room. Follow me."

Jim couldn't believe the magnificence of the interior of the building, trying hard not to let his amazement show as he mounted the large wide staircase, the sparkling tear drop chandelier hanging from the high ceiling.

Finally, Edith entered a room on the first landing and ushered them in. "I hope you both sleep well."

"We will, Edith. This is the room I slept in when John took me out of prison. The four-poster bed, the drapes. I remember thinking, after the cruelty of the orphanage and the stench and noise of prison, this was like Heaven. Now to be back in this room but this time with my husband, it is hard to believe." With the tension disappearing after the reunion with her father, the pure joy of her return to York and the memories involved, a feeling of relief flooded over Ruth.

Edith said, "that's good then, you'll know where everything is. I'll leave you to settle in and find your own way around."

"Thanks so much for what you are doing, Edith. It has made it so much easier for us, hasn't it, Jim?"

"Yes," Jim smiled at his mother. "Thank you, Edith. This is the first time we've been away since getting married. This is our honeymoon."

Edith turned and left the room, saying, "goodnight, see you both for breakfast."

When on their own, Jim whistled quietly. "Never seen anything like this in me life, Ruth. No wonder it broke your heart to leave here."

I wouldn't have left if it hadn't been for his son, Henry."

"Well, we better make the most of this luxury while we can." He drew the drapes closed and quickly grabbed Ruth, pulling her down onto the bed by his side. Grinning, he said, "if we make a start now, we won't be late for breakfast. That would be embarrassing."

Giggling, she kissed him.

Jim and Ruth's special weekend came to an end. Treated like royalty by John and Edith, Jim brought tears to Edith's eyes on leaving, as he held her close and explained just how much it meant to him, knowing he had a mother who cared. Farewells are always hard but as they left the tree lined crescent behind, ready for the long haul back to Roston, both were in good spirits as they waved goodbye.

Well muffled up against the cold, Jim drove and made good progress early on. Each were lost in their own thoughts and, once out of the city, the only sound was the steady plod of the Cob's hooves and the rattle of the wheels crunching over gravel. Once off the busy main road and onto the winding country lanes, the journey became much more pleasant.

Eventually, Ruth broke the silence. "What are you thinking, Jim?"

He turned towards her. She could tell he was smiling, even though just his eyes showed above the scarf.

"I thought they did us proud, Ruth and this was as good as any honeymoon." Jim was thoughtful for a minute. "Just think, Ruth, if you'd stayed there, we might never have met up again?"

"Hard to say, isn't it. I suppose I would have been easier to find in York, than in the middle of nowhere at Gallows Howe." She laughed as she remembered how it had happened.

The miles past quickly. But, as the day wore on and a biting wind rattled the tree tops, Jim decided a rest for the Cob would be a good idea. It would also give them a chance for a bite to eat and to warm up. Eventually arriving at the sleepy, little village of Lastingham, a pub on the right caught their eye and opposite, on higher ground stood a magnificent stone-built church with a beautifully kept graveyard. Appearing small in the shadow of such a building, the cluster of warm coloured sandstone cottages appeared to find comfort from the close proximity of these two buildings, both possibly the hub of this village community.

Jim hung the reins over the front railing allowing the Cob to drink his fill from the stone trough and also graze at the grass verge. After checking the horse's feet, this would give the little fella a well-earned rest before the final pull for home.

After a round of sandwiches and a drink, and a few pleasantries exchanged with the landlady, they took their leave. Ruth was quick to unhitch the horse and take the reins for the last stretch over the moors by Ana Cross, a ride she loved, even though the darkness began to creep in around them. It was a long trek for the Cob but, Ruth knew, the last few miles would prove easier on the descent to Roston.

The night was as black as pitch on arrival and Jim lit the stable lamp and settled the Cob for the night, while Ruth entered the farmhouse and lit the lamp as Meg, Luke's dog, rushed up to greet her. After feeding the dog and fussing her for a minute, Ruth's eye caught sight of the note on the table. Must be from Luke, she thought. Maybe a list of jobs to do. Ruth quickly read it, her heart sinking. The news hit her hard and she grabbed the edge of the table to stop herself falling. She could not believe this. She re-read the note to make sure. Jacob had died suddenly last night. From a heart attack they thought. Luke was at Gallows Howe at present, to see if he could help Josh with anything.

In a state of shock, Ruth couldn't believe that Jacob, the person who taught her how faith and love could turn everything around, had left this world. The tears came steadily as Jim entered. Unable to speak, Ruth gestured to the note and Jim read it slowly. He also read it again. Gathering the still sobbing Ruth into his arms, he held her tight, knowing the love she felt for him. The man who was there in her hour of need. He really had saved her.

Holding her tight until the tears were finished, Ruth said, "I can't believe Jacob's gone, Jim. It happened so quick. No warning. I knew he was a big age, but he was still reasonably fit, looking after himself and the horses." Ruth slumped down in a chair as Jim put a match to the fire.

139

"Well, it's too late tonight for us to help, Ruth. Anyway, Luke's there and he'll look after Josh."

Meg moved to the outer door, a low growl in her throat. She'd heard movement. A moment later, Luke walked in. He could see Ruth was upset. "I'm sorry for the bad news, Mrs Styles but I couldn't think of any other way to tell you once I'd heard. I thought you might want me to help Josh out at Jacob's house. That's where I've been."

"Luke you've done marvellous for us. I'm just so sorry we couldn't be here. How is Josh taking it?"

"Josh was with him when he collapsed. Naturally, he's shocked, but he's handling it well. It was sudden, went out like a light, he said. There was no suffering. Josh got Doctor Rourke there as soon as possible but there was nothing anybody could have done. Well, that's what the doctor said."

"Thank you, Luke. Is there anything left to do outside?" The colour was returning to her cheeks as the initial shock was passing. The grieving, as she well knew, would follow.

"No, all's done, Mrs Styles. In the morning I can take care of things here, as I think Josh will want to see you. He was asking about you tonight, but I said it wasn't possible. He understood."

"You can call as you go to work, Ruth. I'll help Luke, then pop down later." Jim shook his head. "There'll be a hell of a lot o' sorting out to do."

"That's what Josh thinks. He says nothing's been thrown out for years. Well, not since his mother died, anyway."

Ruth was amazed how Luke had settled at Honey Bee, with her and Jim. They sat talking until the early hours of the morning, reminiscing past times as Ruth told Luke how she first stumbled upon Gallows Howe and Jacob Thrall.

"I'm off to bed now, as it'll be an early start tomorrow, and I know Jacob's gone but life doesn't stop for those that's left, does it?

Ruth smiled at the young lad. "That's very true, Luke. Go get your beauty sleep and we'll see what morning brings."

Chapter 26

Ruth thought it appropriate that the final service held in the old tin church would be for the man who gained so much comfort from his strong faith and commitment to the Lord, Jacob Thrall. The old building was full, and many more stood outside as befitted a man so well respected throughout the community and, after the service, just a short journey for the mourners following the hearse to Castle Moor. Josh, Ruth and Jim, stood close, gaining comfort from each other, as the coffin was slowly lowered into the dark recess of the grave and Jacob Thrall was laid to rest. The minister sombrely addressed the throng of people with the final words. "Ashes to ashes, dust to dust."

A handful of soil, followed by the simplest of gestures from Ruth, a white rose floating gently down to lay on the coffin. Ruth grasped Jim's hand for support as the strength drained from her body, fearing she was going to faint. Josh, although upset, appeared to be the same solid upright figure as ever, even in the aftermath of Jacob's sudden death. But he well knew from past experiences, the cost of love is grief.

Slowly, the graveyard emptied and Jim had wandered across for a word with Len Bailes. Ruth and Josh stood quietly together by the grave for a while before Josh spoke. "You know, Ruth, I wasn't even sure of father's age. Not until I came across his birth certificate in his desk."

"How old was he, Josh?"

"He was born in 1845, which makes him eighty years old. I think father knew the end of the road was close as retirement loomed. Luke and I were just going through some of his recent correspondence and found a letter from the diocese asking him to state his intentions for the future." Josh sighed and looked to the Heaven's as if the answer lay among the fast-moving clouds. "But, in all truth, the ambition and the fire had died in him, Ruth. The one good thing is, death came swiftly, he did not suffer. Maybe this was a blessing as he knew in his heart, the fervour of his sermons was no longer there. The words, once spoken from the heart, for God knows how many years in the past, did not carry the same passion. The enthusiasm of his earlier years had gone." Josh hung his head. Without a word, Ruth placed an arm around his shoulders, as he let his tears flow freely to the ground. Eventually, he raised his head. "Yes, this last couple of years, Jacob finally realized age had caught up with him. It was his time to go."

Ruth waited patiently by his side until Josh felt ready to walk away from the grave, then they left together. So much like brother and sister. Josh had done so much to help her over the years, her hope was that she could be there for him now. Jim and Len followed, closing the gate behind them, leaving just the two grave diggers to fill the grave and tidy up around it.

Ruth asked Josh if she could help in any way. "No, thanks all the same, Ruth. I'll move back in for a couple of days, get my mind around what to keep and what to throw out." As Ruth and Jim mounted Dunella, Josh looked up to her and smiling, said, "please don't worry about me, Ruth, I'll be fine." And he at once stood back and waved them on their way. She knew he was man enough for the job ahead, but her heart ached for him at this difficult time.

After the loss of Jacob, Jim and Ruth threw themselves back into work, the following years flying by. The process of clearing the site for the building of the new church had started and the stone from Gallows Howe was already on site but much more was required. Up on the high moor, Brownhills quarry was brought into use again, a track already snaking its way up from the roadside watering troughs to the main entrance. A workman's hut, rebuilt in stone, was built for shelter and the safe keeping of tools. Laid dormant for more than seventy years when these farmsteads were formed, Ruth was excited that the old quarry would, once again, ring to the sound of working men carving stone from the rock face.

On her rides, Ruth had time to think, clearing her mind of negative thoughts. As Luke said, a life had ended but life goes on and although her heart was heavy, she knew Jacob would not want her to be unhappy. At least she could grieve properly, which had not been possible on her mother's death. A sudden chill caught her unawares as memories of Sarah, her mother, flitted into her mind. But the images were of happier times. Sarah, smiling, her hair blowing in the wind as, hand in hand, they strode out along one of her favourite walks, the historic stone barricades of York city and enjoying the beauty of the swirling water of the Ouse. It brought a smile to her face. Yes, she missed her mother, and she would miss Jacob, but both would always be fondly remembered.

Arriving home, she dismounted and Jim could see she was still deep in thought, said, "a penny for 'em then, Ruth."

Wistfully, she said, "I'm just so sad at the loss of Jacob, Jim. I know that's selfish, as it is only thinking of my feelings. But, I'm relieved he will not suffer the indignities of old age in hospitals, or old people's homes. Josh, I know, will say goodbye in his own way and get on with life, as we are going to get on with ours." Ruth appeared pleased with her attitude to the way forward. "Now, do you want me to do the yard work, or put the kettle on?"

He winked at her. "I'll be inside with you for a cuppa, before you know it."

"I'll look forward to that."

Chapter 27

The winter of 1926 proved harsh with temperatures constantly below zero. Heavy snow falls cut many outlying villages off, including Roston and deliveries could only be made by horse and sledge. Schools closed, to the children's delight and it also afforded Ruth more time on the farm. What with frozen water pipes to continually thaw out, keeping up with the log store for warmth and the animals needing more feed and bedding, it all proved hard work but Ruth loved it.

The one thing missing for Ruth was the reassurance and solidarity that Jacob always appeared to have in abundance. As though a cog had gone missing from a well-oiled machine and could not possibly work as well, ever again. But life was beginning to work again. She also realized this would have been a difficult winter for him, on his own at Gallows Howe.

March brought a rapid thaw, once again revealing the hidden greenness of the valley. After so long under a blanket of white, the transformation brought fresh enthusiasm to the community and at the end of the month, spring finally arrived, bringing new life bursting from the ground. Trees and hedgerows responded, branches unburdened of snow, slowly rose in the warmth of the sun and the birds and wildlife of the countryside came to life.

With such an improvement in the weather, Albert also broke from hibernation and arrived in the yard on Honey just as Ruth brought Dunella from the stable. Luke and Jim were already into their second week of stone leading from Brownhills, so Ruth was relieved to see Albert.

"Morning, Albert." She smiled at him. "It's good to see you back out. It's been a hard time. How's Martha stood it?"

"We've been good, Ruth. Didn't go far, kept warm and well-fed and here we are."

"You did right. Now, could you feed the hens and gather the eggs, maybe check the bedding for the young beast, that would be good and maybe bring a few logs." She gave him one of her best smiles. "Thanks Albert," Riding off, she shouted back over her shoulder. "Oh, there's some breakfast on the table if you're hungry. Bye."

Never a minute to spare that one. He shook his head, wishing he had half her energy, as he led Honey to the trough for a drink. By dinnertime, Albert had caught up and was repairing a small gate into the paddock when the postman arrived.

"Just one letter for 'em this morning, Albert."

"Thanks, Jack. I'll take it. Have you any for us? It'll save you a call."

Jack Linus rummaged through his bag. "Yep, just the one." He wiped the sweat from his brow. "Damn it all, Albert, these hills get steeper every day. Either that or I'm ageing faster than I thought."

"Nonsense. There's a lot o' young 'uns couldn't cycle these hills like you, Jack. And that's a fact."

"Oh, I better push on a bit longer then, eh?" Jack turned and wobbled his way along the track. Albert stuffed the letters in his pocket, then brought the logs in to save Ruth a job. He placed Ruth's letter behind the clock on the mantlepiece, before setting the table for them when they returned from work.

Beckoning Honey towards the steps and speaking to himself as he was apt to do nowadays, or so Jim was keen to tell him, "Well, that'll save 'em a bit o' time, old girl. They'll be ready for a rest." But then, he realized, he wasn't alone, the horse was paying attention. Smiling, Albert stroked her neck, leant forward, and whispered in her ear. "I think you might be the only one that listens to me nowadays, Honey."

Back in Brownhill quarry it was the last load of the day. The top layer of rock was scudded clean and the chase cut to take the wedges. The repetitive clang of metal rang out as the men hammered the wedges deeper until the rock face gave to the steady pressure. "We're clear," the man on top shouted. "Pass the straps and I'll fasten the block and tackle on." Once done, he gave the thumbs up, the winding gear clanking into action. Jim didn't back up, waiting until it was clear of the rock face. It was when the lifting gear was under full strain Jim heard the familiar creak of timber at breaking point. Luke and a workman were waiting to see him back. A crack as sudden and as sharp as a whiplash rang out as the baulk of thick timber cracked like a carrot, the huge stone scraping across the rock face before swinging towards Luke and his mate. Jim shouted, "LOOK OUT!" as he jumped off the cart and lunged forward, hurling the two of them backwards and clear of danger, but the beam swung on its axis as it fell and sent Jim crashing to the ground.

The men shouted, "MAN DOWN!" and ran to lift the beam off him. It took four men to haul the massive timber from the crushed and broken body of Jim Styles. A shout went up, "get a doctor quick. He's badly injured." A man quickly mounted and kicked the horse into a gallop, but an hour passed before Doctor Rourke arrived. The men feared the worst. Giving the doctor room, they backed away, faces ashen with shock. Dropping to his knees, the doctor worked feverishly but he knew Jim was dead. Rising from the prone figure, he said, "I'm sorry, gentlemen, there is nothing more I can do. He would be dead from the head wound before he hit the ground, "Please someone, bring a blanket?" The doctor bent and gently closed the staring eyes that appeared to be studying the sky, then placed the blanket over the body. It had all happened in the blink of an eye. Doctor Rourke walked over to Luke, who was crouched on a rock, shoulders hunched, hands covering his face.

He spoke through the great gulping sobs. "It was my fault, doctor... If it hadn't been for us, he would be alive... Jim saved us but the beam hit him." Silence for a minute. "I'm so sorry. It should have been me."

Doctor Rourke dropped to his haunches in front of the inconsolable boy, taking both Luke's hands in his.

146

"Listen to me, Luke. It was not your fault. Nobody can be blamed. It was a total accident and Jim was a very brave man to do what he did."

Luke lifted his eyes to meet the doctor's sympathetic gaze. "How am I going to tell Mrs Styles, doctor?"

"You won't have to, Luke. I'll do that. I'll ride home with you, and explain everything." He studied the men around him and approached the quarry foreman.

"If some of your men could load the body, please and see it is returned to Honey Bee Farm, Roston, I have my car on the roadside and will take Luke home. I think Mrs Styles will be back from work now."

Luke remained silent on the ride home. Still in shock. The doctor didn't try to talk to him. He thought it best to give him time in coming to terms with this tragic accident. Eventually, he looked across at Doctor Rourke and broke the silence. "Jim and Ruth were the only one's brave enough to give me a chance, Doctor Rourke. Did you know that?"

"I didn't, Luke?" The doctor knew the story from gossip around the village but if it helped Luke's state of mind, he would show the respect of listening. Luke told how Jim kept him out of prison after the sheep stealing incident. By the time his story reached conclusion they were on the farm track to Honey Bee.

On hearing the motor approaching, Ruth quickly finished stabling Dunella and poked her head out of the top door. Expecting Jim and Luke, she was surprised to see Doctor Rourke with Luke. Her heart thumped, knowing this could only mean trouble. Where was Jim? She ran out to meet them as she could plainly see Luke was terribly upset. Trying to keep her voice calm, she asked, "Hello, you two. Where is Jim?"

Doctor Rourke turned off the engine and gently taking Ruth by the hand, said, "we better go inside, Mrs Styles."

"No, tell me now this very minute. Please," she demanded. "It must be serious as Jim is not with you."

"I'm terribly sorry, Mrs Styles but Jim was in an accident at the quarry and died from a head injury." The doctor was ready to support Ruth as her legs gave way. "Come inside now so you can sit down." He led her gently to the kitchen and pulled a chair out from the table, easing her down into it. "There was nothing anybody could have done, Mrs Styles. It was instant." He gestured to Luke. "Please bring a blanket, Luke."

Luke gathered a blanket from the spare bed and placed it around Ruth's shoulders.

Ruth never uttered a word. Her whole world had just shattered into a million pieces. The words repeated over and over in her mind, 'Jim died in an accident.' In a state of shock, she looked to Luke, then to the doctor as he spoke. "I'll see to all the necessary procedures, Mrs Styles. Have you anyone that can help you, or stay with you?"

Her voice was barely a whisper. "I have Luke here with me and I have Sam and Albert. I must go tell them."

"No, you stay here. I shall inform Albert and Martha and Sam can be told when he arrives for work." He asked Luke. "Could you inform Sam, Luke?"

"Yes, doctor. He's in tomorrow."

"That's good. Now, if you can make Mrs Styles a cup of tea and stay with her, I shall let Albert know."

News of Jim's death spread quickly and the offer of support and comfort for the family was tremendous. The loss of a loved one is a always a hard cross to bear, but to lose someone close in the prime of their life makes it so much harder.

Albert and Martha kept their spirits up in public, helping the Reverent Benson with arrangements, the funeral taking place a week later. Albert and Martha walked with Ruth for support, followed by Luke and John and Edith Durville. The Reverend Benson led the service and Jim Styles was laid to rest in the church yard of St Mary's and St Laurence at Roston.

The rest of the day followed in a daze for Ruth, but she did remember Josh and his friends relating the escapades involving Jim in the past. Thankfully, the day drew to a close and the last to leave was Josh.

"Just remember, Ruth, when things get tough, as they will, we can always talk things through."

"Thank you, Josh. You've always been there for me when I needed you, but I never thought we would be grieving for two so suddenly. At present, I'm not sure just how I will carry on."

He held her by the shoulders, the piercing blue eyes trying to hold her despairing gaze. "You'll carry on as you have done all your life, Ruth. You were always a fighter and a survivor."

Ruth looked away, tears breaking through. "I'm not sure that I want to survive, Josh."

"Don't talk like that, Ruth. It doesn't seem like it now, but time is a great healer."

She tried a smile, more to please Josh than anything else. "If you say so, Josh."

When mounted, he waved goodbye and Ruth watched him until out of sight. Standing as if rooted to the spot, her mind going through the motions but no solutions forthcoming. Slowly, she turned and walked back inside.

Luke had cleared the table, washed up and lit the fire. He pulled a chair to the fireside and led Ruth to it. As if in a dream, she sat down, his young features showing the concern he felt for her. He sat down next to her. "Can I do anything else for you, Mrs Styles? Like a cup o' tea, or something?"

A drawn smile crossed her face and she shook her head. "No, you've done more than enough, Luke. I think the best thing for both of us tonight is to get some rest. Although I'm not sure I'll sleep much. It's been a stressful day for everyone."

"Goodnight then, Mrs Styles. Don't worry about the animals, Albert and I are organised with that."

"Thank you, Luke, that is a big help. I just cannot take it in, my whole world has just caved in around me."

Luke came back and knelt by her side. "You know it's all because o' me, Mrs Styles. It was my fault. He pushed me and a mate out o' the way and the beam hit him."

Ruth was stricken by the youngster's guilt and her voice took on a severe tone. "Luke, that was typical Jim. He never, ever saw danger. In fact," a rueful smile curled her lips as she remembered, "he always loved a spark of excitement in his life, whatever he did, so please, do not think like that,

Luke." She reached out and held his hand. "He did the same at the mineshaft. He didn't know any of them and risked been buried alive. He could have lost his life then, but he was lucky." She paused and studied Luke and took a deep breath. "It's just his luck ran out, Luke." She paused. "Also, I fear mine has too."

The next two month were the worst of Ruth's life. Far worse than the cruelty and neglect suffered in her early years. Anguish, self-pity, worry, all these emotions raced through her and continued to drag her into a pit of despair. Luke tried hard but could not break into her world of grief. He wasn't the only one worried on her state of mind, as Albert and Martha had taken note. Luke decided to tell Albert of his worries, he would know what to do. As it was Albert's day off, Luke thought it best to give Ruth some time on her own.

That very night, after doing the yard work. Luke made his chance. Popping his head through the door, he said, "I've finished the yard work, Mrs Styles and the animals are all bedded down. I must ride into the village with a message but I'll be back shortly. You sure you'll be okay?"

Ruth was sat staring into the fire, inhabiting her own little world. "Sorry, Luke, what was that?" He repeated it.

Disinterested, she answered. "Yes, of course I will. Bye."

A heavy blanket of fog began its steady descent toward the valley base from the moor top, bringing the darkness of night earlier than expected. Ruth knew another long, lonely night stretched ahead of her. The desperate gaping hole of grief would not budge from inside her chest, as vivid now as when the accident happened.

Ruth spoke into the now darkening room, the words sounding hollow and useless. "Why, Lord, why did you do this to me? To us? Hadn't we suffered enough in our younger days?" The once sparkling blue eyes stared, unblinking, through the window but did not register with anything. Not even the rolling hills and the open countryside that had so captivated her when becoming her salvation. What had once appeared beyond beauty with its ruggedness, now appeared cruel, lifeless, and colourless. Her life here was finished.

Turning from the window, her reflection in the mirror hanging above the sink caught her eye. She saw a haggard old lady's face staring back. Haunted. The once blond tresses were now straggly and lank like an uncared-for pony's mane. The smooth, healthy skin of youth had wrinkled across the brow and the beautiful elfin face was pinched in constant anguish.

Always desperately tired, a deep sigh escaped her pursed lips, as if trying to dislodge, or soften, the solid block of stone that had somehow replaced her heart. Expecting no respite from another sleepless night again she slumped into the chair by the fire again, as had become her habit ever since the awful tragedy, she waited silently for she knew not what.

Oh, it's not as though she was short of help, or advice. Everyone had rallied round. Sam and Luke had done their best to keep her spirits up and they were doing their best, along with Albert, to keep the farm up and running. Ruth could see what was happening but the fight and determination that had carried her through the previously tough times had left her body. How could life, and God, turn so quickly and cruelly against her.

Reluctantly, she rose and lit the lamp when her gaze was caught by a glint of light flickering on the dull metal of the gun barrel stood in the corner of the room where Jim had left it. Meg, the cur dog that Luke had befriended and brought with him from his home in Copton, lay sleeping at its side. Ruth's heart gave a sudden batwing flutter and she stiffened, her heart quickening on how easy it would be to ease the pain. It was now clear, vivid in fact, on what she had to do to finally end the suffering.

Walking over to the cupboard by the side of the fireplace, she reached in. With thudding heart, her white, shaking fingers eventually clutched the cold brass of the cartridge head. In a daze, she grasped it tightly and drew it out. Although her heart was pounding, her actions were quite deliberate. Stooping to pick up the gun propped against the wall, her arm reached out, fingers ready to close around the cold steel of the barrel, when suddenly Meg's eyes opened and she gave a low throated growl. Ruth drew her hand back, shocked and frightened at this show of aggression by this usually placid, good-natured dog. Not once had she known it show hostility to anyone since Luke brought it home. Once Ruth's hand was clear of the gun

151

the dog quieted, but kept a menacing eye on her.

"Quiet, Meg. Quiet now." Ruth realized her voice had dropped to a whisper in the hope of trying to calm the dog. Once more she reached for the gun. This time, the hackles raised on Meg's neck and the dog rose quickly onto its haunches, snapping and baring her teeth.

"Meg, what the devil has got into you?" Ruth tried again, her hand reaching nearer. Again, Meg snapped sharply, causing Ruth to pull back in shock. Suddenly, a knock at the door and Ruth froze in mid-stride as she stepped back from the snarling dog, her mouth open but no sound escaping as Martha Styles stood in the doorway, the dim light of the fire reflecting in her glasses.

"Whatever are you doing, Ruth?" Martha tried not to show the depth of shock she was feeling but she read the situation instantly. It took a second or two before Ruth stammered an answer. "I... I was just tidying up and about to put the gun away, Martha."

Albert and Luke had followed in on Martha's heels. Although a fire burnt in the grate, the room was cold, the atmosphere uncomfortable. Albert felt a sense of guilt, as if they were stumbling in upon a secret side of Ruth's life. Martha turned to her husband. "Albert, if you would keep Luke company in the front room, I need a word, in private, with Ruth." Martha was not asking, she was ordering.

Without uttering a word, Albert nodded at Luke and they made themselves scarce.

Martha took Ruth by the hand and sat her down. Ruth still clutched the cartridge, not knowing what to do, or how to explain it away. "Now Ruth, are you going to explain what is happening, or do you want me to guess?"

Ruth was stunned. "It's not what you think, Martha." The guilt at what she was about to do was clear in her face but she stuck to her story. "Like I said, I was just clearing things away that reminded me of Jim."

"You're not a very good liar, my girl." Martha's face hardened. She was not about to pull any punches. This was the hardest thing she had ever faced for many years but it must be done.

Eventually, she settled in the chair next to Ruth but making sure there was no physical contact, or comfort for Ruth.

"I'll tell you what I think you were about to do if we hadn't walked in. While on your own you were going to take your own life. End the suffering, the pain, and the grief." Martha waited. "That's not the answer."

Suddenly, Ruth could take it no longer. Defiantly, she stared into the granite features meeting the gaze of the steely grey eyes. "Don't you dare tell me that is not the answer. "I just buried my husband after a terrible accident. How do you know how I feel." Ruth's voice had risen to an almost hysterical pitch. "You don't understand. How could you? I've lost everything and we had our whole lives ahead of us and after fighting so hard." Ruth's head fell to her chest, shoulders shaking but still no comforting arm from Martha. Not yet.

"You think you're the only one that's lost a loved one in life, eh? Albert and I had both taken Jim to our hearts, the son we never managed to have." Martha thought it time to tell a few home truths and decided to tell her story. It might help. "Many years ago, Ruth, before I was married, I was in love, or so I thought and fell pregnant twice. The first, a boy, was stillborn. I felt unworthy. Unable to carry a child the full time. I felt less than a woman. Two years later, I fell pregnant again after I was raped. This time I carried through and gave birth to another boy. I had him for a precious two years before diphtheria took him from me. He died in my arms. Now, Jim has gone as well."

This was proving harder than she ever thought possible but she was not about to stop as Ruth's sobbing had ceased. She was listening. "This was all before I met Albert." Martha's heart was beating fast, reliving the heartbreak of loss. "No one knows how I suffered. It was a different age back then. Bearing a child out of wedlock was a sin. I was treated as an outcast by many, including my family and the church." Martha took several deep breaths before she could carry on. "I have never told anyone this part of my life, not even Albert. That's how I knew exactly what you were going to do and the reason we came up tonight. I wanted you to know that I understand your pain and what you are going through and how hard it is to think straight. Every day, you beg for relief from the pain of loss. No one, not even God can offer a solution to this, Ruth. There is only time and love that can heal."

Ruth remained silent. Martha sniffed and wiped her eyes, the granite features and hardness of voice of just a few minutes ago were now sympathetic and comforting. They pulled the chairs close and held each other. "I'm so sorry, Martha. I didn't know. It was me that didn't understand. I was thinking only of being dragged back into the nightmares of the past, doubting my strength to cope with my own suffering."

"It will take time, honey, and you have a hard road ahead of you. Again." Martha got up to go, "but I do believe, with Luke and Sam's help, the sun will shine bright once again. Now, let me gather Albert up and let you and Luke get some sleep." She tapped the side of her nose. "That is also a good remedy."

Ruth rose from her chair, weary, realizing she still clasped the cartridge in her hand. Martha gently eased it from her fingers. "I'll put this back where it belongs, eh?"

Hugging Martha, Ruth whispered in her ear. "Thank you so much for helping me, understanding what I am going through. Also, just being here for me, Martha. I expect it to be hard but maybe, with help, I will be able to see the way forward."

With that, this matter-of-fact woman turned and shouted through to the front room. "Albert, time to be going, let these people get to their beds. They have a busy day tomorrow."

The men appeared at her first shout and Albert studied Martha first, then Ruth. Went over and hugged her. "We're still here for you, Ruth. Never forget that."

As neither one could speak because of the emotion. Luke broke the silence. "I'll give you a lift back home, you two. If you give me a minute, I'll soon have the cart out."

Martha raised her arm, waving the offer of a lift away "No need for that, Luke. You've done enough, young man." Turning back to them all with a smile now lighting her face, she said, "It's all downhill to Roston. We can both manage that, can't we, Albert?"

"Course we can. We'll enjoy the walk. Anyway, at our age, everything is downhill," he added.

Come on, Albert. It's a good job I'm used to your moaning. Goodnight, everyone." Martha closed the door behind her.

A beautiful, clear night, the sickle moon flitting steadily between wispy clouds as Albert took her arm and the cool of the evening hit them. Eventually, as Martha was not in a talkative mood, Albert asked how the meeting with Ruth had gone. He was curious, hoping she had been able to help.

"Pretty good, Albert. I was right. It didn't want leaving any later."

"What do you mean?"

She decided against telling everything that happened. "I mean, we were lucky that Luke called when he did as Ruth needed a good talking to but I believe she's back thinking straight. It's the shock, you know."

"Understandable, Martha. At such a young age as well. They had all their lives before them. I can't come to terms with it myself. We'll all miss him."

"Shut up. Talk like that is depressing. What's more important is, Ruth's pregnant."

"What?" It sounded loud in the cold night air. "Did Ruth tell you that tonight?"

"Quiet. Albert, it's late. Sound carries at this time of night."

Albert lowered his voice. "Sorry. I was just shocked."

They were almost home now. "No, she doesn't realize herself yet, but, mark my words, this next two or three weeks, when she comes down to tell you the good news, have the decency to act surprised. I'll have too as well." She smiled to herself on opening the front door, satisfied in the knowledge that, given time, Ruth would come through this latest heartache. Now, Martha could enjoy her first decent night's sleep since the awful tragedy.

Chapter 28

The realization at just how close she had been to ending it all frightened Ruth and she made a vow, there and then, to drag herself back into the real world. From the moment of Martha's visit, Ruth somehow mustered an inner strength enabling her to face each day. Not yet back to work at school, the thought occurred to her that time away from the farm may help. Luke had, reluctantly, returned to the quarry and taken charge of leading the stone and Sam stepped up to say he would be glad of an extra day a week, so with Albert back, given time, it should get back to normal. Although Ruth was not sure what normal meant anymore.

It was while sorting through the sympathy cards and letters of condolence that Luke spotted an unopened letter behind the clock. "Look, Mrs Styles, there's one here that hasn't been opened." He handed it across to Ruth.

"How did I miss this one, Luke, d'you think?"

"Not surprising really, Mrs Styles, with all that's happened." Luke handed her a knife from the drawer to open the letter.

Ruth sliced it open and her mouth dropped open. "It's from Toby." Then she noted the date it was written. "This was sent two months ago, Luke." Ruth sat down and began to read the letter aloud to Luke.

Dear Ruth.
I am desperately sorry to hear of Jacob's death, and that I could not

make the funeral. He touched many people's lives, mine included and I'll never forget my days spent at Gallows Howe. I know how much you thought of him and you'll miss him terribly. Please try and stay well all of you. I would like to finish off with what I hope you'll think is good news. I have been asked to visit the Royal Stables in London as there is a possible chance of employment with the horses. What else? Will let you know in due course.

This is where I must thank you for all your knowledge and guidance on these fine animals, Ruth.

Wouldn't that be turn up, a lad from the 'sticks' going to work for Royalty.

Regards to all.

Toby.

Ruth finished reading.

Luke's eyes were wide. "Wow. Royalty. How's he managed that? I knew he was good but I didn't realize he was that good. Fancy us knowing someone who may be looking after the King's horses." He picked Ruth up out of the chair and swung her round the kitchen.

A smile broke out on Ruth's face. The first since Jim died.

Luke put her down, realizing what he'd done. "Sorry, Mrs Styles but I was just so excited, I forgot."

"Don't be sorry, Luke. This is just the news we wanted to hear." The letter had put a sparkle back in Ruth's eyes, but then realized and said, "but there is no mention of Jim's death."

"Well, he wouldn't know, the letter was sent two-month ago." Luke said.

She sat and thought a moment. "You're right, Luke. I suppose Jocylyn might have told him if he's been over to Malton to see his sister."

"Well, now you're starting work again before long you can just sort of bump into him, casual like and find out."

Ruth laughed. "Talking of work, how is your studying coming on." Luke didn't answer but his face screwed up. That said it all. "Ah, I've lost track a bit lately but, another week or two we'll soon catch up." Ruth thought for minute. "No, on second thoughts, Luke, with all correspondence finished, I think we should just break in gently with mathematics for an hour before bed."

"Well, I was thinking of having a read for a while."

"Hmm. No, you can read afterwards, there'll still be time."

"Okay, Miss Styles," he said grinning.

"And just so you don't think I'm being too hard on you, Luke, Ruth gathered her writing materials together, I'll write to Toby explaining what happened, and why I was so long in replying."

Working silently on until the chimes of the clock struck ten, Luke gathered his books and pen into a folder and studied Ruth across the table. "If you don't mind me saying so, Mrs Styles, I was really worried about you before Martha's visit." The frown was now replaced with the hint of a smile. "But you are looking loads better."

"She gave me a good talking to, Luke. Just at the right time." Ruth didn't tell him the seriousness of it. It wasn't Luke's problem. In fact, Ruth was glad of his company. The farmhouse was quite lonely now without Jim's gap-toothed smile lighting the room up anymore. Tears came to her eyes at the thought. She glanced at Luke, who was watching her closely. "Please don't worry about me anymore, Luke. Believe me when I say I still have the resolve to see that we both survive. I know there will be times when I feel down but I will get through them."

"Just don't be frightened of asking me for help, Mrs Styles. I'll be here, like you and Jim were for me."

"Thank you, Luke. That means a lot."

"Right, I'm away to bed. I have an early start. G'night, Mrs Styles."

"Goodnight, Luke. I should be up and about in the morning."

Ruth tried to picture the long hard road ahead before the sun would shine again but she was beginning to believe that it may just be possible to fight back from this disaster.

Chapter 29

As the weeks passed, Ruth gradually began taking hold of responsibilities again, rising early and doing the yard work for Luke, allowing him more time at the quarry. Suddenly, a queasy stomach had her dashing to the kitchen sink as she began heaving with sickness. A few minutes passed before feeling well enough to carry on. Unhooking a cup from above the sink, she quickly sipped the cold water, until the unpleasant taste disappeared. Finally, Ruth dried her mouth, trying to think what could have brought this on, but footsteps on the staircase heralded Luke's arrival and she immediately forgot about it. Once seated for breakfast, they began organising their day.

"I'll leave tea ready, Luke. I should be in first but, if not, you can put it on the boil. Is that okay?"

"'Course it is. I could be late tonight though, as the weather looks good and I might get an extra load in."

Pocketing the sandwiches already made, he said, "right, I'm off, Mrs Styles. See you tonight."

"Cheerio, Luke. Be careful." But he was already out of the door.

With her mind back in survival mode, Ruth realized just how vital the everyday yard work was for her mental state. Twenty minutes later, Ruth walked into the warmth of the stable, saddled Dunella and made the ride up the roughest track out of Roston. Exhilarated by that experience, the rest of the ride to the school at Castle Moor was leisurely. Slightly apprehensive about her first day back, she arrived early and was all prepared for the day ahead when Mr Haigh knocked on her classroom door and walked in.

"Welcome back, Ruth. We've missed you. All of us." His smile said it all. "Just do as much as you can and work yourself back in gradually. I will be in my classroom if you need anything at all."

"Thank you, Mr Haigh. That's very kind of you. I'm sure I will have some difficulties but the children will help me through the day." Trying to keep bright, she said, "In fact we have the gardening days to plan, haven't we?"

"We have that. Come and talk it through when you feel ready, Ruth." He put his ear to the door and pulled a face. "Ahh, get ready for the onslaught, the mob are arriving." He rolled his eyes. "Oh, Ruth, how much longer can I put up with noisy children. Roll on retirement."

Ruth laughed at the face he pulled. A minute later, a tousled head of hair peered around the classroom door. "Come in, Dennis. I won't bite you."

"I know you won't bite, miss, but…"

"But what, Dennis?"

He squirmed in front of her before saying, "Well, you know, I wasn't sure what to say to you."

"How about, good morning, Miss Styles?"

That broke the ice for the youngster. He giggled, then said, "Good morning, Miss Styles." Dennis' brow furrowed. "Me dad said you might not ever come back after what happened."

"Well, you tell your dad, I am back and I intend to teach you the best I can and also keep you in order while I do so." Ruth pointed to a stack of papers on her desk. "These are the lessons that I have prepared for this week."

A glumness settled like a cloud over the boy's features. "Oh, 'eck. I 'ope they aren't too hard, miss?"

Before Ruth could answer, the classroom door burst open and the rest of the children piled in on top of one another, before spotting Miss Styles, who had risen to her feet at all the shouting. She frowned. The noise stopped and, somehow, with a little pushing and shoving, they all managed to filter into single file and sat down.

"Good morning, children."

"Good morning, Miss Styles."

"I'm very pleased to see you all again." She smiled. "I hope you were on your best behaviour for Mr Haigh and the teacher who stood in for me?"

The class answered "Yes, we have, Miss Styles."

"So, what am I to think about all the noise and pushing and shoving when you entered?"

"Ah, well, miss." This was Horace, a rather small, tubby boy but with an angelic smile that could charm the birds out of the trees. This is possibly why he often spoke up for the class. "It was like this, you see. If we'd known you were in here we would have been much quieter." He switched the smile on as if by magic.

Ruth tried not to smile back. "That should make no difference. That is not how you were taught to enter a room, is it?"

All the class. "No, Miss Styles."

"So tomorrow, you will remember, won't you?"

"Yes, Miss Styles."

"Now, History books out children and let me see how your memories are on the Battle of Stamford Bridge."

The day didn't fly by for Ruth but it didn't drag either. Her class were relatively well-behaved, for which she was relieved and only the odd difficult question from the most inquisitive in her class. Ruth was now looking forward to the freedom the ride home offered. But the thought of Jim not there to welcome her brought the tears. As she urged Dunella into a gallop, the wind dried them on her face. The excitement of the ride had helped her emotionally and knew she would be good for when Luke returned.

Ruth didn't dwell in the empty house, quickly changing into her work clothes. As Ruth came out of the hen house with a basket of eggs, Luke pulled into the yard.

"Got an extra load in, Mrs Styles, like I thought. Farmer did good for me today, easily matched the rest of 'em." Clapping the dust out of his clothes. "How did your day go?"

"A bit nervous to start with, Luke but the children were good. I'm pleased the first day is over with, though."

He smiled at her. Ruth wondered just how long Luke would stay at Roston as he was growing into a fine young man. He could make more money at the quarries, or even the new stone venture at Castle Moor.

"I was hoping it went well." He paused, before asking, "Are you okay with the work here, Mrs Styles, 'cos if you are, I'll see to the horses, then be in for a bite o' tea."

"Yes, tea should be ready in about half an hour, Luke."

"Okay, thanks. Oh, by the way, would you mind if I went for a drink tonight. The men from the quarry were asking, that's all.

She looked him up and down, quizzical, head on one side. "How old are you, Luke"?

"Sixteen."

"How old?"

"Well, nearly. Another three month."

"If you get the horses done, we'll talk about it after tea and your schooling is done."

"Thanks, Mrs Styles." Luke turned and led Farmer to the stable. Albert had already stabled Dulcie.

Ruth watched him go. Beams of sunlight were spearing through the trees, flashing distorted shadows across the yard as the sun dipped closer to the horizon. When does a boy become a man? She had no idea but she understood he was maturing fast.

A strange feeling was awakening in Ruth. She couldn't explain it but somehow, she felt older and wiser. More of a woman. Maybe not surprising after all the anguish she had been through. Shaking her head but still groping for the answer, she disappeared inside.

With Luke's schooling over, Ruth promised he could ride Dunella into the village. He was not to ask twice. Hurrying outside, he quickly saddled up and was on his way in a matter of minutes, Meg running alongside. Inseparable. She smiled to herself as she watched them go.

Now this was a chance, while completely alone, to be able to sort through

Jim's belongings and decide what to keep and what to discard. She had put this dreadful task aside long enough and hoped she was strong enough to face it. Beginning in the bedroom, Ruth started with his clothes. Hugging each item close to her chest, the tears flowed freely, as if each one discarded was a piece of her life. A piece of that fragile happiness that she always feared, could and would, be torn from her again.

Well, it had come to pass. Part of her life had gone the way of the four winds, along with Jim. Only memories left now. Ruth spoke to the empty room. "I'm so sorry, Jim. This is the hardest thing I have ever had to face in my whole life. I feel so heartless doing this but if I am to have any chance of moving forward, I must do it. Please, please forgive me." Placing the most treasured memories of him by the bedside, Ruth also kept certain books from his schooling that meant so much to them both. A smile broke out at the memory of him struggling to understand and learn from her teachings. But such was his determination to succeed, the knowledge and confidence gained enabled them to run the farm together.

Once finished, Ruth flopped into a chair, completely drained of energy. It had taken all her will power to finish the job. Once done, the house felt empty again and to escape the loneliness, although still early, Ruth was just on the point of retiring to bed, when the sound of horse's hooves heralded Luke's return, so she hesitated.

But it wasn't Luke as she heard a tap at the door. Glancing at the clock, it wasn't late, not eight o'clock, it could be anybody calling to see how she was managing. On opening the door, Ruth found herself staring into the dark eyes of Jocylyn Dymock. Shocked, a hand shot to her mouth, lost for words.

"I'm sorry to call unexpectedly, Ruth but I was on my way back to Oak Tree and had not seen you since the funeral, I thought it a good chance to offer my condolences personally. I for one will miss Jim greatly. My world was certainly brighter in the short time I knew him."

Ruth bit back the tears, not wanting to break down in front of Jocylyn. "That's very kind of you, Jocylyn." Finally, remembering her manners, she said, "Please come in and sit down." Ruth pulled a chair close to the fire. "Can I get you anything to drink?"

"No, I'm fine, Ruth. Is Luke out tonight?" Jocylyn asked, seating himself in the offered chair, as Ruth threw a log on the fire causing a flurry of sparks.

Ruth settled in the chair opposite. "Yes, he's down in Roston. No doubt in the Tavern. But I don't think he'll come back drunk."

Jocylyn smiled. "You seemed to say that with some doubt, Ruth."

"Well, he is growing up and once with friends and money in his pocket, who knows?" She gave a shrug of the shoulders and lowered her eyes as she felt rather than saw Jocylyn watching her closely.

"That will always be the case with the enthusiasm and coltish energy of teenagers, Ruth. You never know what is coming next." A silence followed before Jocylyn spoke again. "You appear to be coping admirably, Ruth. I realize it is early days but, I promise you, time will heal a broken heart. Eventually." His voice lowered as he added, "I can vouch for that through my own experiences."

Ruth's eyes lifted to meet his steady gaze. She knew he was trying to be kind but thought it highly unlikely that, with his breeding and money, she couldn't imagine him suffering too much discomfort in his life. A life of luxury, never tainted by poverty, cruelty, or uncertainty.

"Yes, I am coping, Jocylyn, and I believe time will help me but you must understand, Jocylyn that we were born into two totally different worlds." Ruth felt the resentment rising within her, not just at Jim's death, but her continuing fight for survival. "For one, while you would enjoy a fine education with a family home and business to return to, I was forced to beg, steal and borrow and eventually flee from the cruelty of the orphanage." Her voice was calm and measured, but inside, her heart thumped with the effort of doing so. "I know your intentions are well-meant but I don't think you will ever be able to understand how my world has just fallen apart."

Jocylyn's gaze hardened, as if a spark had ignited in a part of his brain which had lain dormant. He let these words linger in the silence that followed, before saying, "I came tonight with the intention of trying to explain that, whatever your lifestyle, losing a loved one is the hardest thing in life that anyone must deal with. But I can see, and feel, that you are not prepared to allow that working class chip to drop from your shoulder just yet. As if money and position is a guarantee of no heartbreaks. I thought, foolishly, that I may be able to help but if you prefer to hang on to the belief of life not being fair, then I shall go now."

With no response from Ruth, he rose to go. "If, in the future, you feel that I could help, then feel free to visit me at Oak Tree anytime."

Ruth remained tight lipped, tense, knowing he was right, but not prepared to admit it. But she did manage a curt, "Thank you, Jocylyn."

"Goodnight, Ruth." He reached the door, looked back once, before closing it behind him. Walking out he took a deep breath of the fresh night air and cursed himself for being such a dimwit. Angry at his own clumsiness. Quickly mounting, he rode out of Roston towards Castle Moor.

Once back home, he couldn't believe his behaviour. Whenever meeting Ruth Styles, he acted like a speechless schoolboy, never able to choose the right words. What had made him act so abruptly so soon after Jim's death. Maybe he thought sharing his own personal grief with her would ease Ruth's pain.

Unfortunately, there may not be a second chance at redeeming the friendship. Only time will tell, he thought, fingering the painful black and red scars across his arm and chest.

Returning to Oak Tree, he poured a glass of wine, collapsed into his favourite chair, and thought of how he should have handled it. What the hell had he expected. Was it himself fishing for sympathy from Ruth, as he'd been on the verge of reliving his nightmare. He quickly poured another glass, and slowly but surely, the pain eased but the wine would only offer release for tonight. Come morning, he would suffer. What the hell did it matter, he knew – had known from the first moment their eyes met - that he desperately wanted to be with Ruth Styles. But not in such tragic circumstances. With this thought in mind, the drink induced sleep swept him away, not into the fantasizing vision of the beautiful Ruth Styles, but to a world haunted by his worst nightmares. Images of himself, fighting through the ring of firefighters into the blazing inferno of his home. Once more, bursting into the hallway to see Ellen and his child on the first landing screaming as the flames licked around them, engulfing them both. Suddenly, the huge staircase crashed down, along with woman and child, trapping him by the chest and sending fiery, splintered embers in all directions. Ellen's scream rang in his ears, even above the roar of the out-of-control fire and, ignoring the searing pain of his scorched flesh, he heaved the flaming beam aside and reached for the outstretched hand of Ellen to try and drag her and their child to safety.

Too late. Their screaming ceased, silenced forever, both succumbing to the smoke and fumes of the inferno and the stench of his own burnt flesh made him wretch. With clothes on fire and moulding to his limbs, he watched as his skin changed colour, bloating and swelling into huge, fatty blisters. Suddenly they burst open, changing quickly to a crinkled black parchment. His smoke-filled lungs were fighting for every breath and he began to pray the end would come quickly. With energy and will power totally spent, the end was imminent, the agony and pain receding. As the blackness of death rolled in, an inner peace claimed him, knowing he would die next to his beloved family.

In his dream the fire was finally brought under control, only spiralling wisps of smoke slowly rising into the cool night air. But all that was left of the mansion were the stark brick gables and walls, charred with a blackness that came from the very devil himself.

With a start, the charred and blistered body that lay asleep in the hospital bed, shot bolt upright, a blood curdling scream of terror shattering the tomb like silence of the hospital and the scream brought Jocylyn out of his drink induced sleep. Drenched in sweat, he broke down in tears as he was once again dragged back into the suffering of this ever-recurring nightmare, escape impossible. Eventually the night cracked open, revealing a pale band of light climbing over the horizon to fill the sky. At that moment, Jocylyn realized that he also needed help in erasing his own personal tragedy if he was ever to live a normal life again.

Chapter 30

Toby was far from confident standing on the platform, small case clutched in white knuckled hands, awaiting the train for London; but Victoria had assured him a Mr Jeremy Topham would be there to meet him. Also, she'd promised to look well after Pal.

The sound of the approaching train and a billowing plume of smoke streaming from the funnel set his heart thumping. Everyone inched nearer to the edge of the platform ready for boarding and appeared to be from all walks of life and, as far as Toby could judge, all regular commuters. Mostly office workers, smartly suited. A few young children holding onto parental hands and people with multiple cases packed for holidays, he assumed. He smiled to himself. I bet no one else will be going to the Royal Stables.

With a loud hiss and a cloud of steam, the engine halted and the station master exchanged information with the guard. Toby managed to find a seat with two elderly ladies and a young woman with a small boy.

"Would you like me to put your case up on the luggage rack for you, ladies?" Toby asked.

Well-dressed and in their seventies, Toby imagined them visiting relatives further down the line. "Thank you, young man. That will be much more comfortable for us, don't you think, Ethel?"

"Much," Ethel replied.

Toby smiled and settled, enjoying this fresh countryside flitting by trying to pick out landmarks that he'd only read about. Gazing out, he realized just how much more varied agriculture was to the hill farming he was used to. Different crops, larger fields and many more horses about. So taken up with the ride, Toby was surprised when reaching his first change at York. Grabbing his suitcase, he waved goodbye to his fellow passengers and, all he had to do now was find the correct platform for his train to London. Unsure, he spotted a guard. "Could you tell me which platform I need for the London train, sir?"

"O' course. Number three, just down there and left. If you run, you might just make it."

"Thank you." Toby ran, reaching the last carriage as the train lurched forward. Flinging the door open he jumped on. "Wow, that was close," he said. To himself, he thought. Only then did he notice a passenger occupying the seat at the far side of the carriage. "Sorry, miss. I thought I'd missed it."

She lifted her head from the book in front of her. "You nearly did. Do you usually leave it as late as that?"

Catching his breath, he replied, "No, not usually. But I wasn't sure of the platform I wanted."

"Where are you heading?" she asked.

"London."

"Not running away, are you?"

"God, no. Nothing like that." Proudly, he said, "I have an interview for a job at the Royal Stables."

"My, you must be something special. Where did you learn all this, especially at your age?"

Toby related his story of saving Pal and how Ruth had taught him her special ways to treat animals. And, of course, Winnie's herbal remedies. "So, I hope I can convince them I'll be good enough for the job."

Comfortable in her company, he realized this lady had the ability to turn a five-minute stranger into a five-hour friend and while they conversed, he studied her. Slim, short cropped black hair, a cream-coloured hat set at a rakish angle and a brown jacket and skirt. Possibly a year or two older than himself, but that could just be her confident manner.

A silence followed before Toby asked, "And you? Are you going far?"

"The same, back to work in London, after visiting my mother who is ill in hospital." She peered out of the window, before saying, "I am not sure she will pull through."

"Oh, I'm sorry, Miss. I really am." Toby struggled for the right words to offer comfort but found none.

"You weren't to know. I'm not a Miss, either. I'm a Mrs." Her lips curved into a smile, showing even white teeth, but Toby noticed the dark, luminous eyes betray the optimism she was trying to show.

Their conversation ended abruptly when a family of six boarded. The woman quickly buried her nose back in the book and Toby reached up on the rack for his. The children were well-behaved but his concentration had slipped and was relieved when they arrived at a bustling Kings Cross Station.

As the train pulled to a halt, Toby glanced across at the lady who was putting her book away. "Would you mind if I ask your name, as you've made my journey much more pleasant?"

"Edna. Mrs Edna Smith."

Toby chuckled. "Well, would you believe it. I'm Toby, Toby Smith." He held out his hand and Edna took it, her hand feeling warm and smooth in his.

"What a coincidence, Toby." Then she fell silent. "Well, not really, I suppose. With a name like Smith, there are a lot of us about." As she disembarked, she shouted back over her shoulder, "But my stage name is…" he didn't quite catch the name with all the noise around. Then, she finished off with, "Good luck, Toby," waving her book in the air before being gobbled up by the milling crowd dispersing onto the platform.

"Good God. How do I find Jeremy Topham among this lot. He'd never seen so many people in one spot, all appearing to know where they were going. Edging away from the heaving throng, he jumped up on one of the seats to get a better look. No one stood out as if they were looking for him. You fool, Toby. What made you think you'd be able to spot him among all this lot. Did you think he'd be wearing a crown? You should at least have asked where he would be waiting.

He got down from the seat and suddenly there was a tap on his shoulder. "Mr Toby Smith, I believe?"

Toby couldn't believe his luck. He held out his hand. "Yes, indeed, and you must be Mr Jeremy Topham. Wow, am I glad to see you."

Jeremy smiled at seeing the relief on Toby's face. "Yes, it will appear slightly crowded when not used to it."

"Slightly crowded you say. You mean it's like this every day, Mr Topham?"

"Oh, Today is quiet, Toby, compared to the rest of the week. Right, follow me and we'll take you to your place of stay."

Once out on the streets, it was all hustle and bustle, but Jeremy stepped forward and hailed a taxi. Within seconds, one scrunched to a halt in front of them. Jeremy stepped in, quickly followed by Toby. "To the Royal Stables, Jackie, if you please."

"On my way, sir." The taxi sped off, accompanied by a blast of car horns from behind them.

Toby watched the drivers face in the reflection of the front mirror and their eyes met and in a typical Cockney accent, the driver said, "Don't worry, son," he laughed, "Can't drive any other way in the city, or traffic would grind to a halt."

"I believe you, Jackie, but I'd feel much safer on horseback than riding with you." They exchanged grins through the mirror. Even though it was proving hectic, Toby was beginning to find it exhilarating, exciting. The buzz from the people, the atmosphere of the big city was making his pulse race. God, he hoped he was up for the job. No doubt it would not be long before he found out.

As the cab cut between the traffic of cars, buses and numerous horse and carriages, Toby winced at every near miss. But the driver knew his stuff, finally pulling up close to the Royal Mews.

Jeremy paid the driver and pocketed his receipt. "Follow me, Toby."

Toby had taken to this man. Short, stocky in stature, with quite a direct manner. He was smartly dressed as you would expect and knew exactly where Toby had to go. At first sight of the Royal Mews, Toby was stunned by the architectural frontage of the building. Built in a soft, warm coloured stone, the entrance was through a neo-classical archway topped by a magnificent clock tower. Jeremy was about to speak to Toby, but turned to find him stood admiring the entrance to the stables.

Jeremy waited for him to catch up, saying, "awesome, isn't it?"

"It certainly is. I've never seen anything like it in my life, Jeremy."

"Right, come on. I'll take you to the office where they will advise you on your interview."

They entered a blue cobbled courtyard with a stone flagged perimeter; obviously a training ground as the horses were being put through their paces by the stable hands. Some of the most beautiful animals Toby had ever seen. His heart lifted as he recognised the Cleveland Bay breed from his own territory. The others were mainly Windsor Grey's, he believed.

Following a long corridor, they finally arrived at a row of offices and Jeremy led Toby to a door marked, Mr Gerald Ransome. He said, "this is where I leave you, Toby, and this is the man you need to impress. Best of luck, old son. If successful, I will see you again. If not, you might be back on the train tomorrow. So, think on, do your best. No one can do any more than that."

Toby thanked him and they shook hands. "I'm pretty sure I'll see you about in the future, Jeremy."

"That's the spirit. An attitude like that is what makes this country good. 'Bye, young man." Jeremy turned and walked out of the building.

Chapter 31

Ruth's morning sickness was daily now. Coupled with missing her time, she realized it wasn't just the shock of Jim's death causing a problem. She was pregnant. No wonder all her clothes were feeling tight. If her reckoning was right, the baby would be due toward the end of the year.

Married in her early twenties and now a widow in her early thirties and expecting Jim's child. The first emotion that rushed to mind was one of anger, boiling up inside, forcing her to bite hard on her hands to stop herself from screaming. How cruel life can be. Not quite a decade together before the world they had worked so hard to build was shattered beyond repair. But as the flash of anger diminished, an uncontrollable fear took its place. Fear of what the future held. How in heavens name can I cope with the responsibility of bringing a newborn baby into the world? On my own. What will happen my job at the school and the day to day running of the farm? This is not possible. All this and more, ran in circles through her mind.

The initial panic of knowing a child was growing inside her body was frightening enough but with all the other worries, Ruth was close to panic. Rising from the chair, she made for the stairs in the hope of gaining comfort through the blessed relief of sleep. Undressing for bed, Ruth stood naked in front of the mirror, examining her changing body. Running her hands over the soft swell of her stomach, she imagines, for a moment, that Jim is there, watching over her.

Slipping into her nightdress, she slid beneath the cool sheets, her arm automatically reaching across the bed but touches only the cold, empty space where Jim once lay. This simple gesture which had become part of their sleep routine, instantly triggered memories of their nights spent in a warm embrace, talking, planning, building for the future. Such a short time together.

No tears, Ruth, she said to herself, determined this time not to let them free. Dwelling on the past brings only heartache. Instead, although alone, she closed her eyes, forcing her mind to think of the future. Her future, with their child, vowing that nothing will be allowed to cloud this new vision. A shiver of excitement catches her unawares, a feeling of exhilaration in fact, at this new found strength. Jim has gone, but in his passing, his legacy is left within her, to live on and always be right by her side. This was their promise to each other.

Before sleep takes over, thoughts of Jocylyn's visit dominate her mind and realizes she must apologise for her harsh words at the first opportunity. The sound of the outer door opening disturbed her thoughts and Ruth breathed a sigh of relief as Luke returned. A glance at the clock made her smile. He certainly isn't a night hawk yet. He'll most likely sit by the fire for a while before mounting the stairs.

She listens for the pad of footsteps on the stairs, but she doesn't hear them. Unsettled, she slides out of bed, slips a dressing gown over her shoulders, and goes downstairs to find Luke slumped in a chair by the fire. Lifting his head and giving her a doleful look, he said, "I'm sorry, Mrs Styles. I didn't mean to wake you up."

"You didn't wake me, Luke. I was still awake." Ruth studied him. "Are you all right, you look worried?"

He slumped back in the chair. "Oh, I suppose I'm okay, Mrs Styles, really. It's just I'm a bit worried about things."

Ruth pulled a chair alongside. "Whatever has brought this on. You went out of here without a care in the world and, a few hours later, you return with all the troubles of the world on your shoulders." She smiled, trying to raise his spirits.

"Nah, it's nothing really. I don't want to burden you wi' my problems."

She looked at him in earnest. He seemed troubled. "Is it something we can talk about, Luke, because that is often the answer to a lot of problems. Not all, but a lot."

"Ah, I don't know how to start without upsetting you, Mrs Styles."

"I'm assuming it must be something that's happened tonight, so let's start there, eh?" She was trying her best to encourage him out of his shell.

"Well, as you know, I just went to the Tavern for a drink, but who should be there but my father. I came straight back out, but he'd seen me and caught me outside."

"And?"

"So, before I could mount up, he asked if we could talk. Well, what could I do? I said okay and we sat on the bench outside and talked."

"Well, surely that was good, Luke. To talk to him, I mean. It's such a long time since you'd seen him."

"Yeh, but it's not just that, Mrs Styles." He hesitated, before saying, "He wants me to go back home and help out. I told him I couldn't, 'cos it would leave you on your own."

This was like a kick in the stomach for Ruth, but she was not about to let it show. With great effort, Ruth smiled and said, "That was good of you to think of me, Luke, but surely, this is good news, not bad."

Luke stared at her, astounded. "And how will you manage up here without me, Mrs Styles?"

"Like I have always managed, Luke. I'm a survivor. Didn't Jim tell you about the hard times we went through?"

Luke's face softened and broke into a grin. "He did, yeh. You know what, Mrs Styles, Dad told me he'd pulled his life around. Dick had returned and, if I went back, they were going to try and make a go of it."

"What did you say to that?"

"I told him I couldn't as I was main man for you, leading the stone to the church and I was not going to let you down."

Ruth's head was buzzing with this news. So unexpected. Not a word from his father for years and then a bombshell like this.

"What do you want to do, Luke?" She placed a hand over her heart. "What do you feel in here?"

Luke appeared mixed up and close to tears with this problem. He did not want to let Ruth down, but he saw a chance for his family to reunite. "That's the hardest part, Mrs Styles, 'cos I don't know. Honestly. I know he's done some awful things but, after all, he's still me Dad."

Ruth glanced at the time. "Right, I'll tell you what we'll do. Let's sleep on it, talk it over tomorrow with clear heads and you can make your decision then. How does that sound?"

"You're not mad wi' me then?"

"Of course not, Luke. Just remember this, family ties are strong and very important. It is always worth going the extra mile to try and keep together."

He breathed a sigh of relief as he headed for the stairs. "Thanks, Mrs Styles. Like you say, let's talk tomorrow, eh? G'night."

"'Night, Luke."

Ruth gave him ten minutes to settle before returning to bed and sliding under the sheets once more. The problems were coming thick and fast, but with a good night's sleep she would, hopefully, find a solution in the morning.

A beautiful dawn was breaking as Ruth opened the curtains of her bedroom to a new day. A dull red glow that began to spread above the horizon, suffusing the wisps of mist that lay in the valley base with a pink hue, only the tallest of trees breaking through the surface. It was as if a monumental storm had taken place overnight and flooded the whole valley.

Once the morning sickness passed, Ruth had breakfast on the table; toast and bacon and a pot of tea, for Luke when he arrived downstairs. "Wow, you had a good start, Mrs Styles. I thought I was up early but you beat me." Luke noticed Ruth's empty plate. "You not having anything this morning, Mrs Styles?"

Ruth was wearing a loose-fitting top over her skirt that hid more of her body shape. "No, not this morning, Luke. I'm trying to cut down a bit." She smiled at him, trying to hide her embarrassment at the lie.

"Well, you look the best you've done for months, Mrs Styles. It must be the good weather."

"Yes, and I also had a good night's sleep, Luke. That helps. Now, before dropping to sleep last night, I thought long and hard about our problem and I think there is a solution. The first chance you have, try to get in touch with your father and ask him if it would be possible for you to still have a couple of days leading for me and the rest of the week you can have for your father." She looked expectantly at the young man.

Luke thought about it for a minute, his face brightening. "No wonder you're such a good teacher, Mrs Styles. You always come up with the right answers."

"Well, we don't know until you see your father, but it could work, Luke."

Finishing his breakfast, Luke said, "Seeing it's Sunday, if I get the yard work done, I'll ride over and catch him at Copton today. How does that sound?"

"Great." Once Luke left, Ruth washed and dried the pots, before starting to bake. She was finding days were easier if she kept active and her brain working. No wonder she flopped into bed every night absolutely shattered. Thank goodness she still had Sam and Albert to help on the farm.

With the smell of freshly made bread wafting through the kitchen, Ruth dashed upstairs and changed into her Sunday best. There wasn't a lot of choice in her wardrobe, only the white blouse smart enough, while adding a long dark skirt and a black bonnet. Ruth decided she must buy a couple of new outfits in the next few days. Noting the time, she thought a walk into Roston for the morning service at St Mary's might brighten her spirits.

The last time Ruth attended church was Jim's funeral, his death shattering the faith she once held dear. While dressing and combing her hair into some sort of respectability, she recalled the day hearing the bell ring out while passing the church at Gallows Howe and, on entrance, the feeling of peace that overwhelmed her. Someone, above mere mortals, must be watching over me, she thought. She smiled as the very words spoken by Dan Parkes that day came to mind. "I bet it had more to do with Jacob Thrall than anybody else, Ruth."

Dear, sweet, Dan. Her thoughts turned to how his new life was doing. Would he and Abigail still be together or would the relationship be over due to his roving eye for a pretty woman. The last time they met, all were going to meet for a night out. She sighed at the thought.

Throwing a shawl over her shoulders, Ruth walked out into the strong morning sunlight and a clear blue sky, the brightness hurting her eyes. The soft pink mist of early morning had dispersed into the atmosphere. The air smelled green and fresh; the sun warm upon her face, as if heralding a new beginning. In a brighter frame of mind, Ruth decided to take the footpath meandering its way through the top fields of Honey Bee before dropping into a steep-sided gully shaded from the sun by rough blackthorn bushes either side, forming a natural avenue of nature's choice. Although the pearly white blossom of spring had long since gone, the branches were laden with a heavy crop of berries. Lost in thought, a couple of rabbits shot across the path, startling her as they scuttled to safety.

Once again emerging into the sunlight, Ruth soon reached the heart of the village, arriving at St Mary's and wandered over to Jim's grave and positioned the flowers just picked into the glass jar. Stood by the grave, Ruth said a few words of prayer, but they meant nothing as she realized, Jim wasn't here. His spirit was at Honey Bee, in the surrounding fields, out on the rugged moors, riding. That is where he will always be, she thought. Turning away, she joined the last of the congregation entering the church. She hadn't realized the time. No matter, she was here now.

The church wasn't packed but there was a mixture of all age groups and the Reverend Benson was taking the service. Seating herself near the back, Ruth studied the architecture of the small church. Jim had gleaned a certain amount of history from Albert. That it was once a nunnery and the only remnant of the original building still standing, was a circular stone turret almost twenty feet high in the grounds of the graveyard.

The Reverend Benson did the best he could with his sermon. But it wasn't capturing Ruth's attention, her mind beginning to wander as she spotted the figure of Jocylyn Dymock sat in the front pew. Alongside him was a slim, dark-haired girl who she didn't know. Her heart jumped in her chest as she realized she may come face to face with him much sooner than she expected. Her mind raced. Do I leave early when everyone stands to sing the last hymn, or should I wait and hope he doesn't recognise me? Too late, the organ sounded and as everyone rose to their feet, for some reason, Jocylyn turned to survey the congregation, instantly recognising Ruth and nodded in her direction. Ruth returned the nod.

The service seemed to drone on forever. Ruth never hearing a word, but eventually, the Reverend closed the Holy Book and the elderly wardens shuffled down the aisles with the collection plates. This allowed the Reverend Benson time to walk to the entrance, shake hands with his flock and say a few words. Ruth was one of the first out. Thanking her for attending, he enquired on how she was coping, or if she wanted him to call and offer guidance.

"No thank you, Reverend. I have good friends who are helping me tremendously…" At that moment, without turning around, Ruth sensed Jocylyn stood close behind her. She shook hands and left, hearing Jocylyn thank the man for a wonderful service and, hopefully would see him again in the future.

As Ruth arrived at the heavy wrought iron gate, Jocylyn's hand reached over her shoulder and opened it for her. "Allow me," he said.

Recovering her composure, she dipped a little curtsey and replied, "Why thank you, kind sir."

"I hope you weren't dashing off to avoid me, Ruth."

"No, I wouldn't…" she hesitated. "Well, to tell the truth, I was a little surprised at seeing you here and…"

"And?"

Ruth lifted her gaze to meet his. "And the last time we spoke, I felt I was quite rude and I would like to apologise. I didn't mean to be, Jocylyn. I just wasn't myself."

"No, I should have realized it was far too soon to talk, Ruth. So, please accept my apology and if we could let bygones be bygones, that would be

178

marvellous."

"I would like that. Thank you."

Jocylyn, deciding to keep the conversation light for the time being, said in a very mock posh accent, "Can I escort you to your carriage, madam?" He offered his hand in an extravagant show of elegance, and Ruth placed her hand in his, playing the part of the upper-class lady to the hilt.

Ruth looked about her, as if searching for someone, then said, "I'm sorry, my Lord, but you appear to have lost your companion," she paused a second, a frown knotting her brow but no answer was forthcoming from Jocylyn. Laughing, she quickly added, "It also appears that my carriage has gone without me. I just cannot get the staff to look after me nowadays, so I must rely on Shank's pony to return home."

Jocylyn broke into a laugh. "I cannot believe you are not from the highest aristocracy in the land, Ruth. You play the part so well."

Curious glances eschewed from the dawdling congregation, possibly a few tut-tutting under their breath, but he continued to walk her to the footpath, bowed from the waist and said, "I shall bid you farewell, dear lady. Take care and I look forward to your company when we next meet."

"Thank you, Jocylyn." Ruth returned to the real world. "You know, I had made up my mind to come and see you at Oak Tree to apologise for my curtness. But now, it is over and done with."

"Yes, I agree, but that need not stop you from calling at Oak Tree when passing, does it?"

She realized she was still holding his hand and withdrew it rather quickly.

"Goodbye, Jocylyn. I will call, I promise."

He nodded at the rough path that Ruth was taking. "Is this your route back home, Ruth."

"It is, and a beautiful walk on a day like today." And with that she took to the footpath through the fields. He watched her until she reached the thicket of bushes and was swallowed up in the dense tunnel of blackthorn. On the way back, Ruth not only pondered on their surprise meeting, but also the dark-haired girl with Jocylyn. She was a real beauty. Where had she disappeared to, she wondered. She would ask Jocylyn the next time they met.

Arriving back at the farm, Ruth was shocked to find herself breathing quite hard. She realized it was a hard climb from Roston, up through the gully and then the fields, but she had done it many times before. My goodness, I'm like a broken winded horse, out of condition. I must do more walking. She smiled to herself, recalling the days, oh, not so many years back, spent roaming every nook and cranny of these steep, towering hillsides and when the weather proved too risky for the horses, Nell was always by her side. Such a good-natured dog and I still miss her. Marvellous memories of the past but now, Ruth felt she was losing everything she held dear.

Shaking her head, she tried hard to dismiss such negative thoughts and concentrated on the days ahead. Her pregnancy was noticeable now. Even Luke remarking on how well she looked. Well, if a young man was noticing a change, it must be coming to the point of breaking the news.

Having recovered her breath, she entered the house and began preparing for school lessons in the morning, not just wondering how long she could keep working, but also how long her riding days would last. Once the riding wasn't possible, there would be no more work. Maybe she should ask Doctor Rourke. He might be able to help.

Chapter 32

Taking a deep breath, Toby knocked on the office door of Mr Gerald Ransome. The moment of truth had arrived. Be confident, he told himself, as a voice from within shouted, "Enter."

Rubbing the sweat from his hands, he twisted the large brass handle and walked in, still gripping his suitcase. Mr Ransome peered over the top of his spectacles as Toby approached the desk.

"Good afternoon, Mr Smith. I hope you had a good journey?"

"Good afternoon, sir. I did, thank you."

While Mr Ransome shuffled through the notes before him, Toby took time to study the office and his interviewer. A large desk dominated the room and the gold paperweights holding a stack of files appeared expensive, as did the photo frame holding a photograph of, Toby assumed, a young Mr Ransome and his wife. Pictures of royalty adorned the walls, a prominent one of George V directly behind Mr Ransome. Another was of a Cleveland Bay; one he would like to study more. The man appeared thorough, still leafing through the notes. Where the hell had they got all this from, he wondered.

Mr Ransome was slightly overweight, understandable, Toby thought, given his job, wore glasses with difficulty, his head bobbing up and down as he read the papers. The dark suit would have once been smart but was now past its best. Toby felt Mr Ransome's eyes lift from his notes.

"Quite a list of qualities, Mr Smith for one of your age."

"Thank you, sir."

Mr Ransome will be fine. May I ask, is it Toby or Tobias?"

"Toby, Mr Ransome."

"What qualifications have you got with you, Toby?"

"I have no qualifications at all, Mr Ransome. It appears someone has sent quite a file on me, though."

"Who sent this through, Toby? Do you know?"

"I can only assume it came from my employers at Malton, Jocylyn and Victoria Dymock."

"In this file, it claims you have worked with horses all your life and that you saved a young horse from certain death. It also states you have a unique way of breaking and training horses and can cure abrasions, strains, and cuts with special medication.

"That's right."

"How do you explain this amount of knowledge picked up in such a short time, Toby?"

"It's not a big secret, Mr Ransome, and it was not picked up, as you put it, in a short time. I learnt it from childhood at Gallows Howe stables, where I grew up and had a lot of help from the farming community. Also, the best advice ever given to me was from a young girl who told me if horses are spoken to as we do to each other and treated with understanding and respect, they will respond in the same way we do and try to please."

Mr Ransome shook his head. "I'm sorry, Toby, but I find this... this story," he waved his hand at the notes before him, "hard to believe." Raising himself out of his chair, he placed his hands on the desk in front of him. "I have worked with horses and trainers for many years and this appears to be nonsensical."

Toby's bristled as this man was accusing him of lying. "Surely, there are names on that file as to who sent it, Mr Ransome. If you have any doubts, check it out first before you jump to conclusions."

"Are you trying to tell me my job, Toby?"

"No, definitely not, Mr Ransome, but as I just explained to you, if you treat animals as you would humans, they will respond. If treated badly they dig their heels in, become stubborn, and walk away. My meeting with you is over. Good day, Mr Ransome."

Still clutching his case and trying hard to control his anger, Toby had had enough of this pompous, arrogant man and turned to leave.

Mr Ransome could not believe what was happening. "Come back here, young man, I have not finished the interview yet."

With his hand already on the door handle, Toby turned and said, "No, you may not have finished, Mr Ransome, but I have." With that he left the room and walked back to the reception area where he flopped into a chair to consider his next move. But first, he must let his anger subside.

With head lowered and lost in thought, Toby suddenly noticed a pair of ladies' shoes appear in his vision. Slowly raising his gaze, he took in the nylon clad legs and the immaculate black skirt and white blouse, blond hair flowing over a blazing red cape slung over her shoulders. Lady Florence, in person.

Toby raised himself from the chair, but before he could speak, Lady Florence beat him to it. With a smile, she said, "It is Toby, isn't it. Toby Smith?"

"It certainly is, m'lady. What a surprise to see you here. A lovely surprise though."

"Why, thank you, Toby, but I spend a lot of time here as I live close by. But this isn't just a chance meeting, I have not only come to congratulate on your new job, but to thank you properly for the way you attended to me and Max on the day of that terrifying storm and," she hesitated, for effect, "his leg healed without any scar at all. That was remarkable." Her hand went to her brow before saying, "I was in shock, you know," as if in explanation of her behaviour that day, "and you realized it, the way you treated me. Thank you so much."

Toby couldn't believe the change in her attitude. "Well, I'm glad Max's injury cleared up and you were no worse for your fall," and then he smiled as he remembered the storm, "it was an exciting day, m'lady, wasn't it?"

She laughed at his description of the episode. "If you say so, Toby. Now, when do you start here?"

"Oh, that's not going to happen, m'lady. I've had the interview, and Mr Ransome didn't believe me so I walked out. I'm just figuring out how to get a taxi back to the station."

"Pardon! I don't believe it." Toby saw the dark green eyes flash with anger once again. She placed a hand on his. "Please give me a moment, Toby. I shall only be two minutes."

"I don't want to cause any bother over this, m'lady. If you could advise me..."

"Two minutes, Toby. That's all." With that, she was gone.

Within two minutes, Lady Florence arrived back with Mr Ransome following in her wake.

"Mr Ransome would like a word with you, Toby." She shot a hard glance in Mr Ransome's direction.

"Mr Smith, would you like to return..."

"Right here, and right now, Gerald, if you don't mind."

Toby could see it was close to foot stamping time but he dare not smile and kept a serious face.

"I do apologise, Mr Smith."

"I accept your apology, Mr Ransome."

"Now, if we could start the inter..."

Lady Florence cut him dead, her voice sharp. "There will be no more interview, Gerald. You've made a big enough fool of yourself, and of *me*," she fumed. "See that this young man is taken into our employ by tonight, or I need to know the reason why. That will be all, Gerald." And he was dismissed with a wave of the hand.

There was silence for a while, before Toby spoke. "Thank you, m'lady."

"Well, he wasn't only doubting your word, Toby, he was doubting both mine, Victoria, and Jocylyn's judgement. Now, has anyone shown you where you are staying?"

"No, not as yet." He laughed, clutching his case to his chest. "As you can see, it's all been a bit hectic."

"Come with me, Toby, it is just a short walk along the corridor." Turning, her heels clacking along the tiled floor and red cape flowing behind, Toby had to admit she cut an impressive figure. He could see that he would have to be very careful in how he treated her. He smiled to himself. A true thoroughbred.

"This will be your abode for the present, Toby. I hope you soon settle in. Gerald will call round at eight o' clock in the morning and introduce you to the rest of the staff. He should have told you all this but as he left in a bit of a huff, it fell to me. I hope you don't mind?"

"Not at all, m'lady." On noticing her frown, he added, "And don't look so worried. I will do my best for you," adding, "and the animals."

A smile lit her features. "I know you will, Toby." She placed a hand on her lips and blew a kiss. "Bye for now." And with that she turned and walked back down the corridor, red cape billowing behind her.

Toby couldn't believe his luck. What a turn around. After acquainting himself with his new living quarters, he swiftly unpacked, washed, and tidied himself up and with excitement mounting, walked out to explore and enjoy his first few hours in this vast city of London that he had only read about.

Chapter 33

B ack at Castle Moor, Doctor Rourke was called to the school to treat Dennis who, showing off in front of the girls, had fallen from the high stone wall surrounding the playground and cut his leg badly. Once bandaged up and with no more sympathy on offer, a sullen Dennis limped off out of earshot. This was Ruth's chance to tell the doctor of her pregnancy and ask how long would she be safe to ride. After offering his congratulations, his advice was, if you ride safely and can mount without too much effort, he saw no reason to stop until the final month. He also added, "In the meantime, I believe it would be wise for you to arrange a check-up with me, just to be on the safe side, Ruth."

"Thank you, doctor. I will do as soon as I have time."

He glanced quickly at her as she rose to leave. "Don't leave it too long, Ruth. It is best to be sure."

This was good news as, by her reckoning, the baby would be end of November, so maybe that would be the right time to call a halt.

Once home, Ruth found a scribbled note propped up on the table from Albert. *All yard work done, only the horses to see to.* Alongside, a plate, with her tea already made. "Thank you, Albert. I couldn't see this through without you," she murmured to herself. She realized then just how reliant she had become on others and still she needed more help. Reaching for the kettle, she remembered Patrick's last words to her as she left. "If I can help you in any way, Ruth, please get in touch."

"Well, could that be the answer. Nothing to hold him at York now, apart from his lady friends," she thought. "I'll take him at his word." Forgetting the kettle, she rushed out to the stable and, for the first time, noticed the return of the swallows to the buildings. The glossy blue feathers flashing in the sunlight with their distinctive swooping flight pattern. Ruth saw this as a good omen as she finally finished bedding and feeding the horses, draping her arm around each in turn before giving them each a sweet. She smiled as she heard the satisfying crunch as they ground them between their teeth, then nudged her for more. "No, no more today, my friends. I have work to do tonight."

With tea over, Ruth brought her writing material from the cupboard next to the fire and placed it on the table while enjoying Albert's enormous doorstep sandwich's. She certainly missed Luke's company and looked forward to his return in a couple of days. So, wrinkling her brow in thought she mulled over the words for starting the letter.

> *Honey Bee Nest Farm,*
> *Roston,*
> *Pickering*

Dear Patrick,

I truly hope that you remember the last words you spoke to me when we parted, "if there is anything I can help you with, please write." Well, you may, or may not, have noticed when we met, I am pregnant. The baby is due in, I think around November. I lost Jim in an accident shortly after meeting you. At present, I work part-time at school, and run the farm, along with Albert, Sam and Luke. We also lead stone to the new church at Castle Moor. So, I am asking if you would consider visiting the wilds of the North York moors to help your long-lost daughter through a very difficult time. The wage will not be big but you will be well fed and have a roof over your head. You would also be there for the birth of your first – and maybe – your only grandchild.

I understand if you are not prepared to make that commitment. Once
you have given it some thought, please let me know at the above address.
Regards,
Ruth.
p.s. I am pleased we met once again.

Once finished, she slipped it into the envelope and with a lick of the tongue
sealed it and stuck a stamp on ready for posting. Washing up and tidying
everything away, she smiled as she began to wonder if her father had ever
noticed her slight bulge. Will he be shocked, or pleased. Only time will tell,
she would not dwell on that tonight. Satisfied with her decision, she hoped
sleep came easier tonight as another busy day lay ahead.

With Jim gone and Luke returning home, Ruth coped with the loneliness
by her work but sometimes it still overwhelmed her. Oh, she was pleased
the Clemmit's were trying to make a go of it as a family, Luke deserved that,
at least, and her plan worked, his father agreeing to the two days a week
stone leading. Also, if Luke did have any spare time from the quarry, he
busied himself doing jobs around the yard. She had a lot to be thankful for.

Come Saturday morning, Ruth saddled Dunella and rode into Roston for
her shopping. As she was leaving the village store, she heard a voice she
recognized.

"Hello, Mrs Styles. I haven't seen you for a while. By, you're looking
well. Well, you know what I mean, in the circumstances, like...and-and
all that's happened?" Dave McCloud was tongue tied. Red in the face, he
couldn't quite get his brain into the same thought process that would bring
the appropriate words out of his mouth at a time like this.

"Thank you, Dave. I appreciate that and, please call me Ruth." Ruth tried
to make it easier for him by acting as natural as possible. "I'm really pleased
we bumped into each other as I think you might be the man to help me."

"If I can, Mrs Styles... I mean Ruth." His flat cap was twisted into a knot
in his hands. He felt the truth was the best way forward. "I'm sorry, Ruth, I
never know what to say, but I want you to know I miss Jim. I miss him a
hell of a lot."

Ruth reached out and touched his hand. "Those words are the nicest I've heard in a long time, Dave. You are the best friend Jim ever had."

There were genuine tears in Dave's eyes. "Yeh, we did have some good times together, didn't we." He sniffed, wiped his nose with his cap, then smiled through wet eyes.

"Now, while I have you here, have you two minutes to spare, Dave?"

"'Course I have."

"Would you be interested in making me an offer on my sheep, Dave, as with losing Jim, and Luke going back to Copton, it is work, and worry, that I could well do without."

"I'd definitely be interested. For one thing, I have plenty o' room for 'em and they are a pretty good price at present. I'll sort a price out and call up and see you one night, if that's okay, Ruth?" Dave was back to his natural self now, wheeling and dealing in animals.

"Thank you, Dave. Glad I bumped into you. See you soon."

Pleased with a possible business deal that would mean less work, she carried on to Albert and Martha's house. With a knock on the door, she shouted, "Anybody in?"

"We're in, Ruth. Come in."

Kettle was boiling. Martha poked her head around the kitchen door. "Cup o' tea, love? Albert is in the front room. Go on in."

"Lovely, Martha. Just what I need." Albert was busy replacing the lamp wick and filling it. The room stank of paraffin fumes.

"Morning, Albert. You are looking even younger than the last time I saw you. How do you do it?"

He strode over and gave her a quick hug and then held her at arms-length. "You don't look bad yourself, Ruth Styles. Now it's my turn to ask, how do you do it?"

"Well, the good news may have something to do with it." Albert could see the colour in her cheeks, and although dressed in loose clothing, even he could see the difference in her. As they talked Martha entered with three cups of tea and biscuits.

Once settled, Martha was the first to speak. "You have some good news,

Ruth, we could do with a bit of a lift, couldn't we, Albert?"

"Couldn't come at a better time. What have you got to tell us?"

"I'm pregnant, folks." Albert had to admit, when Ruth said this, she looked radiant, an absolute picture of beauty.

"Good God," was all Albert managed to splutter out.

"No blaspheming in this house, Albert Styles." Martha scolded, then, "Oh, Ruth, that's marvellous. When do you think you're due?"

"By my reckoning, around November, or early December, but after a check-up with Doctor Rourke, he might be more exact."

"This is the best ever news anyone could have after all that has gone before."

"Are you pleased for me?"

"Over the moon, dear girl. I'll start knitting straight away."

After advice on what to do and what not to do, Ruth left and mounted Dunella in high spirits. This was the most positive feeling since Jim's accident. She just hoped it would continue.

Watching Ruth leave from the front room window, they sat down in their chairs opposite each other and Albert said, "You were right, Martha." He shook his head.

"Yep, I was. And you know what, I think the girl will come through this, Albert, now she has this little bundle of joy to look forward to."

"Just think, Martha, if we hadn't called that night." He shivered at the thought. "Well, it doesn't bear thinking about, does it?"

"No, it paid off and," a hand went over her heart, "Ruth has suffered enough heartache. Let's hope this is the turning point for her."

They lapsed into a comfortable silence for a while, before Albert asked, "By the way, how did I do, then, with the acting, I mean, Martha?"

"Well, I didn't think you had an acting bone in your body, Albert Styles, but you nearly convinced me that you'd forgotten I'd told you."

"Yeh, I was good, wasn't I?" They sat back in comfort and laughed until tears rolled down their cheeks.

Chapter 34

W ith Josh employed at Castle moor quarry, news reached his ears that someone was needed in the loading bays, so he put Barney's name forward. Gaining an interview, Barney pulled out all the stops and got the job, his injury never a problem.

Barney had kept in touch with Maria by letter over the years, but as time passed with no reply, he was beginning to think the worst. Arriving home after work, hot and dusty, a letter lay on the doormat waiting for him. He gave a whoop of joy, it must be from Maria, and quickly slit the envelope open to read.

Manor Stables
York Road
Riccall
York

Dear, Barney.

So sorry for delay. Our move did not go as smoothly as we thought but we are now at the above address and settled in. I am very excited to be in your part of the world and look forward to receiving your next letter.

Au revoir (goodbye)

Maria Madison.

Barney reread it to make sure this was really happening and recalled the kindness and bravery of the whole family. How many years had passed since they first met? Times change, people change but Maria had replied. If it hadn't been for his damaged leg, Barney could have done cartwheels, he felt so happy.

Going into the back kitchen, he stripped to the waist, washed away the dust of the day and changed into fresh clothes before considering his reply. Once finished, and quite pleased with his neat writing, he would post it first thing in the morning.

Although his parents had passed on, he inherited the house and small-holding, as he was their only son, and Barney continued to keep a few pigs, hens, and a couple of cows on the ten acres of land. The cottage, a small rubble-built, thatched building, set in the lee of the rocky moor side was close to the old mill race. Many years ago, the race used to power and run the now disused mill below Castle Moor village. Although the cottage appeared desolate in appearance, Barney kept a surprisingly tidy vegetable and flower garden at the front and was almost self-sufficient. The thatched roof hung low at the eaves and the narrow-latticed windows were deeply inset. Inside, just the two rooms on either floor, proved adequate for him. Furniture was sparse, but suited Barney's lifestyle. To the rear of the building the steep rising moor was kept at bay by a stone retaining wall and, high on the hillside, when the gorse was in full bloom as it was now, the vast moor side became a brilliant shimmering yellow in the strong sunlight.

With animals fed and watered, Barney settled down for his tea, already prepared before going to work that very morning, when interrupted by a knock at the door. A quick glance outside gave him a clue, as a beautiful Cleveland Bay was tethered to the railings. It could only be one man.

Barney swung the door open and Jocylyn stood on his doorstep. "Good evening, Mr Dymock. Have you time to come in." Barney stepped back to allow him entry, then closed the door. his heartbeat just a little bit faster, wondering if it was about his job. Well, best find out straight away. "What can I do for you, Mr Dymock?"

Jocylyn noted the plates on the table. "I'm sorry, Barney, I have interrupted your meal time. I can call another time if you would rather."

"No, it's fine, that can wait. I would rather know if it concerns my work?"

Jocylyn put Barney's mind at ease. "Definitely not, you are a valued member of our workforce. My problem is, the man who replaced our close friend, Jim Styles, is not reliable, therefore we are missing a good leading man. I am asking if you know of anyone who could fill the gap."

He pulled a chair out for his boss. "Please, sit down," Barney sat in the other chair, scratching his head. "There is one lad that might fit the bill, Mr Dymock, but it would depend on Ruth Styles." He thought awhile, as Jocylyn gave him time. "You see, Ruth and Jim took Luke Clemmit on when the lad was suffering a difficult time at home, but he's as honest as the day is long now. He works a couple of days a week leading for the new church." He hesitated again. "But, that'll soon change as they are almost finished the building. He could be your man, Mr Dymock."

"Thank you, Barney. Do you think it better to be in touch with Ruth?" He was hoping Luke replied in the affirmative, "Or should I see Luke in person?"

"Definitely see Ruth first, Mr Dymock as she might have him lined up for something else. Does that help you?"

"That is marvellous, Barney. Now, I will leave you in peace to enjoy your tea." As he reached the door, he turned and asked, "When I first came, you asked if it concerned your work. Is there anything you are unhappy with, or not sure about?"

"No, I thank you for giving me a chance. Not everybody would do that with the injury I have."

"You have nothing to worry about, Barney. Thank you for your time." And with that he was out and mounted, waved goodbye to Barney stood at the window and was soon galloping across the old clapper bridge spanning Piper beck.

Chapter 35

T he thunderstorm was at its worst as Patrick ran from the market stall to what he called home. Drenched to the skin, he almost slipped down the steps to his cellar abode. Flinging the door open, he was in such a rush he almost missed the letter lying in a pool of water. Picking the dripping envelope up he cursed, "Damn the weather. What a time to come a downpour."

Placing the sodden letter by the side of the range, he lit the fire to help dry it out in case of damage. Hanging his wet clothes on the piece of string above the range, he changed into dry clothes and waited impatiently for the warmth of the fire to heat the room. Boiling the kettle, Patrick decided to have his tea before opening his precious mail.

Careful not to cause damage, he eased the letter out, hoping to God it was still readable. Luckily, all was well and he couldn't believe the news. Learning Ruth had lost Jim and was now pregnant was devastating news. But she was reaching out to him for his help.

The letter had shocked him. Could he be of any help with the farm work? Also, how would he cope with a newborn baby? In his own mind, useless, as he never looked after Ruth as a child. But surely, he could still baby mind. True, Ruth had given him a choice to say no, but he never gave that a second thought. She needed him.

A big challenge. Could he pick up the pieces of his guilt-riddled life and find out if he was man enough to help Ruth at this stressful time in her life. A grandchild on the way and Ruth had asked for her father. "Good God, of course I can," he said into the empty room, then smiled, aware he was talking to himself. How do I get there? I have no money to speak of, maybe just enough to buy food. Well, Ruth did it as a young child. I'll do the same. First thing in the morning, he decided to call at St Catherine's and inform the ladies that he was moving on to be with his daughter.

That night, Patrick fell asleep in the old, battered chair by the fire and was woken by an almighty banging on the door at the break of day. Bleary eyed and cold, he jumped up and stuck his head close to the window just as a bowler hatted man decided to look in. They both leaped back in shock, Patrick knowing he shouldn't be there and the bowler hatted man, not expecting eyes staring back at him.

Patrick opened the door and was greeted by a fierce growling voice. "What the hell are you doing in here. Can't you read the notice?" He gestured to the boards with the large red lettering, DANGER. KEEP OUT. Full of his own importance, he carried on. "These are all due to come down and it's my job to check they are empty and ready for the demolition crew." He didn't give Patrick a chance to answer. "I'm going for the police this very minute and have you thrown in prison."

"To be sure, I am sorry, mister, but I'm homeless. Nowhere else to go, you see."

"That is no excuse. What's your name?"

"Michael Donaghue." The lie quickly sprung from his lips.

"Ah, Irish, eh. That explains a lot. Wait there, I'll be right back with the law."

"Very good, sir." Patrick sounded quite obedient.

The fellow puffed his way up the steps, Patrick followed. As soon as he disappeared around the first corner, Patrick dashed in, threw his clothes into his kit bag, put a few belongings in his pocket, and as an afterthought pulled a flat cap well down over his eyes. Slinging the bag over his shoulder, his first port of call was St Catherine's which, luckily, was in the opposite direction to which the bowler hatted do-gooder had gone.

Arriving at the café, he was pleased to see activity inside. Rushing in, Jenny was just boiling the kettle. "Ah, an early bird. Cup of tea, Patrick?"

No, not this morning, Jenny. Haven't much time. I'm off to see my daughter. Now, if the police call looking for a Michael Donaghue that fits my description, remember, it's not me. Must go, Jen. Thanks for everything. Tell the others for me, please and don't worry, everything is going to be all right." He hugged her hard, then left Jenny open mouthed in astonishment.

With no real idea where he was heading, his only thought was to keep well clear of the area the police would be searching. He tried to recall his journey through the bombed areas of York after the war and, once on the outskirts of the city and feeling much safer, he pondered the direction to travel. The road he was on led away from the city, so that was good enough for now and he began to stride into... into what? The great unknown.

With streets almost deserted, the sun threatened to break through the early morning barrier of low cloud. Such was Patrick's spirits at this moment, the kit bag felt like a mere feather upon his shoulders and his old army boots comfortable companions once again, ready for the long walk ahead.

Once leaving the cluttered streets and terraced rows of houses behind, the road stretched before him, as if winding him closer and closer to Ruth with every stride taken. As the day wore on and the heat of the day bringing sweat to his brow, he halted to stuff his overcoat in his bag, and spied the sign he wanted, to Malton. Sticking to this road, bypassing the small villages at present, he strode on until a small thicket of trees caught his eye by the roadside. A small stream trickled and burbled nearby, where he knelt and drank his fill. His next problem would be food. Maybe, as surroundings turned more agricultural, the chance of food would be more likely.

Patrick hadn't realized but his stride became more purposeful with every mile covered, the walk effortless, his morale rising with every step. It was only on the steep climb near the village of Whitwell where he became aware of blistering feet and calf muscles tightening.

Lost in his own small world of pain, Patrick never heard the rattle of the cart approaching until it drew up alongside.

"Whoa, there." The man pulled on the reins. "Goin' far, young fella?"

196

Patrick smiled at the introduction. "Yes, I'm heading towards the ironstone mining village of Roston, in the North York moors."

"Well, the way you're limping, it's going to be one hell of a trek, fella.' And it'll be a waste o' time, there's no jobs going there. It's almost shut down nowadays, just a few hangers on left."

"No, I'm not looking for work. You see, my daughter runs a farm there and she's expecting a baby, so I'm going to help her."

"Jump aboard then, I can drop you at Malton. That'll save your legs a bit."

Patrick hesitated. "Thanks all the same but I have no money."

"Don't expect any. Are you getting up here, or not?"

Patrick did not need a second asking. Throwing his kit bag into the cart, he jumped up alongside the man and they shook hands. "Brennan. Patrick Brennan."

"Dowson. Jack Dowson."

Patrick studied the man. Well in his seventies he thought, but it could just be the weather-beaten features that made him appear older. "You farming out Malton way, Jack?" Patrick asked.

"Used too, when younger. When I retired, I hung onto this old girl and now I just do a few deliveries for people I know."

Jack was a man of few words and they travelled in silence for a while, only the crunch of gravel under the cartwheels and the steady rhythmic plod of the horse's hooves breaking the quiet country air. Patrick tilted his head back and gazed at the brilliant blue of the sky, only the odd wisp of a mare's tail cloud visible. With the sun comfortably warm upon their backs, Patrick felt a contentment that had been absent from his life for many years. With only the odd car passing and all other traffic agricultural or on foot, Patrick's mind had wandered, until Jack spoke.

"Do you intend making Roston today, Patrick, or will you find somewhere to rest up?" The older man glanced across at him.

"It's unlikely I'll make Roston, Jack." Patrick started to massage movement back into his legs. "Guess I'm not as fit as I used to be," he said with a rueful smile. "Once you drop me off, I'll head to Helmsley, or Pickering and maybe find shelter for the night." Patrick peered at the sky. "The weather looks like holding out, so it shouldn't be too bad."

"Well, if you stick on the track that runs alongside the river Rye for as long as possible, then look out for the Kirkbymoorside signs, you're almost there, Patrick. Best of luck."

"Thanks for the lift, Jack." They shook hands and, with kitbag over his shoulder once again, Patrick hit the road. Following Jack's instructions, he soon left the market town behind, the houses thinning out as he struck out alongside the winding route of the river, buying bread and cheese at a village shop with his last few coppers before they closed for the day.

As the sun dipped, his legs screaming for respite, Patrick searched the open fields for shelter and just before darkness fell, spied a tumble down stable, almost hidden from the road. Heaving the field gate open, he slipped through the partly open door and in the dull light made out a manger and stack of hay in the corner. Couldn't be better, he thought. Checking the night sky for any bright stars and the manger for newborn babies, he settled himself under the hay and drifted off to sleep.

The early morning sun broke his slumber. On opening his eyes and blinking into the strong sunlight, a bunch of hungry black and white cows were trying to nose the stable door open. Not expecting visitors so early, Patrick shoo'ed them away, grabbed his belongings and made his escape.

The weather was kind for his walk, the grass, sparkling with dew, felt soft beneath his feet and kind on the painful blisters. The rising moors were now before him and the terrain grew tougher as he hit the lonely road over to Roston. Following Jack's advice, Patrick found the rough track climbing out of Hutton towards Lastingham and, eventually, after miles of nothing but heather, the ancient route marker of Ana Cross came into view and in the distance, the towering ironworks chimney at the head of Roston.

Sitting down to rest his aching limbs and rap an old rag around his sore feet, he took note of this wild unforgiving landscape. Although used to the country surroundings of his homeland of Ireland, this was a ruggedness that he'd never experienced. Beautiful, yes, but daunting also. Farms clinging precariously to the steep sided valley as they rolled ever deeper to the small, lush green pastures at the base. A long meandering line of trees clung to either side of a small stream, where the natural fall of the dale, formed in glacial times, took it to its final destination. Horse and carts were moving slowly to and fro across the dale and the rough dry-stone walls running haphazardly, separated the fields from moorland. The occasional tumble down shed provided shelter for stock, or for the unfortunate traveller, thought Patrick. It also flitted through his mind on just how did these hill farmers eke a living from this land? But they appeared to be doing so and through the hardest of times as well.

Knowing he was nearing the end of his journey, Patrick's heartbeat quickened. He expected easier going dropping into the village but the tortuous twisting descent, littered in loose, rolling rocks and deeply rutted, made every step painful. As he stumbled his way down, a man on horseback was even finding the gradient difficult. Patrick asked him for directions.

"You're almost there, mister. That's Honey Bee." He pointed back over his shoulder. "And it looks as if it's not a moment too soon as I watched you come down that hill."

"Yes, it's rough and steep to be sure. Is there anyone at home, do you know?"

"Yes, Mrs Styles has just arrived back from work."

"Ah, that's good to know. Thank you."

"See you again." And the horse continued to scrabble its way to the top.

A short walk along the track and Patrick stopped to survey his daughter's property. Stone built, overlooking the valley with a large orchard at the back, housing a couple of wooden sheds, hen houses he assumed. A range of low, tidy stone buildings lined the rough track, with hens, pigs and horses roaming free in the fields, the rising moor steep and rugged behind it.

"Hello. Anyone there?" Patrick shouted into one of the outbuildings and out came Ruth, mopping her brow.

Her face, red with exertion, showed her surprise. "My goodness, father, I had no idea you were coming. This is a complete shock. Is this just a visit or can I take it you're here to stay?"

"I'm here to stay, if you'll have me, Ruth?"

"Well, I was expecting a reply by letter but, now you are here, that's wonderful."

"Ah, well, you see, where I was living, I had to leave pretty quick as they were about to demolish my abode," he said with a wide grin on his face, and he related his story.

Laughing, Ruth said, "It sounds like the same old Patrick, nothing running smooth yet, I take it?" Wiping her hands on her skirt, she asked, "When did you begin walking?" She threw a questioning glance at him as he limped towards the house. "I take it, you did walk?"

"I did that, but I have to admit a kind gent gave me a lift into Malton."

"Have you eaten, or could you do with a cup of tea and a bite to eat?"

His eyes lifted to meet hers with a smile upon his lips. "I thought you would never ask."

Albert was working most days now, but shorter hours and had lit the fire before leaving knowing it would save Ruth time. Ruth eased the crane over the fire and while uncovering Albert's special sandwiches, the kettle came to the boil. Replacing it with a larger cauldron, Ruth said, "When that boils, Patrick, it's for a bath and it'll also help soothe your feet. They look painful. There's a bottle of antiseptic on the windowsill," Ruth nodded over to the sink. "The bath is hung up in the stable. While you make yourself attractive, I'll do my schoolwork and then we'll talk." She looked directly at him. "How does that sound?"

"That sounds good, Ruth."

Patrick settled quickly into their routine and eased the workload off Ruth's shoulders. It also meant Albert could spend more time with Martha. Ruth was organised with help for the birth of her baby by having Martha stay at the farm for a fortnight, as Doctor Rourke thought November would be likely.

With torrential storms blighting the end of harvest, it left Sam and Patrick just a couple of loads to lead home to finish off. They were on the last load and had been gone awhile when Ruth realized they were late. Albert had left as they would unload first thing in the morning. Ruth heard a clatter of hooves in the yard and dashed out. It was Josh. "Sorry I'm late, Ruth. Got held up at work. I just thought I might be able to help with the last load."

"I'm pleased to see you, Josh. They haven't arrived with the last load and I am just about to ride down and check what is happening."

"Okay. I'll come with you, ' cos I always enjoy your company."

"Likewise, young man." She giggled at the riposte. He always gave her a lift.

Riding into Roston, Ruth saw the horse and cart outside the Tavern. Her face was like thunder as she slid down from Dunella, Josh instantly at her side. "It may not be what you think, Ruth?"

"We'll soon see, Josh."

Josh rolled his eyes heavenward, fearing the worst and followed Ruth into the bar.

"Good evening, Ted."

"Evening, Ruth. What can I get you?"

She strode straight past him. "Nothing tonight, Ted." And stopped at the table where Patrick, Sam and Dave McCloud were sat drinking.

With her ice blue eyes staring directly at Patrick, she spoke to Sam. "Sam, please get that last load up to Honey Bee before I get back up there." Josh stood just behind Ruth and he gestured to Sam to get a move on. He was not to ask twice. Never taking her eyes off Patrick. "Patrick, I had given you a chance to salvage a relationship with me again. I say the same words to you. If you are not back at Honey Bee before me, the door will be locked and your belongings on the doorstep."

"Ah, Ruth, me darling, I'm just going to have another, then I'll be up."

Ruth, blazing with anger turned, and walked out without another word. She'd said her piece.

Once the door had closed, Josh, containing his anger, bent down to pick Patrick up out of his chair but Patrick swung a punch. Josh ducked and delivered such a haymaker of a left hand to the offered jaw that teeth and blood flew across the room. Before the unconscious Patrick had even time to drop back in his chair, Josh grabbed him by his coat collar, hoisted him over his shoulder, fireman fashion and stormed out, telling Ted he would pay for any damages caused. Dave McCloud sat open-mouthed, his pint still half raised to his mouth, it had all happened so fast.

Slinging Patrick over the saddle, he quickly mounted and passed Ruth half way up the bank.

"See you up at the farm. Don't worry, all's well."

Josh dismounted at the stable, dragged Patrick to the water trough and shoved his head under water. A second or two and he started to struggle. A few more seconds he was fully conscious. Shaking the water from him, he stared long and hard at Josh.

Josh grabbed him roughly by the collar once again, his rage never subsiding and whispered menacingly in his ear. "Just remember this, Patrick, if you ever treat Ruth like that again, it will be the last thing you'll do, I'll make sure of that. At that point, Ruth rode into the yard, scrutinising the pair of them. Josh smiled up at her. "He did well, didn't he? He got back before you. Now, I'll just see him into the house before stabling Dunella, then I'll help Sam with Dulcie." He walked Patrick, a little unsteadily, to the house and bundled him over the doorstep. "Don't worry, Ruth. Everything will be fine from now on. Now, you go get your beauty sleep."

Ruth dismounted and let Josh lead Dunella to the stable. Watching him go, she realized just how lucky she was to have such a true friend as Josh.

Chapter 36

The very next day, Ruth called Patrick and Sam into the kitchen for a clear the air talk. The atmosphere was strained to say the least. Patrick appearing to have been hit with a sledgehammer, which he had. Josh's fist. The purple and blue bruising covered the right side of his face up to his eye and a tooth had gone missing. Sam also held Patrick responsible for the episode but was man enough to admit, he should have known better.

Ruth sat them down at the kitchen table and began. "I would like to explain to you Sam, why I flew off the handle in the Tavern last night. When I was just nine years old, I suffered heartbreak from the damage that drinking can do. The memories are still with me and I do not intend visiting those dark days ever again. I am not trying to rule your life, Sam, but all I ask is, please, keep your drinking time separate from the hours you are working for me. Understood?"

"Understood, Mrs Styles. It won't happen again."

"Thank you. That is all I wanted to say. You can go now, Sam."

Ruth was now alone with her father. "Patrick. I'm sorry I put pressure on you by asking for your help. I thought it might lead to some reconciliation for us both, but I can see now, I was expecting too much. It was not the right thing to do." She paused, Patrick waiting expectantly for Ruth to say her piece, knowing it would be bad news. "So, I've decided, once you pack your belongings, you are quite willing to move on. You are under no obligation to stay. I will manage."

Patrick leant forward over the table, his dark eyes searching Ruth's for some compassion. "Will it make any difference if I give you my word it will not happen again. Will you believe me if I tell you that is the first drink that has passed my lips since we lost Sarah. And can I explain why I cracked?"

"Go on."

"It was because I was so thrilled to be with you, to be part of your life and to be given a chance to make amends for my mistakes in the past." Tears welled in his eyes, his voice cracking with emotion. "I am so sorry, Ruth. I realize now, drink is a danger to me and I can never go down that road. But I am begging you for one last chance."

Ruth managed to keep her steely defiance in place on the outside, but inside her resolve was softening. What were Josh's words, last night. "Everything will be all right." Ruth rose from the table. "I want to believe you, Patrick, only I'm not tough enough to withstand such nightmares again."

"I will never, ever put you in such a position again, Ruth. Please do not refuse me this, my last chance of finding happiness with my family."

Ruth turned away, swayed by emotion. "Very well, Patrick. Let us see if we can get back to normal. Albert will be here by this time and Sam will be waiting to unload. No doubt, Sam may have told Albert what happened to your face. If not, you will have some explaining to do." She dared a glance in his direction, knowing her eyes would betray her real emotions. "Think you can handle it?"

"I can, Ruth." He waited until she looked directly at him. "Thank you." With that he went to work.

Eventually, with every passing day, moods improved, Patrick's dark good looks were almost back to their best, minus a tooth, and a certain normality returned to everyday life. Ruth was finding her pregnancy difficult, her bulge restricting how much she could do. Doctor Rouke advised less manual work but to keep walking every day if she could as this all helped towards an easier birth.

Ruth had arranged with Martha to come and stay for a fortnight and be there for the birth. But come the end of October, Ruth had risen early, unable to sleep due to backache, gone downstairs for a glass of water and her waters burst. It was still dark. Shouting Patrick from his bed, he rushed downstairs to find her crouched by the sink, glass in hand. "Please, Patrick could you bring Martha for me. I think the baby is on the way."

Seeing the shock on his face, framed by a white woollen nightcap, would have been laughable at any other time, but she was frightened. "Quickly now, if you would." Patrick leapt back up the stairs, nightgown flapping around his spindly white legs and returned wearing his army boots, an overcoat covering his night attire and a flat cap pulled well down over his head.

"Take Dunella, Patrick."

"Will do." Patrick was out of the door and gone within seconds, dreading knocking Martha up at this time of morning. He needn't have worried. Martha took it calmly. "Give me five minutes to get dressed, Patrick and I'll be with you."

Once outside, Patrick got Martha mounted, then mounted himself. "The baby has decided to come a bit early, Patrick. Another week I was coming to stay at the farm with Ruth. You say, her waters broke."

"Yes, I think so. She just asked if I could come for you."

"You did right, Patrick."

Arriving back at Honey Bee, Patrick lifted Martha down and they hurried inside. Ruth sat at the table with a glass of water.

"How are you feeling, honey?" Martha asked.

"A bit nervous, Martha, but a lot better now you are here."

"Ah, no need to be nervous. You've seen plenty of births to know how natural it all is. Any pains?"

Ruth nodded.

"Tell me when they catch you. That'll give me some idea what time we've got." Martha looked for Patrick who had rushed back upstairs to get dressed. "Now you're decent, Patrick, can you go knock Doctor Rourke up. You'll find him at the old mill in Castle Moor. You needn't rush, I think we have plenty of time," explaining where to find the old mill. "Oh, before you go, make sure I have plenty of water handy, light the fire and bring some blankets and towels." Patrick did as he was told, then dashed out once more, this time properly dressed.

Martha lay the blankets down next to the old settle and made a comfortable bed, swung the kettle over the fire in readiness and then sat beside Ruth and held her hand. She was shaking and the pains were causing her more discomfort. "The little fella', or girl, is on the way. It should just be right for Doctor Rourke to arrive and tell us what a good job we did, Ruth." Martha smiled encouragement. Ruth met Martha's confident gaze, the firelight flickering in the warm brown eyes of the older woman.

"I'm frightened now, Martha. Frightened I might not be able to stand the pain. Frightened that the baby might not be... you know, healthy."

"Everything's as it should be, Ruth. Now, how are you and your father getting along together. Seems to be working well after that first little upset." Martha gave a slight chuckle that made Ruth smile. "Worse things happen, Ruth. As we well know." They chatted, Ruth squeezing Martha's hand as the pains became more regular until Patrick returned.

"Just right, Patrick. What timing. If you can pass me a bowl of water and towels, we are ready and waiting."

Ruth suddenly screamed. It sounded loud in the small room. Then silence again. A few minutes later, Ruth, sitting in an undignified position on the blankets, threw her head back, sweat standing out on her brow, screamed again, long, and hard.

"Hold her hand, Patrick. This is going to be an easy birth."

"This is not... AARRGH, easy, Martha. It's bloody painful, she sobbed."

"Squeeze Patrick's hand hard with every pain, Ruth. Try to crush it."

"AAARRRRGHH."

Eventually, "There, I told you it would be easy, Ruth. You are such a fit girl."

At that very moment, a face, topped by a bowler hat poked around the door. "May I come in?"

"Of course, doctor. By, you did well to get here so quick."

"Patrick just caught me on my way out, so we were lucky."

Ruth lay back exhausted on the pillows after the effort. The newborn baby opened its mouth and screamed for what seemed an age. Patrick continued to mop Ruth's brow with one hand as he tried to free his other from Ruth's strong grip and Doctor Rourke helped Martha to her feet, then took her place by Ruth's side.

"Have I produced a boy or a girl. Martha?"

"A beautiful dark-haired boy, Ruth. Everything is as it should be and he is the spitten image of you know who."

These were the most beautiful words to Ruth's ears and a smile of satisfaction spread across her face. As the child quietened, Doctor Rourke placed the small bundle of new life with Ruth and it immediately snuggled into the crook of her arm and fell asleep. As did Ruth.

The very next day, when the children trooped into school, Mr Haigh brought them to attention and asked for quiet. "I'm delighted to say I have good news for you this morning, children. Doctor Rourke has informed me, Miss Styles has given birth to a healthy, baby boy." Whoops of joy and clapping followed, before he shushed them to silence to start their lessons.

As Doctor Rourke left the school to make other calls, after recent events, he began to consider his own future. Freda had been his companions for many years, yet they were no nearer to a decision on marriage. He believed himself to be a patient and understanding man. In fact, he thought it one of his main strengths but the time for indecision had passed. He was determined to ask Winnie for her daughter's hand, this very evening.

On finishing work, he made a quick change of clothes, spruced himself up by trimming his beard and moustache, he hurried out, excited at the prospect of what he was about to do. As darkness descended, Michael drove up to the old mill and noticed lamplight in the front room. All the better for the job in hand. Drawing to a halt and gathering the small posy of wild flowers off the front seat, he gave a quick rat-a-tat-tat on the door and walked in. The table was all set and a pleasant aroma of cooking wafted through from the kitchen "Good evening, Freda, Winnie. Something smells good." He nodded to both women in turn. "These are for you, Winnie." He handed the bunch of flowers to her. "Not only for all the special treats you have done for me over the years, but tonight I am about to ask you the biggest favour ever."

"Why, thank you, Michael." Winnie looked thoughtful. What might that favour be, exactly?"

"I am asking for your daughter's hand in marriage?"

This was so unexpected that Freda's hand shot to her mouth. After a short silence, she blurted out, "Michael, you should have told me you were going to mention it."

Before Michael could answer, Winifred answered for him. "What a load of bunkem, Freda. If you didn't know anything about it, what have you two talked about all these years? The weather." Winnie snorted with laughter as she rose from her chair and found a suitable vase, filled it with water and placed it centre of the table.

"Now, let us have dinner together and discuss this business of your marriage."

When all had eaten their fill, and the small talk was finished, Winifred eased back in her chair and the next question shocked the pair of them. "What took you so long, Michael?"

Michael was lost for words, but thought the truth must be best. "Well, to be honest, Mrs Grey, Freda and I thought you may not be able to manage on your own."

Winnie's penetrating gaze settled on Freda. "You what? You two thought I wouldn't be able to manage?" She puffed her cheeks out in rage. "What you really mean is, you were too scared to leave home, tell the truth."

"No, it wasn't that mother…well, okay, a bit of it was that. But I do worry about you."

"Well, don't. I'm not ready for the old folk's home just yet." She held her glass out for a fill up from the wine bottle. "We've been lucky, Freda. Spent a lot of time in each other's company, seen the tough times and the good. Now it's time to flee the nest girl and allow each of us to get on with our lives." She paused before saying, "You've got a good man there who thinks the world of you, Freda, do not let him get away." She smiled at Michael. "You have my blessing, Michael Rourke. I look forward to the wedding. Make it soon."

When Michael and Freda had left, Winnie turned her chair to the fire, content. Yes, she would miss Freda but, over the last few years she realized just how much her possessive ways had stifled Freda and was now trying to make amends. If her daughter could marry and settle with Michael, it was not too late for her to enjoy a long and happy life. With a sigh of contentment, Winnie dozed by the fire, before retiring to bed.

Chapter 37

Ruth found the transformation in her father hard to believe. Following the episode in the Tavern, Patrick became the doting grandad, on hand when the baby cried, or if he was ill or teething, so Ruth did not lose her sleep. It was then, Ruth realized, he must have spent time with her as a baby, as Sarah was quite ill giving birth but Ruth could not remember that. Also, Martha did not intend missing out on the newborn child and often rode up on the cart with Albert, allowing Ruth the opportunity of beginning work again at the end of January. Christening him James, after his father, he was a good baby, but also headstrong, which brought a smile to Ruth's face.

Ruth had only just arrived back home and lit the lamp when a knock at the door disturbed her. Carrying James on her hip, she shouted, "Come in." The door opened and Jocylyn entered.

Slightly flustered, Ruth said, "Jocylyn, how good to see you again."

"Likewise, Ruth." He stood back and admired her. "You are looking exceptionally well, and the little one... James, isn't it, is coming on a treat. Can I help?"

"Thank you, could you just hold him a minute while I hang these clothes up?"

Handing James over, Jocylyn handled him expertly, sat down and placed James on his knee. Ruth could not hide her surprise. "My goodness, it's not your first time with a little one, Jocylyn."

"No, I am quite used to handling a baby."

Jocylyn dropped his gaze, but not before Ruth noticed tears spring to his eyes. To break the moment, Ruth spoke lightly, "Patrick will be in any minute and he spoils him terribly, along with Martha. But then, I wouldn't have it any other way." She pulled a chair out and sat next to him by the fire just as Patrick entered, a smile on his face. "Thought I recognized that mount outside." They shook hands. "I'll just tidy myself up, then take James up to bed for you, eh?"

"That would be a big help."

A few minutes later, Patrick returned and eased James out of Jocylyn's arms and retired upstairs with him. "Goodnight, everyone."

After a few minutes silence, Ruth spoke. "Is this unexpected visit for business or pleasure, Jocylyn?"

"Well, both, Ruth. I haven't seen you since the day at Roston Church and I have come to ask about someone to lead stone at the quarry. Barney Stopes thought you might be able to spare Luke Clemmit."

"Yes, Luke came to us after trouble at home, but as the church nears completion, he could well be your man."

"Will you see him soon, Ruth?"

"His leading days are every Thursday and Friday. I shall ask him to call at Oak Tree to see you."

"Marvellous. I spend most of my time there. It is a beautiful setting and close to the village. Also, I take great pleasure knowing you are just over the next ridge of moor at Roston."

Ruth coloured slightly, not sure how much she should read into this statement, so just nodded in agreement. "Yes, a place of privacy where you can be yourself." She smiled at the thought. "That is if you ever have time."

Ruth began to relax in his company. "By the way, your new project is taking off in a big way. You have a daunting task ahead but you appear to be relishing the challenge?"

"I am. It is hard work running both the business and renovating Oak Tree."

He leaned forward in his chair. "You must call down this summer and see the improvements."

"I hope to, as Mr Haigh is keen on the gardening project."

While Ruth put away the ironing, she asked Jocylyn to swing the kettle over to boil for a cup of tea.

"Nothing stronger?" he asked.

"No, I'm afraid tea is the strongest drink I have. Sorry."

"Don't be. Tea has a certain soothing quality when drunk in the right company." His eyes caught hers as he said this. Oh, she was old enough to realize he was flirting but, annoyingly, she still felt the burn in her cheeks.

Returning from her chores, Jocylyn had a pot of tea made and poured a cup for Ruth as she sat down. "Thank you, Jocylyn." While sipping her tea, Ruth asked, "Have you visited Roston Abbey recently?"

"I have. I try to go every six weeks if possible as Victoria calls on a friend from this area, whom she met when at college."

"Ah, so your lady friend isn't from Roston, Jocylyn?" She meant it to sound casual but it sounded as if she was prying.

"My lady friend?" A frown creased his brow for a second. "You mean the lady at the service. That was Victoria, my younger sister. Victoria lives at Malton, running the stables there. Her friend lives at the very head of this dale and they have kept in touch over the years. You may know it, a beautiful stone farmhouse, surrounded by a few arable fields and rough, rocky moorland. Access is along the narrow, twisting farm track that peels off in front of the pub halfway up Chimney Bank. Very isolated, especially in winter months."

"Yes, I know the place well, have ridden past it many times. Exciting rides." For some silly reason, Ruth felt a sense of relief that Victoria was his sister.

"When was the last time you heard from Toby, Ruth?"

"The last I heard from him personally was not long after Jim's accident. I received a letter telling me he was going to London to attend an interview to work at the Royal Stables. How did that come about, Jocylyn?"

"Well, it is a long story and I promise I will tell you all one day, but suffice to say, Victoria and I both realized Toby possesses a special ability, especially with horses, that can never be taught, Ruth. Luckily, due to Lady Florence, he survived the interview, is fully employed at the Royal Mews and causing consternation in some quarters with his unique methods of handling and training horses." Jocylyn smiled. "Before I go, I must tell you this, Ruth. Winifred Grey's remedies will live on as Toby uses her ointments to treat all superficial injuries that occur and they work a treat. Many, I'm sorry to say, are caused by overzealous whip use by the grooms."

Ruth felt a surge of happiness for Toby, as she knew he would win through in the end. "What marvellous news, Jocylyn. I'm so pleased for him."

"I knew you would be. You were right when you said he was special." Jocylyn looked at the clock. "God, look at the time, Ruth? I must be getting back." Picking up his hat and gloves, he said, "Please call when passing. Goodnight, Ruth."

"Goodnight, Jocylyn."

With the fire dying, Ruth lifted the spark guard across, grasped the lamp and headed for bed. Leaning over the sleeping figure of James, she tucked the covers in around him, planted the customary kiss on his forehead, before undressing and sliding into bed.

Chapter 38

A fter his so-called interview, Mr Ransome appeared eager to please, introducing Toby to the staff and the head groom who, for some reason, had earned the nickname, Sir Tim. Once Toby began to interpret the different accents, he enjoyed the work and the challenge. There were only six horses in his stable block, but all were to groom, feed, exercise and bring on with the utmost patience to obey commands. He loved it. The only problem was the night life. Or, not so much his night life, as the other occupant in the small flat.

Jack and Toby worked together and got on well, only Jack was going out most nights and kept asking him along. "I can't afford just yet, Jack. I need my first pay packet and then, I promise, I'll be the first to come for a drink with you. In fact, I'll look forward to it."

"Shake on it."

They shook hands. "See you in the morning. Don't wait up for me, Tobe, because I know the girls are all waiting for me."

Toby laughed as the young lad oozed confidence. "God, you've got some bottle, Jack Tate. You really have."

"Don't worry, Toby, when your settled, I'll show you country lads just what you've bin missing out in the sticks all those years." Toby could see Jack been a hit with the ladies. Medium height, but with a shock of black hair slicked back and a ready smile always playing about his mouth, he certainly held a roguish charm. Toby thought he would be a similar age to himself but was years ahead in confidence.

"Get yourself gone, Jack, or your mates will have snapped your date up while you just talk about yourself. Have a good night, mate."

"See you, Tobe." And with that the door banged shut.

A fortnight later, Toby drew his first pay packet, he couldn't believe the amount. "Is this right, Jack?

Jack looked over his shoulder. "Looks about right, Tobe. I think I started on that."

"How long have you worked here now, Jack?"

"A couple of years." Jack was dressing ready for work. "You've fit in well up to now, Tobe, but you need to be careful with this new head man they've brought in, Tim Oliver. The girls tell me he's a nasty piece o' work. They refer to him as, 'Sir Tim.'" He chuckled at the thought. "Behind his back, of course."

"Nasty, what, with us, or the horses?"

Jack smiled. "Both."

For the first two months, everything ran smoothly. The stable block where Jack was in charge was spotless. Six stalls all hosed out first thing every morning and new bedding every night. The girls in all the different blocks worked hard and were good to get along with. Toby quickly adapted to the night life and was pleasantly surprised having money to spare at the end of the week. He did miss Pal, but a letter from Victoria assured him he was in good form and getting plenty of exercise.

It was towards the end of the year when trouble blew up. A new horse had arrived, headstrong and, it appeared, never broken properly. Tim Oliver took charge of bringing it to order. Toby was concentrating hard on a difficult Cleveland Bay, when a shrill whinny and clatter of hooves across the yard caught his attention. Sir Tim was holding onto the reins as the horse reared dangerously, kicking out with its front legs. Sir Tim had lost control of the situation, and also, his temper.

Toby turned to Jill. "Take care of this one, Jill, I'll give Tim a hand," and rushed over but he was too late. Sir Tim let fly with the crop across the horse's neck, swiftly drawing blood. Terrified and in pain, the animal reared again knocking Sir Tim backwards. Toby managed to grab the reins and held firm as the horse came back down.

Sir Tim gathered himself up off the floor, the red mist still burning bright in his eyes, saw Toby talking quietly to the horse and, for whatever reason, he swung the crop again, catching Toby across the face, slicing his cheek open like a razor. Toby felt the warm rush of blood run down his face. Grabbing hold of Sir Tim with his other hand, he lifted him off his feet. Luckily, Jack arrived. "Leave it, Toby," he shouted. "I saw what happened. Don't hit him. It'll be instant dismissal."

Jack handed a towel to Toby to staunch the blood, but Toby continued to talk softly to the animal although in considerable pain. The frightened animal began to quieten, the fear leaving its eyes. Toby knew he'd won. The trust was there now. Confidently, he said to Jack, "I have the horse under control, Jack. You'll find a bag in our room, with dressings and ointment in. Could you bring it for me, as the horse needs treating."

"You need treatment, Toby."

"Please, Jack. Do as I say. I'm okay."

Within two minutes, Jack returned as Toby continued to lead the frightened animal, gently around in circles, but all the time never stopping talking. While Toby held firmly onto the reins, he told Jack what to do. Once the horse was seen to, Toby then returned to his flat and got cleaned up, bandaged his cheek, and returned to wash the blood from the cobbles. Sir Tim was nowhere to be seen.

The very next day, Toby was called into Mr Ransome's office, along with Jack and Tim Oliver.

"Right, I have a report telling me of an altercation between some of you. I want the full story from each of you and it better be the truth. This is a serious matter. There is an injured animal that will have to be explained, also an injured person. If this gets out of this block, all three of you could be on the way home." Silence fell in the room before he spoke again. "The truth. Now."

Tim Oliver was first to speak. "I was having trouble with the new horse,

Mr Ransome. The next thing I knew, Toby Smith flew over and bundled into me, causing me to catch the horse's neck with the crop."

Mr Ransome turned his attention to Toby. "Is that right, Mr Smith?"

"No, not at all, Mr Ransome. Yes, I ran over to help as Mr Oliver had lost control of the horse, but I was too late to stop him striking the horse and drawing blood. While I held the reins, still in a rage, he caught me on the face, slicing my cheek open."

Ransome turned his attention to Jack. "What was your view of it, Mr Tate?"

"Exactly as Mr Smith told it. Mr Oliver lost his temper with the new horse and lashed out. The horse first and then Mr Smith. There was blood everywhere." He waited for a response. None was forthcoming.

"That will be all. I will make further inquiries with the other staff and see you all first thing in the morning before making my decision. Thank you. That will be all."

Later that evening as Toby bathed his face and put a new dressing on, he was amazed at the healing power of the ointment. "God, I hope this ointment heals the new horse as well as it has me, Jack. It really is good stuff."

"Ah, but tha' knows, lad, there's still a lot o' witchcraft out in them there hills."

"You are a cheeky sod, Jack Tate." Toby held his hand out. "Thanks for standing alongside me, Jack. Let's hope the other staff back me."

"They will, they all saw what happened. He's finished here."

Jack was right. The very next morning, only Jack and Toby were called to Mr Ransome's office.

"Thank you both for your honesty on the incident. Your account was fully backed by all the staff who witnessed it. Mr Oliver will leave at the end of the week and that will be the end of the matter. That will be all, Mr Tate, you may go. I just want a word alone with Mr Smith." Toby's heart missed a beat. Surely there cannot be anything else.

"Thank you, Mr Ransome." Jack left the room.

"Sit down, please, Mr Smith." Toby did as he was asked.

"It's true to say, we didn't see eye to eye on first meeting," this said quite grudgingly. He appeared to be a man who did not like his judgement questioned but he carried on. "The word is, among the staff, that you are a truthful, reliable member of this establishment and there is a lot of support for you to be the next head stable man. Would you feel comfortable with the extra pressure?" Mr Ransome sat behind his desk, waiting for an answer.

After giving it some thought, Toby answered. "At present it would be a step too far, Mr Ransome. I would appreciate more experience before taking on that role."

"We do have an immediate replacement for Mr Oliver who you will meet this next week. This will only be temporary, maybe a year, before the job will be offered to yourself. How does that sound?"

Toby's face broke into a grin. "That sound fantastic. With a year's experience and learning from the staff here, I look forward to becoming established at the Royal Mews. Thank you."

They rose, shook hands, but before Toby left the office, he turned and faced Mr Ransome.

"Mr Ransome, you may not be able to help but I would like to ask you a big favour?"

"And what would that be?" Mr Ransome asked guardedly.

"Well, my horse is stabled at Malton and I do miss him. I was there when he was first born and nursed him through ill health. Then, I thought I'd lost him forever when taken for the war effort, but a friend rode him home from the war and we were reunited. If I am to stay on here, I would appreciate it if a stable could be found for Pal."

"It's a little unusual, and I cannot promise anything, Mr Smith, but I'll see what I can do?"

"Thank you." Then, before leaving, added, "I'm sure Lady Florence will vouch for his good behaviour, if need be."

Mr Ransome gave a small cough to clear his throat and cover what Toby thought was maybe embarrassment. "Er, no, that will not be necessary. Leave it with me. Good day, Mr Smith."

Toby left the office a happy man. If Pal did arrive here, then it would be more like home.

Chapter 39

1930

10, Darwin Court
York

Dear, Ruth.

I hope this letter finds you and our grandson, James, in good health. John and I would dearly love to visit as soon as possible, but John is in poor health and needs me by his side, at present. Will keep you informed on his progress.

With love

Edith.

With heavy heart, Ruth reread the letter. As promised, Edith wrote at regular intervals advising Ruth on John's health and, eventually, she had good news to deliver. Edith wrote, explaining after specialist treatment, John had made a strong recovery and was determined to meet his grandson and to gaze once more on the wonderful moors that he had come to love. Ruth replied that any weekend was suitable.

A smile eased the worried features of Edith on receiving the letter. "Good news, John. We can call and meet our grandson any weekend." She paused before asking, "will you be up for driving, or should we take the train?"

"No, I'll drive, Edith." The black pearls lifted and held Edith's gaze. "This is a great incentive for me."

Edith remained hopeful. With the loss of Henry, followed so quickly by Jim's death, John had found it hard to bear, but the treatment, and this visit, had certainly lifted his spirits.

A brilliant blue sky greeted them as they chugged their way out of York and John became quite nostalgic and in good spirits. "Remember our first trip together out to these moors, Edith." He held a faraway look in his eyes as he carried on. "I recall everything so clear. The bleak ruggedness, the colours standing out so sharp. It changed my life."

"Mine too," replied Edith, clutching his arm. That was the day I met my son." Breaking away from the main roads which were in much better condition than John remembered, the car laboured its way through the small picturesque villages before beginning the steep rise along the spine of the moors, the deep lush valleys peeling off and plunging down into the valleys at either side of the road.

"Glorious, Edith. Absolutely glorious. Look in the distance, there," he pointed ahead, "the old cross where you told me you loved me." Her eyes misted with tears. They pulled up at the old monument and John held her by the shoulders and studied her, before taken her in his arms. "I may never get this chance again, Edith, so I just want you to know, these last few years together, with you, have been the happiest days of my life.

"John, what has got into you. We have a lot of good years left in front of us. Neither of us are going anywhere yet. We have too much to look forward to. Now, enough of that talk, we'll eat our sandwiches out in the wild, then we'll be ready to meet out grandson."

After stretching their limbs with a walk through the heather to 'Old Ralph' and enjoying the spectacular view into the deep basin where a thin, glittering rivulet, no more than a gutter, was where the river Esk's journey to the sea began. John pointed to the farmhouse close by, surrounded by a few fields, the tumble-down walls already tangled with undergrowth over the passage of time. "No longer a living to be made at some of these outlying farms now, Edith. As the hardy characters of these dales die out, the young ones are realizing there is a more prosperous life out there."

Shaking his head and holding tight to Edith's hand, they made their way back to the car. As John started the motor, he said, "What a wonderful day for our trip, Edith. Thank you." They kissed before easing the clutch out and turning towards Roston.

In the early afternoon, Ruth heard the trundling sound of a motor drawing nearer. She stood at the gate stroking Dulcie with James and as the car neared, John gave a toot on the horn. James held his ears and the horse shied away. John was all smiles as he stepped out.

"What a transformation in you, dear girl. Motherhood becomes you." He took Ruth in his arms and gave her a bear hug, while Edith bent low to speak to James.

"You must be James Styles, is that right?"

"Yes, and this is where I live." He threw his arms wide as if he owned the whole valley. Dressed in short grey trousers with braces and a brown shirt, he showed Edith his scrubbed knees as John and Ruth looked on.

Edith felt the prickle of tears but she was not about to cry, even though they were tears of joy. She strode over to Ruth and the two women hugged.

James studied Edith with dark, sharp eyes. "Why are you crying?"

"Because I am so happy to see you, James. They are tears of joy, not sadness."

"I don't understand," he said shaking his head. "I cry when I hurt myself, don't I, mam?" The dark eyes sparkled again as he stared earnestly into Ruth's face.

"Yes, you do, which is quite often isn't it?"

"Mmmm, yes." He nodded in agreement.

Ruth lifted him up onto the top bar of the gate and held onto him. "There's no need to hold me, mam. I won't fall."

"Oh, how many times have I heard that?" He smiled at her. Now I would like you to meet your grandmother, Edith, and grandad, John, properly."

"Hello." He held a small hand out to shake, which they duly did.

"Edith is your father's mother and she lives in York. Now, will you be a good boy and ask grandad Patrick to put the kettle on for our guests."

James suddenly jumped free from Ruth's hands making her gasp. He giggled. "I didn't fall, that was a jump, mam."

As James ran to the house, Ruth escorted her guests to the garden. "Come on, we'll sit in the garden until Patrick shouts us for tea. It would be a shame to waste a day like this, wouldn't it?"

"It certainly would," they both agreed.

Patrick's handiwork paid off. He'd made a shaded area in the garden with a couple of wooden benches and a table. He duly came out with tray, teapots and cups, James followed carrying a tray of sandwiches with freshly baked bread, which smelt delicious.

After introducing Patrick, Ruth began explaining her future plans. "There are a few old hands around this dale can't see me managing this farm on my own but with the help I have, I intend proving them wrong."

John nodded his approval. "Maybe they don't know you well enough, Ruth, and also what you have been through."

She smiled at him. "Maybe not." She looked across at James. "I also have a lot to fight for."

As the day wore on, John said, "now we have taken up a lot of your time and we must make tracks for home." They rose together, and James rushed to hold Edith's hand as they walked to the car. Lifting him up, Edith gave him a kiss. "You are just one adorable child, James Styles. I look forward to next time. Bye, everyone." The motor chugged into life and they waved until out of sight.

John had enjoyed his day, but was tired on arrival home, slumping in his favourite chair with a huge sigh. Edith brough a tot of brandy which perked him up.

He held his arms wide for Edith to come towards him. "Edith, I cannot believe that I have been lucky enough to know two women with such an unbelievable fighting spirit. For you and Ruth to suffer the loss of one so young but still be looking to the future, you have my admiration."

"Thank you, John, but, don't forget, it was you who inspired me to carry on and, in doing so, won my everlasting love."

They embraced in the low lamplight and comfort of their home and relived their day, before retiring to bed.

Chapter 40

The next year saw James begin his education at Roston and liked nothing more than a ride on Dunella, when Ruth would drop him off at school before heading to Castle Moor to teach for the day. When class was over, Martha, although in her eighties, met him out of school and they had tea together. James adored Martha, and Ruth knew the feeling was mutual as James gave her a reason for living after the loss of Albert the year before, dying during the night. Martha had roused briefly during the night and all was well but, as dawn broke, she reached across the bed and felt the cold hand of death next to her. The fear of God swept through her, instantly knowing Albert had gone, quietly and peacefully. Without a word and without pain. The story of his life. No suffering, no hard words, no fuss. She was thankful for that. Rising and dressing quickly, her first thoughts were to find someone to help her and, although early morning, the owner of the shop across the road took charge and organised everything for her.

All in the past. A lifetime together, snatched away by the grim reaper. Martha was now looking over her shoulder, knowing full well her time was numbered but watching and looking after James made her life worthwhile.

Ruth was determined James would receive a solid education, to be given more of a chance in life than she, or Jim, ever had. James enjoyed riding with his mother and developed a love, not only for horses but all animals. Happy feeding the pigs, hens, or ducks and gathering eggs from the nest boxes, he certainly enjoyed an outdoor life from an early age.

The hot summer of '32 was late arriving due to a very wet spring, so nature walks and gardening began later in the year than normal. Pupils were impatient to be clear of the stifling hot classrooms, keen to enjoy the outside world. With sandwiches and a drink packed into their satchels, or paper bags, Ruth led her charges past the derelict stone buildings opposite the school and soon entered the cool, dark footpath leading to Oak Tree farm across the fields. Ruth was always aware of keeping the children interested, be it learning in school, or identifying wild flowers, or bird song. "Listen, children." She put a hand to her ear. "Can anyone identify that bird call?"

"Oh, that's easy, miss. It's a blackie," David answered.

"You mean a blackbird, David?"

"Yes, miss. A blackie." He then cocked his head on one side, listening intently to a bird call further away. "There, can you tell me what that one is, miss?" Well into the game now, the children's chatter ceased and all were listening.

"I think so, David," she said. "It sounds to be coming from the patch of reeds at the base of the moor over there," and pointed into the distance.

"Do you know it, miss?" He asked again, impatient.

"I'm not sure, David. Could it be a woodcock or a snipe? Beautiful birds and both quick in flight."

David appeared impressed. "Hmmm, not bad, miss. In fact, you're pretty good. It's a snipe. That low rasping call gives it away. The woodcock is more of a soft croaky call, heard more at dusk and early morning."

"Now, tell me, David, where have you gained such knowledge on birds?"

"Me dad's a gamekeeper, miss, and he sometimes takes me out on the moor and I learn all sorts."

Arriving at the garden, Mr Haigh had acquired the help of two retired farmers to prepare the garden ready for planting seeds, so all Ruth had to do was peg the lines straight and the children duly raked the drills and watered the base from the water butt. Once planted, they were covered and watered once more. By this time, Ruth called a halt, taking the children out of the strong sun. "Sandwich time, children," and they all made for the relative coolness under the spreading branches of the huge oak tree. Suddenly, a figure appeared at the five barred gate into the field, wiping sweat from his brow.

"I thought I heard voices. Hello, everyone."

In working clothes, sleeves rolled up and his dark hair hanging loose, Ruth thought he appeared even more attractive than ever. A shudder of excitement ran through her, the strong sunlight highlighting his tanned features. The outdoor life certainly suited him. But the scars and discolouration of the skin on his forearms and neck, had her wondering what could have caused it.

"Hello, Mr Dymock," they all replied, the older pupils remembering him from his day at the school.

"I hope Miss Styles is not working you too hard in this hot weather?"

"No, we're okay." Joseph, a newcomer to the village, rose to his feet and strode to the gate. "I'm Joseph."

"I'm very pleased to meet you, Joseph."

"Is this where you live, Mr Dymock?"

"It is. This is my home and we are busy making the farmhouse more comfortable." He studied the other children, then spoke to Ruth, puzzled. "You haven't James with you?"

"No, James attends Roston, then Martha takes him home as she seems to enjoy having him." Jocylyn was pleased of the excuse of speaking with Ruth, but he needed time alone with her to explain his true feelings towards her. This was not the time.

"I'm sure she does. Well, next time you are here, the children can pick a few conkers and I can show you the progress on the building work." He made an elaborate bow in front of Ruth. "Good day, children, and until the next time, Miss Styles." It didn't escape the notice of the boys.

"Goodbye, Mr Dymock." She watched him go and said, "Right children, enough sun for one day, we must get back, or Mr Haigh will think we've got lost. When all was tidy, Ruth led the band of weary children home and all was quiet until Joseph sidled alongside. "You like gardening, miss?"

"I do, Joseph. I like being out in the open air."

Joseph sniffed and wiped his nose on his sleeve.

"Please, don't do that, Joseph. Use your handkerchief."

"Don't have one, miss."

Ruth rummaged in her bag and found a spare one. "You can have this one. I have another."

Joseph blew his nose hard, and then out of the blue, said, "Do you like him, miss?"

"Who, Joseph?"

"Mr Dymock, whoever?"

"Well, yes, I do, Joseph. He is a kind man who allows us to grow vegetables on his land."

Joseph thought about this for a while, then lifted his face and gazed at her. "He fancies you, Miss Styles. I can tell."

Ruth coloured. "Don't be silly, Joseph. I am now a widow with a child, and by the way, that's enough talk about that."

"Yeh, well, I was just saying, miss, in case you hadn't noticed." He walked away, still sniffing.

God, she would be glad to be safely back in the classroom. Unbelievable what young children noticed nowadays.

Once back at school and the children on their way home, Ruth undid the gate where Dunella stood waiting, nuzzling into her, as if looking forward to the ride home as much as Ruth. She mounted easily, marvelling at the strength of this fine animal, taking the fiercely rising road with such ease, it set her pulse racing. Once out on the open moor and the wind in her face, the ride was over all too soon, as they began the steady descent into Roston. Such an exhilarating ride in beautiful weather. Once home, Patrick was there to greet her and with most of the yard work done, this left Ruth special time with James before bedtime.

The decision to have Patrick come and help at the farm had worked. Ruth now was finding time for herself, as her workload eased. Over the last few years, a true father, daughter relationship had developed and James worshipped his grandad, following him everywhere, copying his ways and mannerisms.

With James in bed, Ruth and Patrick settled down to read as the last remnants of daylight lit the far side of the valley. After a while, Ruth rose and lit a spill from the slumbering fire to light the lamp, then noticed Patrick with eyes closed. "Are you enjoying that book, Patrick?"

His eyes flickered open. "To be sure I am, Ruth. Why do you ask?"

"Well, you're holding it upside down."

Flustered, his features broke into a grin. "Ah, Ruth, I must have dropped it when I nodded off. That'll be why." His eyebrows lifted. "I can read, you know?"

"I know. I've heard you read to James." She studied him closely, before saying, "strange, how there is so much we don't know about each other, such as not knowing you could read, Dad." Ruth placed her book by her side. "When did you learn?" she asked.

"I had a lot o' time to fill in prison, Ruth. I had to try and stay sane. Days, and nights, were long and lonely and the guards treated us like dirt. Learning to read and the thought that, in the future, you may find some way of forgiving me kept me going."

Ruth, deep in thought, closed her eyes. Patrick thought she had dropped to sleep, but eventually, her head turned to meet his gaze. "You know," she said into the quiet of the room, "at one time, I would never have thought this possible. To be able to forgive, I mean. But, as time passes, life moves on and we learn from it. I see you and James together and it brings tears to my eyes. Tears of pure joy, and I wonder, how can this be, after all the heartache and suffering we have both been through." She paused for breath and took a sip of water. "And here we both are with a beautiful boy asleep upstairs, you coming to help me in my hour of need, enabling me to keep the farm running, maybe God willing, for my son to inherit." She sighed. "Are you happy here, dad?"

Patrick rose from his chair and took both her hands in his. "These last few years have been the happiest of my life, Ruth. I cannot imagine where I would be now if I hadn't received your letter. If it's possible, I will do all I can to help you keep the farm profitable and make a living for us all."

Ruth stood up, threw her arms around Patrick, and with her voice breaking with emotion, she said, "I do love you, Dad. I really do." And she buried her head in his shoulder. "It's a love that has been buried for so long, I was never sure if it could, or ever would, resurface."

"I'm not sure that I deserve it, Ruth, but I promise I'll try to make up for not being with you in your darkest hours and be with you every step of the way from now on."

Ruth was relieved by this support from Patrick. "Thank you, Dad. That does mean a lot to me." Choosing her next words carefully, she said, "While talking so openly about relationships, father, do you think it would be a betrayal of my love for Jim if I happened to meet someone else?"

Patrick could not hide his surprise at the question. "No, of course not, Ruth. The years since Jim's death have left their mark but you have a life to live. You have mourned and grieved enough. It is time to pick up the threads of life again, if you can, and move forward." He thought for a while, before saying, "Also, I think James would benefit from a father figure in the household. That would be my advice."

Ruth's features lightened, as if pleased by his words. "I'm pleased you think that way, Dad. I must mention there is someone who, I feel, has taken a liking to me" She waited for a response from Patrick. Nothing forthcoming. "Imagine, me, middle aged with a child at school, thinking of romance."

Patrick smiled. "Do not turn away from it, Ruth, as love can, and will, make your heart sing again. Make the most of your life. That is all I am saying."

"Thank you, Dad."

Chapter 41

Edith couldn't believe how John's health improved after his visit to see Ruth and James and spent as much time together as possible over the next two years. But, in the last few months, Edith noticed him deteriorating, as if he had resigned himself to old age. Against all Edith's cajoling and optimism, John began sorting their last wishes out together, agreeing that the business and properties were to be sold, but the family home retained for as long as Edith needed it. The only other issue was a monthly allowance to be set up for Ruth and James.

His business in York and the orphanage, which had been his life, were rarely mentioned now. Top of John's priorities were buying and sending presents to James and Ruth and a night at home with a glass of good wine in Edith's company. It was after one such night, mid-evening, that John passed peacefully away. Edith returned from the kitchen to find him slumped in his chair, head forward, wine glass smashed on the floor beside him. Quickly ringing their doctor, he was on the scene within the hour to pronounce John dead.

The shock did not hit Edith at that point. Until the funeral, she remained in a dream world, but afterwards, on entering the large empty house alone, it hit hard. Over the next few days, with no close relatives or family to confide in, Edith relied heavily on the kindness of neighbours and acquaintances who offered company and support but, she still found the loneliness hard.

How cruel life, and death, can be, she thought.

But, through the tears and the mind-searching, Edith realized, yes, she may be alone in this house but John had left her with no house, or money worries. And really, neither was she alone, as her daughter-in-law and grandson lived in Roston. To keep herself occupied, Edith began dealing with correspondence and settled down to write to the relevant people and the most difficult one was to Ruth and James. But this one was softened by John's last wishes, thus making it easier to write, as she knew it would ease Ruth's burden.

> *10, Darwin Court,*
> *York*

> *Dear Ruth and James.*
>
> *It is with sad heart that I write this letter. John passed away recently and is buried at St Michael's Church, York. Our visit to you and to meet James did so much to lengthen John's life. It gave him a purpose for living again.*
>
> *I hope this finds you well and there will be some pleasant news from our solicitors, hopefully in the next few months. "I am not sure when my next visit will be now, as I am uncertain about travel now John has passed on. But, if you can find the time to write or visit again, Ruth, that would be wonderful.*
>
> *Please take care and I will write again soon.*
>
> *Love you both.*
>
> *Edith.*

Wiping the tears from her eyes, Edith replaced her writing equipment, leaving the letter ready to post first thing in the morning. Turning the lights off, Edith climbed the stairs to bed with a determination to overcome this dreadful loss as she believed she had something left to fight for.

Although sleeping fitfully, Edith was up, washed and dressed as it was the day for her weekly help to arrive. She had no need for employing servants anymore, with only one person in the house and the one day a week suited Mary as she was not getting any younger.

Always punctual, there was a tap on the door and in she walked, as rosy cheeked as ever. "Morning. Mrs Durville."

"Morning, Mary. If you could take care of the downstairs today, mainly the kitchen, that would be a big help. I have a few chores to take care of but I should be back about lunch time." She smiled at Mary. "Then we might make time for a cup of tea together. What do you think?"

"I think you are looking a lot brighter, Mrs Durville. And so you should be. You still have a lot to look forward to, and given time…" her voice tailed off.

"Thank you, Mary. Yes, I need to think positive and look to the future."

It was a case now of taking each day as it came. At least John had left her in a position where she could live comfortably.

Chapter 42

With Jim and Albert's death, followed by Luke's return to family roots, the workload at the farm had increased considerably, although Luke did keep his word to fulfil his two days a week stone contracting. The last few years had proved hard for Ruth, the mere thought of debt frightening her, but after receiving Edith's letter, quickly followed by confirmation of the monthly allowance for her and James, her money worries lifted considerably.

Ruth could see a way forward. Part of the money would be placed in a savings account for James and the other would pay for an extra pair of helping hands with a bit left over. I'll miss you terribly, John Durville, Ruth thought, and I would rather have you here than all the money, but James and I have so much to thank you for.

There was many expected her to fail, especially a neighbouring farmer who had first called one evening just a few months after Jim's death while Ruth was feeding up in the yard. She recognised him but kept working. It was Reg Pattinson from an adjoining farm in the base of the valley. With shoulders rounded from a lifetime of work and head bent, she watched his laboured gait up the last field. A mass of grey hair had blown free from his cap on the walk up, and his jacket swung loose. With a low centre of gravity, he hung onto the top bar of the gate like a drowning man, unable to talk until his breathing eased.

"Evening, Mrs Styles. You still busy this time o' night?"

"Afraid so, Mr Pattinson." She flashed him a smile as she carried on brushing the horses down. "Unusual to see you out and about this time of night."

"Just bin neighbourly, like."

"That's real nice of you, Mr Pattinson." Apart from a passing nod in the village, the man had never visited before. Ruth guessed his purpose.

Ruth waited for him to break the ice and after a short silence, he asked, "how are you managing now, short staffed as you are. Things must be hard?"

"They are that, but we're coping. Thank you for asking."

"You know, Mrs Styles, you'll never manage to mek a living here now with two main men gone. You, a *woman* on her own," he emphasised woman, "in this remote part of the world." He paused, hoping his words would have the desired effect. Ruth waited for more. "Now, if you were interested, I have a couple of young lads aiming to tek on more land and I would be willing to mek you a good offer, lock, stock and barrel. As it stands."

Ruth knew poverty was still gripping parts of the country, the depression hitting families hard, but in the farming world, prices were holding steady and with the stone leading, her wage from school, plus the allowance, they were managing better than most. But for how long, she did not know. Only one thing for certain she was not open for offers on the farm.

Straightening up from her work, Ruth left Dulcie by the trough and wandered over to Reg. Smiling, she said, "Thank you, Mr Pattinson, and I appreciate your concern. I will certainly keep that in mind but, this is my home, my life, my refuge and where I intend staying. I have been through tough times before and, no doubt I will visit them again in my lifetime." Polite but firm. "But, at present I intend going forward."

"Pah, I should o' known you wouldn't listen. You realize the offer 'll not stand if out else crops up. Money doesn't grow on trees, 'round here, you know?"

"I realize that, Mr Pattinson. Goodnight." Mr Pattinson didn't know it yet, but his words had completely the opposite effect on Ruth. *A woman on her own!* How dare he. She was boiling inside and more determined than ever the farm would go forward. He had turned without another word and made his way back down through the fields towards home.

Ruth never told anyone of the offer because she knew, for the farm to work out, the decisions must be hers. And hers alone. But she did have someone to talk it over with. Patrick.

One evening, enjoying the last remnants of the evening sun in the garden, Patrick wandered in with tomorrow's lunch after been out shooting. "I'll just skin and paunch these then I'll join you, Ruth. Is James asleep.?"

"Out like a log."

Half an hour later, Patrick sat opposite her. "Couple o' good rabbits tonight, Ruth. We can have them tomorrow night."

"That's good." She paused. Patrick could tell her thoughts were elsewhere. He waited. "I've been doing a lot of thinking lately, Dad."

"Have you now? That sounds dangerous." His eyebrows raised, not knowing what to expect.

She ignored his stab at humour. "Hmm, yes. I'm thinking of taking someone else on if we are to keep our heads above water. Hay time was hectic, harvest 'll be the same. Potatoes need picking and sorting without the fencing, draining and everything else we must do."

"Are you asking my advice?"

She smiled across at him. "Yes, I am."

"Right. At present, Ruth, I don't see how we can run the farm effectively without another pair of hands, even just to keep up."

"My view entirely, Dad."

"But who to get? The younger generation are leaving the villages. The Pattinson lads are full into their own farm. Barney and Josh are working overtime at the quarry in Castle Moor. Unless you can come up with a Prince Charming that can fit the bill, I think we are stuck."

"Yes, difficult every way you look at it, Dad. Maybe we just need to be patient and see what happens."

He gave her a quizzical glance. "And if it doesn't?"

"Then we'll make it happen," she replied in determined tone.

Grinning, Patrick said, "I like your attitude, Ruth. Now, I'm going to bed.

Goodnight."

"'Night, Dad." She listened to him pad quietly upstairs and then the click of the door to check on James before he himself retired. A smile broke free on her lips. Such a doting grandad.

Chapter 43

As Dan Parkes rode closer to home and his roots, the usual optimism that had seen him through life so far had taken a severe battering these last few years but he felt a turning point had been reached and a smile was back on his face. His new life in Pickering had not gone well. In fact, it was a disaster. Yes, he'd made the move; and yes, he and Abi, although not married, moved to a lovely house on the outskirts of the town and he enjoyed his job. So, what went wrong. Well, he had to admit his affair with Lucy, the housemaid had not gone down well but, to him, the biggest problem was the difference in cultures. Abigail was brought up in a world dominated by money, education, parties, and comfort. In other words, spoilt rotten.

He tried hard to adapt to begin with, but her parents didn't help. In their minds he lowered the tone and was an embarrassment to them. This was when Lucy stepped on the scene. He smiled at the thought of her. Bright, cheeky, and up for it. Also, the typical Hooray Henry's that attended the social gatherings became too much and after five hard years of trying to live a lie, he felt relief when making the decision to walk away.

That very night, Abi's father thrust an envelope in Dan's hand as he packed his few belongings into a saddle bag. He immediately hit the road out of Pickering early the next morning as Abi slept, leaving only a short note on the calendar wishing her well. Sunday. What a day to leave a life of luxury and ride into the unknown. No job, no prospects in the near future as far as he could see, but he did have a hundred pounds in his pocket. Well, he felt he'd earned that, and more. With a pack of sandwiches and his treasured gun strapped to the saddle, he led the horse quietly away from the house on a bright but sharp morning. Mounting, he hit the road out of town as the birds began their dawn chorus.

He was apprehensive on what lay ahead but as the day wore on, he felt pretty sure there would be work around these outlying villages, either with farmers, builders, or sawmills, maybe a chance of a bit of vermin clearance on some of these estates. Mile after steady mile passed under the hooves of his only other valuable possession, his horse, Midge.

Dan called a halt when the sun began to dip, losing its warmth but his despondency was lifting. Midge was quite happy, having spotted a patch of grass and a nearby watering trough, wandering over to help himself to a well-earned drink. Dan sat on the grass verge opposite the pub, watching the world go by. There was very little trade, only a small amount of horse traffic at this time of day, and he nodded to the passing farmers, or hikers making their way to whatever business they had.

While Midge happily grazed, Dan nipped into the pub to ask if they knew of anyone offering work and was quite shocked when a lady came through from the back room. Not at all what he expected. In her late thirties, he reckoned. Long blond hair but tied back and equally as tall as himself. Hard green eyes studied him closely before she spoke.

"What can I get you, young man?"

Dan leant on the bar and said, "Well, I was going to ask if you knew of anyone wanting a man to help out for a few days, but I'll rephrase that now." She softened and smiled. Encouraged, he carried on. "My name is Dan Parkes, I've just walked out of my job and I'm looking for work. I thought you might know of somewhere?"

She eyed him up and down. "Can I ask why you left?"

"Certainly. I was gamekeeper on the Ventriss Estate at Pickering." He paused. "And I was a friend of their daughter, Abigail Ventriss."

She could not believe what she was hearing. "Are you sure you are right

239

in the head? Walking out on a job like that, you must have had good reason."

"I did."

She held a jewelled hand out across the bar for Dan to shake. "My name's Helen, Dan. Pleased to make your acquaintance."

"Likewise." His spirits lifted. Whether it was because she hadn't dismissed him straightaway, or it may have been the glance she gave him when shaking hands. He couldn't be sure.

She shouted through to the back room. "Joe, can you spare a minute, please?" A few seconds later, Joe sauntered through. Slightly balding and gaunt with grey, pallid features, Dan guessed he was a sick man. "This fella's looking for work, Joe. You know of anyone wanting a gamekeeper?"

Joe shook his head. "I don't know of any keepers been taken on. You need to be with the shooting men for that."

Helen shook her head in exasperation. "Joe, we know that. He's just left the gentry in Pickering."

"Well, he needs to be out on the moors, then," Joe answered, nodding in that direction. "Plenty o' shooting out there. And I'll tell you something else, there's brickworks and quarries out in the sticks and they're employing."

Helen looked amazed. "How did you find that out? You're never behind the bar."

"Course I am. You have to eat, don't you? Who do you think looks after things then, eh?"

"Yes, I stand corrected, Joe."

"I'm from that part of the country, Joe. Did they give any indication as to where, 'cos I know the ironstone mining is gone."

"Yep, they did. Brickworks at Colmondale and quarrying at Castle Moor, couple o' little villages out towards the coast."

Helen had a look of disbelief on her face. "Who told you all this, Joe."

"A fella and his sister call regularly, mebbe once a month, and we have a chat."

"You've never mentioned it before." Helen scowled at him.

"You've never asked before."

Dan laughed. "He has a point, Helen. By the way, you two sound as if you are married. Are you?"

It was Helen's turn to laugh. "Good God, no. We're brother and sister."

"Well, I certainly got that wrong, didn't I?"

"We could do with you for a while, Dan, just 'till Joe's health improves. He's bin under the weather lately, can't seem to get picked up. We have a spare room where you can lay your head and food to fill your belly. What do you say?"

"I say that would be good and when Joe gets better, I'll make my way to where the work is. Thanks to both of you."

"Bring your things in and Joe will show you your room."

Was his luck about to change. The next week or two were hard as he helped Joe with the everyday chores, log splitting, lifting the kegs of beer and mucking the few beasts out and milking. It wasn't gamekeeping, although they had land that was good for shooting, which was put to good use on the table. The problem was, Joe was soon bedfast and Helen needed more time to look after him. Dan could not see an easy way to move on. Not that he was too bothered, Helen was an attractive lady and he could see the way things were going.

After a night serving on in the bar, Dan lay dozing in his room, with just a flicker of candle lighting the room when a soft tap on the door roused him. "Who is it?"

No answer. The door opened quietly and Helen entered. "Am I intruding?" she whispered.

"Not at all," he smiled, raising himself up on one elbow. "I was feeling lonely." He patted the bed beside him.

Helen lay down beside him, her face wet with tears. "I think we both need someone to be close to tonight, Dan. Do not think too badly of me, will you?"

"There is no need for explanations, Helen. I understand." He did understand. Sometimes the only answer was human contact. Gently wrapping her in his arms, they became as one in this small bedroom filled with emotion and passion, finding release from the pressure of the real world.

The next morning, Dan woke to an empty bed but the aroma of a fried breakfast wafted up from the kitchen. Washing and dressing, he was wondering what sort of a reception might be waiting from Helen. Would she be full of regret and tell him it best if he left. He needn't have worried. Gone were the worries of the night before. She greeted him warmly. "Are you ready for breakfast, Dan?"

"I certainly am," he said as he settled at the table. Helen came across and planted a kiss on his cheek.

"Thank you for last night, Dan, "for understanding me." She was silent as she poured the tea. "You realize Joe is dying. Maybe a month at the most, the doctor says."

"Yes, I know he's an ill man, Helen."

Her face was serious now. "The question is, how long are you prepared to stop with me, Dan?"

He answered truthfully. "As long as you need me, Helen."

Brushing away a tear, she said, "Thank you so much."

"I told you before there is no need for thanks. We all need a little help as we go through life. You helped me and I will be with you to see you through this, then take it from there."

As Helen became more and more reliant on Dan, they enjoyed their years spent together before Dan moved on, something inexorably drawing him home. To the open moors he'd enjoyed so much in his youth.

On the day of his departure, it was almost mid-day, later than he intended and Helen caught him at the doorway.

"Thank you for helping us out, Dan." She quickly put her arm around his neck and kissed him.

"Do you think we'll manage to keep in touch, Helen?"

"I hope so, but if not, please look after yourself."

"I will."

She laughed. "I hope you find what you are looking for, Dan. If not, head back this way. There will always be a bed for you."

"You really are a fine woman, Helen. I may take you up on that."

Mounting Midge, he rode away from the village towards the open moors.

Before he turned the final bend, he reined Midge to a halt and took a quick look over his shoulder. Helen was a small figure still stood in the doorway of the pub. She waved her goodbye. With a smile on his face, he did the same, then kicked Midge into a trot.

Chapter 44

Walking the well-trodden path to Oak Tree, Ruth could see her two gardeners, Bill and Eddie, had left the children plenty of weeding to do. She heaved a sigh of relief when noting the difficult job of netting the fruit bushes all done.

"Thank you, Bill and Eddie," she said under her breath and as she turned to bring the tools out of the shed, Joseph, stood close behind her with a frown on his face and said, "you talking to yourself?"

Slightly embarrassed, she said, "yes, I suppose I was, Joseph. I was really pleased when the fruit bushes were covered."

He took the rake from her as Ruth handed out the other tools and they set to work. Joseph followed her and stood beside her.

"Yes, Jacob, what is it?

Unable to stay silent for long, he asked, "will we see the builders today, miss?"

"No, not today, Joseph, we have a lot to do. We mustn't leave it all to Bill and Eddie."

"Just asking, miss?" He waited a few seconds. "If he asks us, will you go, miss?"

"Joseph, do you mind not pestering me. He may not even be at home."

Again, Joseph waited, then, annoyingly, said, "he is, miss. That's his horse in the field," nodding in the direction of the horse.

Joseph was right. "So it is, Joseph. You are very observant?"

After an hour's work, Jocylyn appeared, this time wearing a headband to keep the sweat from his eyes.

"Good day to you all. Your hard work is really paying off now, I see."

Ruth called a halt for a drink. Jocylyn had also brought a sandwich along, the children crowding around him, asking if they could gather conkers.

"Good idea, kids." Quickly finishing his sandwich, Jocylyn jumped to his feet and, like the pied piper, led them to the heavily wooded area at the rear of the house. "There you go, a couple of trees, so you should find plenty."

While the kids scoured the ground in the depth of the wood, happily breaking open the shiny brown chestnuts from the spiky, leather jackets, Jocylyn and Ruth settled on the grassy bank to keep an eye on them.

Jocylyn, eager for an excuse to see Ruth on her own, asked, "I suppose it's not possible to leave the children for a moment, Ruth?" He tried to hold her gaze but the children were her responsibility and she watched them closely, in case of accidents, or upsets. Sat close enough to hold her in his arms was almost too much to bear for him as he waited for an answer.

"No, Jocylyn, I couldn't." Ruth turned, finally recognising the desire in those deep, brown eyes. With heart suddenly hammering in her chest, she realized this man wasn't just flirting, or playing with her emotions, he was serious. Ruth was glad to be seated as her legs felt weak. Struggling to speak, she spluttered out, "if anything happened, I would be responsible."

"I understand that, Ruth." A short silence followed as he stood up, then offered his hand. Ruth took it and his touch roused emotions in her that she thought she would never experience again. Feelings, laid dormant ever since Jim's death. "But, I might be able to persuade you to accompany me on a trip to visit Victoria. I need to see her on a few business matters." Hurriedly he carried on before Ruth found her voice. "Mr Haigh tells me you are free this Monday, so, no excuses please, as Patrick is quite capable of taking care of James and everything else. What do you say?"

Ruth was caught off guard. "I'll have to make sure with Patrick, but, if he is happy with that, I would love to, Jocylyn." His smile was infectious and she could not help but return it.

"Wonderful." His dark eyes held her gaze again and his voice dropped to no more than a whisper. "I believe you realize my feelings for you are more than mere friendship, I cannot deny it any longer, Ruth."

Her heart thumped madly and realized that, if she accepted this invitation, it would be a chance to love, and be loved again. "Well, we certainly cannot talk here." She glanced across at the children, still happily playing. Relieved, she said, "I will look forward to our ride on Monday, Jocylyn."

"So shall I, Ruth. Pick you up at 8 a.m."

"I'll be at the end of the lane." She turned to her charges who were still engrossed in their search. "Right come along children, you must have enough chestnuts by now."

There always had to be one, Ruth thought, and it was Joseph. "Yes, but these aren't for roasting, miss. These are for conker fights."

"I'm not sure Mr Haigh will allow that, Joseph."

"Nah, we'll do it after school, miss."

"Well, I think you have far too many, Joseph. What will you use the others for?"

"Oh, these, you mean?" He held up his bag of chestnuts, laughing at her ignorance. "These are for next year when they're hardened up."

"My goodness you are a well organised young man, Joseph, I can see that."

As Ruth led the way up the steep climb out onto the main road, Joseph caught up with her again and walked alongside quietly, before asking, "Have you enjoyed today, miss?"

"I have. It was a lovely afternoon, Joseph."

"Hmm, thought you had, miss." He looked at her knowingly.

"Now, why would you say that, Joseph?"

"Well, you just look a lot happier, that's all." He went quiet but not for long. "Did he ask you out, miss?"

"That is not a question to be asking your teacher, Joseph." She looked away, smiling, before saying, "also that is none of your business."

"I know it isn't but I think that's why your happy, miss."

She stopped and regarded him seriously. "My goodness, do you always have to have the last word, Joseph?"

Deadly serious, Joseph remarked, "Yeh. My mam says so."

Ruth couldn't help but laugh and put her arm over his shoulders. "You are a very perceptive person, young man."

Joseph looked up at her and smiled.

Chapter 45

It was late afternoon when Dan recognized home ground. After the relatively flat going, Midge began to labour on the undulating hills through the outlying villages from Pickering and Dan was relieved on arriving at Roston but he was shocked. It was more like riding into a ghost town. Many cottages were standing empty. Some of the timber-built ones were in ruins. Deciding to give Midge a breather on the village green, Dan sat in the shade offered by the overhanging branches of the oak tree and ate his meagre snack.

Suddenly, the noisy clatter of hob nailed boots and shouting of excited school children caught his attention, running from the nearby school into the shop. Minutes later, smiling broadly, some appeared with a bag of sweets, some with ice cream. A few came and sat on the green to enjoy the last of the sun and one small boy took particular interest in Dan's horse. He kept taking a sly look over as he tried to wrap his tongue around the fast-melting ice cream, as the elderly lady scolded him on the rudeness of continual staring. Eventually, ice cream eaten, face wiped, the pair made their way to the row of stone cottages opposite.

Having sat longer than he intended, Dan was trying to figure out his next move when a woman on horseback rode into view and his interest picked up. Something about the body line appeared familiar to him. The straight back, the easy, upright riding style. He studied her but she was too far away to recognise. Dismounting, she gave a quick knock on the front door and entered the stone cottage. Dan was still admiring the horse, a thoroughbred certainly, when the lady stepped out with the youngster and hoisted him onto the front of the saddle. Leading the animal over to the mounting steps on the green, Dan tried to get a better look but with the sun behind her it was difficult. Once mounted, he watched the pair ride off, the boy giggling with delight as the horse made light work of the climb up Chimney Bank.

Deciding to seek more information, Dan entered the shop, now quiet after the school children's departure. He spent a few coppers on a freshly baked loaf to last him over the next day or two and wandered to the counter to pay his money.

"Anything else, sir?" The girl was young, in her teens, Dan thought. Dressed in black with white pinafore and a simple bonnet hiding a shock of dark hair."

"No, that's all for today, thank you." He hesitated, before asking, "unless you know of anyone in the area wanting an extra pair of hands?"

"Just give me a second, sir." The girl disappeared into the kitchen for a minute, then returned. "There is a couple of places. The Pattinson's about a mile back along this road, or Honey Bee Nest Farm, heading towards the moor top just after the pub. They'll be worth a try, mother said."

"Thank you kindly, young lady." Dan doffed his cap in her direction and the peaches and cream complexion took on a rush of colour. The name Honey Bee struck a chord. That must be Ruth and Jim Styles. If they are still there. Damn it all he should have asked before leaving. Not to worry. He would find out soon enough as he urged Midge into following the thoroughbred into the fierce climb.

Approaching the sharp hairpin on the first steep rise, the cart track veered off left across the moor. Dan knew this moor well, roamed every part of it with shooting teams in the past. Happy days spent out in the wilds. Allowing Midge time, they arrived at the front of the farmhouse. Dismounting, Dan sat on the mounting steps for a while, studying the well-maintained outbuildings, hen houses, a cluster of ducks around the pond and a well-kept orchard. The yard and stackyard all tidy and windows and doors of the farmhouse all recently painted. An awful lot of work had gone into the place.

Suddenly, a child's voice full of excitement reached his ears. Dan turned as a young boy and an older man approached the house from the fields. The man eyed Dan quietly. "Can I help you, young man?"

"Maybe," said Dan. "I asked at the shop and they'd heard you might be wanting an extra pair of hands. I was just passing through to Castle Moor and thought I would ask the question."

"That's right, we are wanting extra help but the lady you need to speak to has just dashed out but will be back shortly. If you can wait, I'll put the kettle on?"

"A cup of tea would go down well, sir." Dan smiled and held out his hand. "Parkes, Dan Parkes."

"Pleased to meet you, Dan." The dark eyes surveyed the younger man, taking in his appearance, weighing him up, Dan thought. "I'm Patrick, and this is James my grandson and my right-hand man." Patrick settled on his haunches. "We do everything together, don't we, James?"

"Yep, we do. Grandad would struggle on his own. That's why he needs me to help him out."

Patrick tousled the boy's hair as he asked Dan into the kitchen. "Take a seat, Dan," and waved him to a chair. He was about to make the tea as Ruth entered.

"Oh, hello," she said. "I saw we had a visitor but I didn't recognise the horse. Is Patrick making you welcome?"

"He is indeed, and also his right-hand man."

Dan recognised her voice as soon as she spoke. As Ruth came closer, Dan rose from his chair. "It can't be, can it?" she said in disbelief.

"It can and it is. Dan Parkes at your service, Mrs Styles."

Ruth put a hand to her mouth. "Good God, I can't believe it."

James suddenly interrupted. "You told me not to use that word, mother."

"I'm sorry, James." Ruth bent close to the young boy to explain. "I shouldn't have done but I was so shocked." She threw her arms around Dan's neck and hugged him close. Patrick brought the tea, grinning at the reunion. "I take it you two know each other pretty well, eh?"

"Dad, you'll never believe this, but this is the man who was there for me when I most needed someone. He saved my life." Lost for words she fell silent, suddenly realizing she was still hugging Dan.

"Sorry, Dan," She laughed to cover her embarrassment. "I can't believe it. After all this time, what will it be, eight or nine years. Oh, Dan, it's unreal. I have such a lot to tell you." She felt like the young girl who had suddenly ventured back into Dan's life.

Chuckling at her excitement, he said "Yes, we have a bit of catching up to do, but remember, there is a lot of water run under the bridge since we last met."

When all were sat around the table, Ruth asked, "Where are you heading, Dan?"

"Believe it or not, I'm out of work, Ruth." And he told his story. Ruth and Patrick exchanged a quick glance.

Ruth's face said it all and she reached and took his hand in hers. "I'm sorry it didn't work out for you and Abi, Dan, but Patrick and I were just discussing taking another man on. With what's happened it has left us struggling to cope."

Patrick got up and said to James, "Come on young man, we'll let these two have a talk while we read a story before bed, eh?" James jumped into Patrick's arms and they disappeared upstairs.

Ruth and Dan continued to catch up, recalling the early days, what had happened in their lives, the hard times, the happy times, the tragedies, and everything in between until darkness descended. Ruth lit a spill from the fire and lit the lamp. Dan watched her closely. "You know, Ruth. I carried a flame like that in my heart for you over many years. Still do. I don't think you ever realized just how much I loved you." Ruth began to speak, but he put a hand to her mouth. "No, let me finish. I am not about to spoil things by acting like a lovesick teenager, but our nights spent alone in that little cottage, all so innocent, were the happiest of my life. Now, please be honest with me, Ruth, you must have felt the same spark when we were together?"

Ruth reached for his hand and grasped it tightly. "I did, Dan. More than

I care to admit. But, when you think, we really were still just kids. Our emotions were all over the place. I am not saying they weren't real. They were. I'm just saying that, with the passing years, lives change. Other things take priority. And, as life changes so do we. We must, to survive."

Dan smiled, covering her hand with his. "Well, I'm pleased you felt the same way, Ruth." He shook his head before saying, "there may be a chance for me yet."

Unable to stop a smile, Ruth withdrew her hand and replied. "Do not start down that line, Dan Parkes. I'm older and wiser now. I have a child at school and…"

Dan interrupted "and grown into a very charming and beautiful woman."

Ruth felt her cheeks colour and smiled. "I thank you for those kind words, Dan, but our lives have changed dramatically. We have survived and, who knows what lies ahead. Let's just take it from there and see what happens."

"Sounds good, Ruth and if there is work for me at Honey Bee for a few weeks, all the better. And I promise, those special moments we had together I will treasure until the day I die."

"We both will, Dan." Sighing, she said, "the reality is, I cannot pay as much as gamekeepers earn, but it will be a living wage and a roof over your head. Do you want the job?"

Dan was eager to stay. "You bet I do."

"That's settled then. Your room is first on the left upstairs and Patrick, or Sam will keep you right tomorrow with what's to do."

Chapter 46

Ruth was already at the lane end when Jocylyn came to collect her. "What, no chauffer today, Jocylyn, she said with a grin. "I expected to ride regally in the back, waving at the crowd like the Royals do."

"Sarcasm doesn't become you, Ruth Styles," he remarked with a grin.

"It must be that working class chip surfacing again, my dear?"

"I'm afraid so. It is something I will have to work on."

"Is that a promise, Jocylyn," she replied with a flirtatious smile.

"It certainly is. If you allow me to, that is."

"I think it might be a lot harder than you think, Jocylyn Dymock" She stuck her chin out in mock determined mood before the grin appeared back on her face.

"There is nothing I like better than a challenge, especially with a beautiful lady involved."

Ruth's spirits were high. A beautiful day, a handsome man by her side and time away from work. Why shouldn't they be. He was still admiring her. She had to admit, although pushing forty, a quick glance in the mirror when dressing and preening herself, filled her with confidence.

"Well, are you going to start this motor, or stare at me all day?"

He broke out of his trance. "I'm sorry, Ruth. Your beauty took my breath away."

His flattery was working its magic and she was enjoying every minute.

253

Finally dropping the clutch, they set out along the low road through Copton out onto the main road to Pickering, Ruth pointing out the significant landmarks she'd noted while out on Dunella.

"You appear in good spirits this morning, Ruth. Have you had good news, or is it just the break from work that you can enjoy?"

"Well, it's everything really. I mean what a fantastic morning for a ride out, a day away from work and in the best of company. I also met up with an old friend last night. A friend who helped me through the difficult years when I first came to this part of the country."

"Oh, and who might that be?"

A gamekeeper called Dan Parkes. It's amazing really, when I think back. I found him laid unconscious with a broken leg after a fall and I helped him recover. I think he may have left the area before you settled here, Jocylyn."

"Hmm, I don't remember the name, but it sounds a compelling story. Will you carry on, please?"

She laughed. "Only if you promise to stop me when I'm boring you?"

"I promise."

Ruth related her life story, pulling no punches, right up to the present day.

He shook his head in disbelief. "I knew you were a strong woman the moment I met you, but I didn't realize just how strong and at such a young age."

"As a child, when tragedy strikes, it either destroys you, or makes you stronger. I was lucky, I gained strength." Ruth was silent for a while, then, "You realize, Jocylyn, this is the first time I have ever related my life story without becoming emotional." She turned and studied him as he concentrated on his driving. My goodness he was a handsome man. Why on earth had he taken a shine to her. There was no mistaking his intentions now. This trip would finally answer a lot of questions for them both.

Although Ruth enjoyed the comfort and luxury of the drive and the company of Jocylyn, there was something missing. That frisson of excitement that only horse riding could give her. All too soon though, they were pulling into the stone pillared driveway of Greythorpe Manor on the outskirts of the old market town.

Passing the small cottage, where Toby had stayed before moving to London, they followed the long winding drive past the line of stables up to the Manor House itself. A square, brick built Georgian mansion with marble steps leading up to the front entrance. The Manor had a panoramic view out onto the vast green fields, with possibly a dozen or more horses grazing and a forest of trees in the far distance. A picture of money and elegance and a sign of the lifestyle that Jocylyn had left to forge his own way at Castle Moor. Why? Ruth wondered. She was about to find out.

Rather than leading the way into the Manor itself, Jocylyn took her by the hand. "Come with me, there is something I want to show you, Ruth."

In the distance, Ruth saw he was leading her to the blackened remains of a former house. Elegantly built like the Manor itself, but smaller. The roof had caved in, charred and blackened brickwork left just as it had collapsed. Fungi, bushes, and small trees were sprouting from the debris on the base.

Ruth's nerves were on edge, uncertain at what Jocylyn had in mind.

"Why have you brought me here, Jocylyn? I'm sure it is not just to look at a burnt down property."

Jocylyn took a deep breath before replying. "No, it is more than that. This is where I used to live, Ruth. This was my home when I first married." He threw his arms wide, his eyes wet with tears, but he was determined to hold it together as Ruth had done when opening her heart to him on her former life.

This statement, out of the blue, hit Ruth hard and her shock showed. "I..I didn't realize you were married, Jocylyn."

"I am no longer married, Ruth. I'll try and explain." He continued to speak quietly but still very articulate. "I married Isobel when I was a young man. We were very much in love; I had everything I ever wanted; Money, business, and a splendid lifestyle. As you say, the silver spoon in the mouth helps. We moved in here and were blissfully happy and had a baby daughter until she was four years old." This is where Jocylyn began to struggle. Ruth went to his side, to hold him close and offer comfort.

Gently, she said, "you don't have to go through this, Jocylyn, we can walk away now."

He turned to face Ruth, grim determination on his features. "No, I must face this, Ruth, as you did, or I will suffer forever." He paused, before saying, "but I know I can only face it with you by my side. Do you understand?"

"Completely, Jocylyn." Still with her arms around him, she asked, "Are you still suffering nightmares from what happened that night?"

He nodded, unable to speak.

"You must tell me the story now, Jocylyn. Please. However hard. It is the only way for you to find peace of mind. Believe me, I know and I will be right by your side."

A minute or two passed. Ruth was beginning to doubt his strength to carry on.

"I returned home that night to find the fire crew fighting a losing battle." His voice was calm. "It was as if the whole sky had set on fire." Jocylyn was now back at the scene, the horror playing out before his eyes. "The firemen tried to stop me. I screamed at them that my family were inside and I fought through them. Kicking the front door open, the searing heat belched forth. I pulled my coat over my head and dived in. I could hear their screams, could see them at the top of the stairs." He raised his head to the heavens, his arms outstretched, fingers clenched claw like in front of him as if trying to save them once again.

"The smoke and heat were unbearable. The stairs and the upper floor were a raging furnace. As I ran towards them the whole staircase and upper floor collapsed, the heavy timbers crashed down, crushing me to the floor in that searing heat. I could smell the burning flesh of both myself and my family and knew that was the end."

Jocylyn had sunk to his haunches now and Ruth was by his side to support him the best she could as he rocked to and fro in anguish. She stayed there, wiping the beads of sweat from his brow, soothing him as you would a child. Eventually, he found the strength to straighten up. Ruth led him to a stone bench at the side of the drive and sat him down.

His story wasn't finished. "Only it was not the end, Ruth. The nightmare was just beginning. The constant hospital treatment, the guilt. Why had I been spared? With my family dead, I wished I had died in the blaze alongside

them. Time passed, ten years of depression, guilt and nightmares followed."
He hung his head as Ruth gripped his hands tightly, as if it was possible to
instil an inner strength from herself into Jocylyn.

"Over those ten years, I have never thought of another life, or another
woman as I always felt it would betray my love for Emma and our child."
He paused and looked directly into Ruth's eyes. "That is, until I met you. I
only needed those few precious moments together with you at the school,
to realize I could find a new life. The only thing that has driven me on,
until now, is moving to Oak Tree and the new business venture." He took
several deep breaths before speaking again. "But now, I need to know if
your heart beats with the same intensity as mine whenever I see you, or
even think of you." His gaze was still locked on Ruth, although he stared
through red-rimmed eyes, the hurt there obvious. And Ruth understood
fully what he was suffering. A lonely man lost in a wilderness of emotions
never experienced before.

Ruth searched her brain, willing herself to find the right words to soothe
his troubled mind, but it was impossible. Eventually, she replied as evenly as
she could. "Jocylyn, please believe me, I do care and I admire your strength
and courage even more so now, knowing how you have suffered. My day is
always brighter when in your company, or I know that I will see you, even
just for a little while." She paused, considering her next words carefully.
"But you must understand, this is not the right time for either of us to make
a rational decision after such an emotional moment, Jocylyn. We both carry
a lot of baggage from our earlier lives and it takes time to adjust. Let us see
if we can settle the nightmares first, then we'll meet, talk, and spend time
together over the next... well, however long it takes."

"I'm truly sorry, Ruth. I should not have expected a decision from you
but I had to say what was in my heart." His face creased into a smile. "And
from your words, there may be a chance in the future for us. You are right,
though, this is not the time, as you say, but please don't take me to your heart
based on sympathy. I've had enough of that."

"I assure you my decision will not be based on sympathy." She placed a
hand across her chest. "It will come straight from the heart, Jocylyn." Was

this a time for her to move forward, and lose the feeling of guilt that she was betraying her love for Jim. Her inner demons were saying no, but her heart and her head were shouting yes, you must move forward.

Placing her hands on his cheeks, she gently drew him to her and she felt the warmth of his body and the thud of their heartbeats. The kiss was filled with passion, a passion locked within them, both starved of that special love between a man and a woman for many years. Finally, Ruth grudgingly eased her lips away. Smiling, and in an unsteady voice, she asked, "Will that do until you return me safely back home?"

Rising, he grasped Ruth by the waist and raised her easily from the bench. "I am already looking forward to the journey home and also, to the future, Ruth." Turning, they walked steadily away from the charred old building, leaving it in the past, where it rightfully belonged and returned to the car.

Chapter 47

Ruth kept the conversation light on the way home, talking of Jocylyn's renovations at Oak Tree and of her work at the farm, even imitating Mr Pattinson's statement of, "a woman 'll never mek a go of farming."

Jocylyn rocked back with laughter. "I can imagine your answer."

"Deep inside, I was fuming, Jocylyn, but I kept my temper, saying I would keep his offer in mind but my intention was to stay there."

"I expected nothing less from you. I'm sure Mr Pattinson does not know you very well."

"That's true, but sometimes, I believe we become too attached to buildings, or surroundings, and forget that it is about the personalities and characters who abide there that make them special." She sat back in her seat, enjoying the philosophy of her words as the cool night air rushed past her face.

Jocylyn grabbed a quick glance at her as they joined the moor road. Relaxed, eyes closed, hair, although shorter now than in her youth, sweeping clear from her face. God, how has she retained her beauty after all she has gone through. He shook his head as they drew up at Honey Bee.

"You can drop me here, Jocylyn. I'll enjoy the walk along the lane a night like this."

"Are you sure, I can soon take you along?"

"No, quite sure. I need to clear my head after today." She reached over and they kissed again. "Until the next time, Jocylyn, and thank you."

"Goodnight, Ruth." She watched until he disappeared from her view and then began to walk home. The moon was up and not a breath of wind, only her, surrounded by the silence of night. She sat on the mounting steps outside the stables before going in, hoping to make sense of all that had happened. Jocylyn suddenly expressing his innermost feelings so openly. Was it just an emotional outburst on re-visiting his former home? Is he lonely, that can play a big part on the mind? All these thoughts ran through her mind. If he really did think they had a future, what about the cultural differences? It hadn't worked for Dan, why should she be any different.

Finally accepting defeat on all the unanswered questions that only time could solve, she raised herself from the steps, took one last look at the moonlit valley and then, a smile breaking across her features, asked herself, "but where else would I want to live?"

The clock struck nine as she walked in the door. Not too late back then. Patrick sat reading at the table, closed his book. "Have you had an enjoyable day, Ruth?"

"Wow, Dad. Very emotional but enjoyable. I'll tell you all about it tomorrow as I'm tired out. Has James behaved himself?"

"To be sure, he has. He takes after his Grandad."

Ruth rolled her eyes heavenward, then her face softened in a smile. "God forbid."

"The child is growing up fast, Ruth, doesn't miss a thing but a bit headstrong occasionally."

"Well, I suppose that is understandable, knowing his pedigree." She looked around. "By the way, where is Dan?"

Patrick picked his book back up. "He's ridden into Castle Moor to see if Josh, or any of the lads are about." He was thoughtful for a moment. "It appears to me he's wanting to turn the clock back but he'll find things have changed. Some have moved away, Pete's health is bad, Josh is becoming a bit of a miser they say. I think Dan will find village life somewhat different since he last roamed these hills."

"Hmm, you're right, Dad." She yawned. "As usual." She leaned over and kissed him on the forehead. "But if we don't learn to embrace change, we would soon become extinct, like dinosaur's in a modern world."

Patrick gave her a surprised look. "Quite the philosopher tonight, are we? What's brought this on?"

"Today's experience has brought this on, Dad. A simple day out with Jocylyn. My heart is telling me, I've fallen for him in a big way." Patrick could see the difference. Her gaze was misty-eyed, her face glowing, even in the dull lamplight. "I believe I need to be brave and grasp this opportunity if I want to spend the rest of my life with him." Ruth took off her coat and hung it on the chair back. "Now, if you'll excuse me for not sitting up to chat with you, Dad, I have a busy day tomorrow, so I am away to my bed. Goodnight."

"I don't know, you youngsters can't last the pace."

"Aw, shut up, Dad," she said climbing the stairs. Halfway up, she turned back with a smile on her face, and said, "anyway, you should know by now, God works in mysterious ways."

About the Author

John lives at Castleton, a small rural village set in the spectacular heart of the North Yorks moors. Inheritance is his second novel and continues to follow Ruth Brennan's life, and also that of all the characters created in his first book, A Journey of Hope.

This is his third and - possibly - final book to complete the Ruth Brennan trilogy on her life. His next book will tackle a totally different genre of writing.

Also by John F. Watson

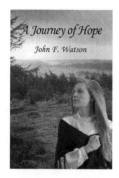

A Journey of Hope

Ruth Brennan, born into abject poverty in the City of York at the end of the 19th century, develops into a character of great courage, passion and determination, possessing a more indomitable spirit on every turn of the page, as she desperately tries to flee the demons of her past. Follow Ruth on her epic journey from birth and early carefree schooldays, through the tragic loss of her parents and cruelty suffered at the Orphanage, before fleeing to make the long, arduous trek toward the coast in search of work. But, by chance, along the way, she stumbles upon a small hamlet set in the very heart of the wild, untamed beauty of the North Yorkshire moors where, at barely sixteen years old, she finds true friendship, religion and love.

Inheritance

The year is 1911 and Ruth Brennan, reunited with Jim from their orphanage days together, now looks to the future with a new found confidence. But first, she must banish the haunting memories from her early childhood if she is to find true happiness.

As Ruth battles with her own demons, Joshua Thrall learns that he must leave Freda, his first true love and as the horror of the 1st World War begins, Josh, along with close friends Barney and Pete, they decide to leave the hardship and poverty of the countryside to fight for King and Country.

A hard, emotional story of love, romance, family conflicts and bravery set around this close-knit rural community with the rugged, stunning scenery of the North York moors as its backdrop.

'Inheritance' is a sequel to 'A Journey of Hope.'

Printed in Great Britain
by Amazon

29390462R00150